BEIRUT NOIR

EDITED BY IMAN HUMAYDAN

Translated from the Arabic and French by Michelle Hartman

This collection is comprised of works of fiction. All names, characters, places, and incidents are the product of the authors' imaginations. Any resemblance to real events or persons, living or dead, is entirely coincidental.

Published by Akashic Books
© 2015 Akashic Books

Series concept by Tim McLoughlin and Johnny Temple
Beirut map by Aaron Petrovich

Front cover photo © Samer Mohdad. Reconstruction phase at the seafront in downtown Beirut, Lebanon, 1995. From the series *Beirut Mutations*. www.arabimages.com.

ISBN-13: 978-1-61775-344-2
Library of Congress Control Number: 2014955099

First printing

Akashic Books
Twitter: @AkashicBooks
Facebook: AkashicBooks
E-mail: info@akashicbooks.com
Website: www.akashicbooks.com

ALSO IN THE AKASHIC NOIR SERIES

PARIS NOIR (FRANCE), edited by AURÉLIEN MASSON
PHILADELPHIA NOIR, edited by CARLIN ROMANO
PHOENIX NOIR, edited by PATRICK MILLIKIN
PITTSBURGH NOIR, edited by KATHLEEN GEORGE
PORTLAND NOIR, edited by KEVIN SAMPSELL
PRISON NOIR, edited by JOYCE CAROL OATES
PROVIDENCE NOIR, edited by ANN HOOD
QUEENS NOIR, edited by ROBERT KNIGHTLY
RICHMOND NOIR, edited by ANDREW BLOSSOM, BRIAN CASTLEBERRY & TOM DE HAVEN
ROME NOIR (ITALY), edited by CHIARA STANGALINO & MAXIM JAKUBOWSKI
SAN DIEGO NOIR, edited by MARYELIZABETH HART
SAN FRANCISCO NOIR, edited by PETER MARAVELIS
SAN FRANCISCO NOIR 2: THE CLASSICS, edited by PETER MARAVELIS
SEATTLE NOIR, edited by CURT COLBERT
SINGAPORE NOIR, edited by CHERYL LU-LIEN TAN
STATEN ISLAND NOIR, edited by PATRICIA SMITH
STOCKHOLM NOIR (SWEDEN), edited by NATHAN LARSON & CARL-MICHAEL EDENBORG
ST. PETERSBURG NOIR (RUSSIA), edited by NATALIA SMIRNOVA & JULIA GOUMEN
TEHRAN NOIR (IRAN), edited by SALAR ABDOH
TEL AVIV NOIR (ISRAEL), edited by ETGAR KERET & ASSAF GAVRON
TORONTO NOIR (CANADA), edited by JANINE ARMIN & NATHANIEL G. MOORE
TRINIDAD NOIR (TRINIDAD & TOBAGO), edited by LISA ALLEN-AGOSTINI & JEANNE MASON
TWIN CITIES NOIR, edited by JULIE SCHAPER & STEVEN HORWITZ
USA NOIR, edited by JOHNNY TEMPLE
VENICE NOIR (ITALY), edited by MAXIM JAKUBOWSKI
WALL STREET NOIR, edited by PETER SPIEGELMAN
ZAGREB NOIR (CROATIA), edited by IVAN SRŠEN

FORTHCOMING

ACCRA NOIR (GHANA), edited by MERI NANA-AMA DANQUAH
ADDIS ABABA NOIR (ETHIOPIA), edited by MAAZA MENGISTE
ATLANTA NOIR, edited by TAYARI JONES
BAGHDAD NOIR (IRAQ), edited by SAMUEL SHIMON
BOGOTÁ NOIR (COLOMBIA), edited by ANDREA MONTEJO
BRUSSELS NOIR (BELGIUM), edited by MICHEL DUFRANNE
BUENOS AIRES NOIR (ARGENTINA), edited by ERNESTO MALLO
JERUSALEM NOIR, edited by DROR MISHANI
LAGOS NOIR (NIGERIA), edited by CHRIS ABANI
MARRAKECH NOIR (MOROCCO), edited by YASSIN ADNAN
MISSISSIPPI NOIR, edited by TOM FRANKLIN
MONTREAL NOIR (CANADA), edited by JOHN McFETRIDGE & JACQUES FILIPPI
NEW ORLEANS NOIR: THE CLASSICS, edited by JULIE SMITH
OAKLAND NOIR, edited by JERRY THOMPSON & EDDIE MULLER
RIO NOIR (BRAZIL), edited by TONY BELLOTTO
SAN JUAN NOIR (PUERTO RICO), edited by MAYRA SANTOS-FEBRES
SÃO PAULO NOIR (BRAZIL), edited by TONY BELLOTTO
ST. LOUIS NOIR, edited by SCOTT PHILLIPS
TRINIDAD NOIR: THE CLASSICS (TRINIDAD & TOBAGO), edited by EARL LOVELACE & ROBERT ANTONI

MEDITERRANEAN SEA

CORNICHE

AIN EL MREISSEH

RAS BEIRUT

BLISS STREET

MANARA

CARACAS

BEIRUT

RAOUCHÉ

MEDITERRANEAN SEA

TALLET AL-KHAYYAT

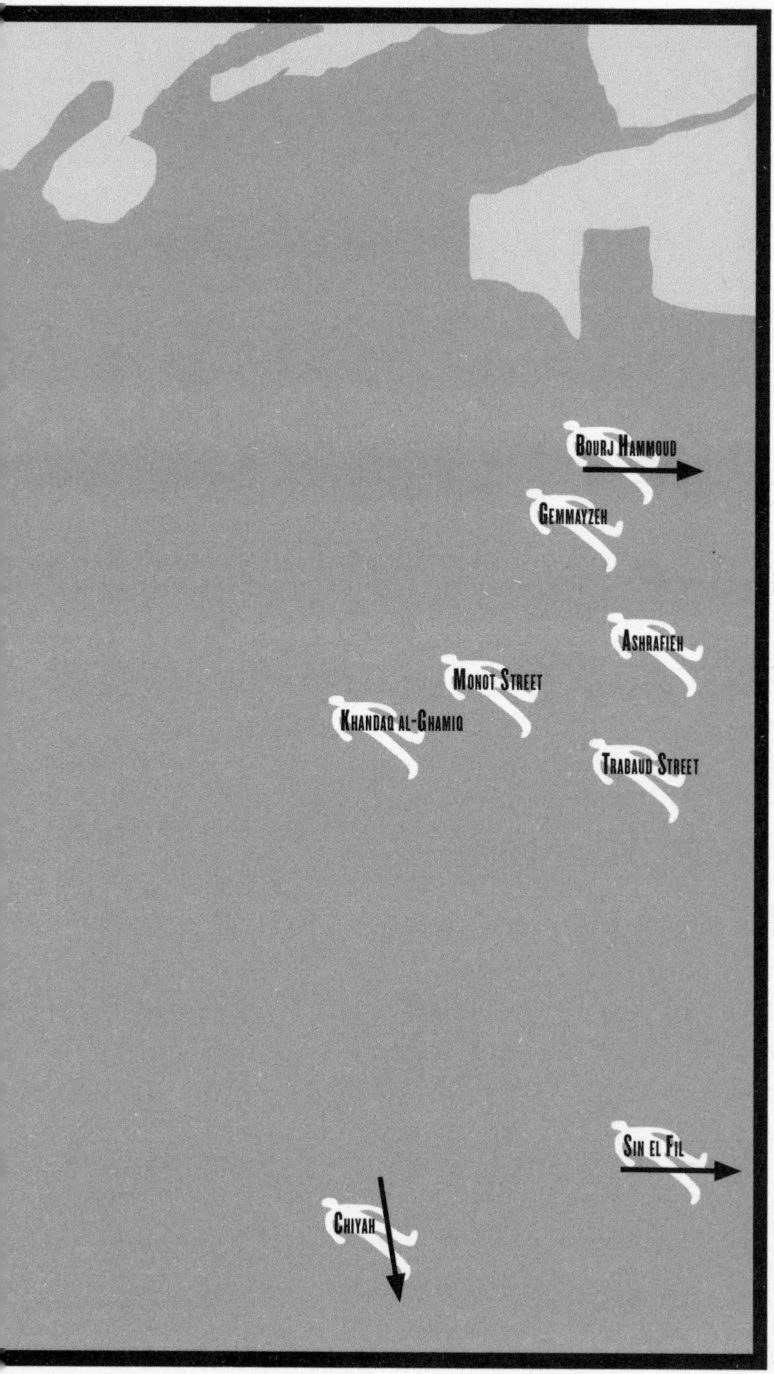
Bourj Hammoud
Gemmayzeh
Ashrafieh
Monot Street
Khandaq al-Ghamiq
Trabaud Street
Sin el Fil
Chiyah

TABLE OF CONTENTS

PART III: WAITING FOR YESTERDAY

Dedicated to the memory of Bachir Hilal (1947–2015)

INTRODUCTION
VIOLENCE OF LONELINESS, VIOLENCE OF MAYHEM

Beirut is a city of contradiction and paradox. It is an urban and rural city, one of violence and forgiveness, memory and forgetfulness. Beirut is a city of war and peace. This story collection is a part of a vibrant, living recovery of Beirut. *Beirut Noir* recovers the city once again through writing, through the literary visions of its authors.

Assembling this collection was an ambitious experiment for me; editing it was fascinating and full of challenges. It is by no means easy to bring together a book of fifteen short stories by writers with such different perspectives on Beirut. Fourteen Lebanese writers, and one Palestinian writer born and raised in Beirut, contributed to the book you are holding today. Taken together, their stories reflect the city's underworld and seedy realities. Each story is only one tiny piece of a larger mosaic; they all coalesce here to offer us a more complete picture of the city.

There are so many clichés we must confront when examining Beirut. It is difficult to write about it without describing it as a city that never sleeps, as the center of life, and also as a city that is the companion of death. These two descriptions are inextricably linked, though they may seem contradictory. Those of us who live here and know the city well recognize these powerful characterizations that we hold in our collective imagination. Elsewhere, I once described Beirut as "the city that dances on its wounds."

We know that Lebanon is a country with a long and rich history of diverse cultures and religious traditions, as well as a wealth of languages. Every school in Lebanon teaches three languages—

Arabic, English, and French; I kept this trilingual background in mind when choosing the stories for this collection. Michelle Hartman, who has previously translated two of my novels, meticulously translated these stories from both Arabic and French into English; there are also three stories originally written in English.

From within this collection of stories, a general attitude toward Beirut emerges: the city is viewed from a position of critique, doubt, disappointment, and despair. The stories reveal a vast maze of a city that can't be found in tourist brochures or nostalgic depictions that are completely out of touch with reality. Perhaps this goes without saying in a collection of stories titled *Beirut Noir*. But the "noir" label here should be viewed from multiple angles, as it takes on many different forms in the stories. No doubt this is because it overlaps with the distinct moments that Beirut has lived through.

All of the stories are somehow framed by the Lebanese civil war, which lasted from approximately 1974 until 1990. The war here serves as a boundary between the memories of the authors and the memories of their characters. Indeed, whether the stories include time frames during, before, or after the war, all of them invoke this period somehow—even if only to recall other times of which nothing remains.

Some of the stories explore the memory of people wounded by Beirut during the war, who have not yet healed. These works include Mohamad Abi Samra's "Without a Trace," Leila Eid's "Beirut Apples," Marie Tawk's "Sails on the Sidewalk," Abbas Beydoun's "The Death of Adil Uliyyan," Bachir Hilal's "Rupture," and Hala Kawtharani's "The Thread of Life." Other stories are told by new and fresh voices born amidst the violence of this war. These brim with playfulness within their dark visions, such as Hyam Yared's "Eternity and the Hourglass," Najwa Barakat's "Under the Tree of Melancholy," and "Dirty Teeth" by a young author writing under the name of The Amazin' Sardine. Some suggest the complexities of class issues in a society marked by sectarianism, like Tarek Abi

Samra's "The Bastard" or Mazen Maarouf's "The Boxes."

While the tales might be playful, the characters' lives can be unstable, and they often have no confidence whatsoever in the future. Despite this, we laugh darkly while reading Bana Beydoun's "Pizza Delivery"—its melancholia takes us right to the limit of what we can find humorous. This is also true of Rawi Hage's "Bird Nation," as well as the stories by Hyam Yared and Bachir Hilal. Beirut is like that. So much gloom and wasted lives; we weep even as we laugh. In Beirut, chaos is a way of life.

This is not all there is to Beirut though. The city is still crowded and on the move; indeed, it can be boisterous at night. But these crowds and mayhem are not the same as those during the day. Beirut nights are different. It's as if in the absence of day, the city is freed from its severity. Nighttime somehow softens its harshness and anxiety; the city can be seen in its lights reflecting off the sea, its expansive sweep under the nearby mountains, and its truly beautiful vistas. The contributions from Bana Beydoun and Mazen Zahreddine offer portraits of the city at night, through the lives of young people born after the war. This is a Beirut where the violence of loneliness and the violence of mayhem come together.

Chaos reigns here—it is the source not only of violence but also the diversity and dynamism of every aspect of the city. Most stories in the collection confirm this—but especially those by Rawi Hage, Zena el Khalil, and Alawiya Sobh.

And yet time is precious in Beirut. Hyam Yared's story, centered around an hourglass, is a reflection of the fear people have of time flowing through our fingers and being lost, just as Lebanese people lost fifteen years of their lives during the civil war.

Through the eyes of the dead child who is the eponymous narrator of el Khalil's "Maya Rose," we see a panoramic scene of Beirut's coastline from above the Corniche by the lighthouse and beyond. This story, like the entirety of *Beirut Noir*, allows us to glimpse beautiful things in Beirut, even as it wakes and sleeps in violence and disorder.

Beirut lives through time, always oscillating between war and peace; these moments make *Beirut Noir*'s scenery as naked as the edge of a knife.

Iman Humaydan
Beirut, Lebanon
September 2015

PART I

WHEN TIME DOES NOT EXIST

THE BASTARD

BY TAREK ABI SAMRA

Chiyah

1.

They were born on the same night, of the same father but different mothers.

That day, unusual disorder in the hospital meant that they were confused with one another. When their progenitor grumpily leaned over to examine this pair of twisted-up, crying red faces, he hesitated for a moment—they definitely resembled him, but not their mothers. Then, deciding at random, he designated which was to be the bastard with one disdainful gesture of his hand.

One was the offspring of his wife, a sickly woman who died in childbirth. The other was the maid's, a beautiful young peasant woman who was vigorously healthy. Thanks to his many ties to the ministry, he was able to get both children recognized as legitimate. Nonetheless, at home each one forever occupied the position assigned to him by that paternal gesture.

2.

As children, they liked each other well enough and often played together, but at the same time they were jealous of one another for completely opposite reasons.

From the most tender of ages, the so-called bastard was aware of the total dishonor of his status; his mother's smiling eyes hardly compensated for the contemptuous pity, mixed with slight disgust, that he inspired with every look from a friend or stranger. He experienced this contemptuous pity viscerally: he experienced it like a cramping in his abdomen; he experienced it like an urgent need to vomit.

As for the supposedly legitimate son, you could have attributed his small stature to the fact that he was completely flattened by his father's tyranny. Though his father was uneducated, the boy was destined to become a doctor—a great doctor. And according to a magnanimous decree, he was always meant not just to be near the top of his class, but among the top five. Fear and determination offset his mediocre intelligence and he almost always succeeded at keeping himself in the third or fourth position, even at the cost of the most beastly indignities.

3.

Though he was rich, the father resided in the bustling neighborhood of Chiyah, on Assaad al-Assaad Street, where he owned a building and lived in an apartment on its top floor. Adjacent to the building, a low, little house of two excessively narrow rooms—built in a rush a few months before he was born—served as the lodgings for the bastard and his mother. The bastard never entered his half-brother's bedroom. In fact, the whole apartment was off-limits to him, their father being unable to stand anything that might unite the two children. It was the same for the legitimate son: crossing the low, little house's threshold was absolutely forbidden. The possibility of any exchange between this child and his other potential mother—the maid who had been his mistress—terrified the father. Nonetheless, even the laws of the universe were unable to stop them from killing time together. And they often played together in the mud behind the low, little house.

There was a small sandy enclosure just behind the bastard's house where they met daily—at dawn during vacations, in the afternoon on school days. The father often sent the building's doorman to bring the legitimate son home, dragging him by the ear.

Usually, they filled buckets with water that they mixed with earth to make mud projectiles to throw at each other. You would have said that each one was relieved of his shame by splattering his half-brother's face with mud. In fact, each aspired to the other's misfortune: the scorned one coveted respect; the slave, his freedom. One evening, when they were twelve years old and amusing themselves by smearing mud beside their house, the so-called bastard said proudly to the supposedly legitimate son, "You don't have to worry about anything, your life is so easy! Your future is secure, you have money and a father."

Wounded, his brother didn't know how to respond at first and started to cry. Finally, he stammered through his tears, "But at least you're allowed to play when you want. And you also have a mother."

4.

The bastard enjoyed an unprecedented popularity at his school . . . their school. His ugliness—unlike his brother's—didn't at all prevent him from being popular among the female students: whenever he'd appear, it was as though their clitorises transformed into claws and tore viciously into their flesh. By the time he graduated with his baccalaureate he'd already deflowered a dozen—the other was still even less than a virgin.

The one, according to plan, enrolled in medical school. The other, leaving the low, little house a few months before his mother's death, was hired as a waiter and began studying law. They didn't see each other for three years.

5.

The Communist epidemic was palpable in the air; from one day to the next, it intoxicated a significant number of student brains.

Every evening, the local bar transformed into a forum for heated political debates. One particular Friday, the controversies grew so ferocious that people came to blows with fists, glasses, bottles, and chairs. After the owner was finally able to evict this thunderous crowd, drunk on alcohol and ideas, two young men recognized one another outside in the dark. They each walked alone, on opposite sides of the wide street, their footsteps drawing parallel paths. It was dark, but a few weak moonbeams surreptitiously pierced through the heavy cloud, and then two giant, thin, infinitely stretched-out shadows were drawn at a diagonal behind each of their backs. They pretended not to notice each other but from time to time shot over quick, furtive glances.

This farce had already lasted a good while when the bastard had an idea that made him stop cold. So he crossed the street. Seeing him approach, the other one, paralyzed, nervously chewed on his lower lip and stared: unspeakable hopes were aroused in his heart that left him nonetheless vaguely sensing a tragic outcome. When they were face to face, the bastard—putting on a somewhat ironic grimace—exclaimed with affected surprise: "But someone might say that this is my brother!"

"Or rather your half-brother," the other one immediately corrected him. Still, he found it impossible to pull himself away physically, but believed instead that the extreme precision of his comment could at least establish a certain distance in their kinship.

"Whatever," said the bastard, calm and condescending, instinctively seizing upon the futility of his brother's gesture. Using his old favorite childhood way of teasing, which despite its terseness reminded the other one of the full extent of his subjugation, he said, "So then, *doctor*, sir, how are you today?" After a moment of mutual discomfort, he sharply added, "Let's walk a little," to put an end to the brief silence.

The sun had already risen and the two brothers were still walking. They had spoken feverishly all night long. After they separated, each one, desperately trying to fall asleep in his own bed, tried in vain to repress some bits of this long nocturnal conversation.

In his head, the legitimate son mostly replayed their discussion about communism, which fascinated him to no end. The subject had somewhat concerned him during this past year, but until now he had been content to simply pay it modest attention without getting carried away by the general frenzy which had gradually gained ground inside the universities. Yet just a few hours had been enough for his brother's eloquence to, quite simply, ignite him. He was taken by a boundless admiration for the People, and henceforth considered himself a devoted supporter of the cause. For the first time in his life, this freedom that he so coveted but rarely knew became incarnate; it took form, nearly flesh and bone. He was possessed by unprecedented pleasure, but soon he found himself tumbling into a terror that grabbed him by the neck and strangled him.

Ideas from the same conversation, but utterly different in content, scuttled through the bastard's mind while he lay in bed, staring at the ceiling. The enthusiasm he knew so well how to inject into his brother had clearly shown him the true extent of his capabilities. In truth, possessing a superior mind as well as a highly independent and excessively reckless character, he never once missed out on exercising a certain influence over this submissive being. Meanwhile, his brother could offer no resistance to the absolute domination that the bastard knew he was now capable of: he would steal this son away from his father. Moving back into his old house was the first thing that he intended to do.

6.

The father had sold his building on Assaad al-Assaad Street two years before, and the new owner, with the intention of building a much bigger structure there, planned to demolish it at the same time as the low, little house that had once served as lodgings for the so-called bastard. But the outbreak of the civil war had caused him to postpone his project.

It was the very inevitability of its destruction that compelled the bastard to rent his old house three years after having left it, when his mother died and he started at university. He wanted to recall bits of his past, but didn't really know which ones.

Just like an old man whose still-recognizable features have been ravaged by the passing of time, when his feet first trod upon Assaad al-Assaad Street after these years of absence, it still seemed familiar to him. Yet at the same time it was so disfigured by the war that he felt a vague but intense pity toward everything there—the buildings riddled by machine guns, some of which had lost sections of their walls and even entire facades following bombardments, the asphalt cracked and full of holes, the smashed sidewalks that had almost disappeared, the burned-out cars, the bored, smoking militiamen weighed down by Kalashnikovs.

He found all of the old furniture of the low, little house well preserved but faded and smelling damp. He moved in right away, cleaned a little bit, but changed nothing, not even the furniture.

7.

Another meeting took place, others followed it, and then came a time when the two half-brothers could hardly do anything without one another. Nonetheless, a vague sense of apprehension stopped the legitimate son from visiting the bastard's house; he imagined a sort of curse hovering above Assaad al-Assaad Street.

And all this time, the bastard's influence over his brother, which he received as sincere affection, was increasing: he gave him lessons in Marxism-Leninism, pushed him to join the Communist Party, introduced him to his circle of friends—all of this without any of it coming to their father's attention.

Yet it was the issue of women that finally sealed the legitimate son's dependence once and for all. One day, walking quickly toward Assaad al-Assaad Street for the first time in years, he glanced anxiously at a little scrap of paper that he held in his clammy hand, on which he'd hastily scribbled a few notes the evening before. A certain favor he'd wanted to ask of the bastard had left him in a state of extreme anxiety for the past several weeks. Every time they met, while he was thinking about it, he'd hesitate, his ideas would become blurred, and he couldn't manage to say a single word. He tortured his brain searching for the precise words he wanted to use; then, when he finally found them, he recorded them immediately on paper. His memory—highly developed thanks to the arduous retention of barbarous medical vocabulary—preserved them as is, but now while walking, doubts started encroaching, giving him the feeling that he'd forgotten something. Every time he looked at the paper, however, his writing reflected the same text that his mind had been repeating relentlessly back to him.

Obsessed with these exhausting mental rehearsals, he didn't realize that he'd reached the street on which he'd spent his childhood and adolescence until the exact moment when he found himself right in front of his brother's abode. His anxiety about forgetting his memorized speech then gave way to that of remembering his past. And it was for this reason that until now he'd avoided coming to his brother's place—so as not to give in to the temptation to remember a horrible secret, or perhaps even to discover one. But ultimately he'd understood that he'd only be able to ask this favor that he so coveted if the two brothers could find themselves in a spot completely cut off from the rest of the world—not on the street or in a café or bar, their sole meeting places—so he'd resigned himself to visiting his old neighborhood.

He threw a quick glance around; the state of near-ruin of Assaad al-Assaad Street aroused no emotion in him. He rang the bell, entered the house, and when the actual moment occurred, his memory betrayed him. However, having realized what was happening long before, his brother said to him abruptly: "You want someone to fuck, right?"

Noticing that he was stunned, blushing all the way to his scalp, the brother continued with a soothing, protective smile: "Don't worry, we can arrange everything."

Then, in a wavering, barely audible voice—as though he wanted to hide away somewhere and never speak again—the legitimate son stammered, "You should . . . you should . . . you should . . . It would be better if you came with me to . . . to the brothel?"

The other one tried to get ahold of himself, but it was a bit too much to ask, this shy, startled virgin being so irresistibly comic. So he burst out with a loud, sardonic laugh. Then, somewhat calmer, he said, "A brothel . . . ? No, no, no, that's totally out of the question; you'll get a woman, a real woman, not a whore!"

Women were what the bastard especially enjoyed and what he despised above all. He picked them up everywhere: in streets and bars and at the university. There were more than a few in whom he inspired an intense repulsion, though his successes were by far more frequent: he mistreated them terribly; they suffered but took great pleasure in him. He had one who delivered notes to him at home from classes he never attended, but in which he always succeeded in getting the top mark; another who, every time they spent the night together, put his shoes and socks on in the morning; a third who he often made cry; a fourth who he insulted; a fifth who he beat up; and finally a sixth who he managed completely according to his will. He thus handed this one over to his brother.

A few days later, barely able to stand up on his own two legs but unable to sit still either, the legitimate son paced in his brother's house, tripping all over the furniture. He could hear nothing but the beat of his own heart. Big drops of sweat amassed on the edges of his glasses, trickling onto the lenses. He took them off to dry them with his shirtsleeve. He noticed his face in the little mirror nailed to the wall: he found himself uglier than ever. Sitting in bed, calmly smoking a cigarette, the bastard followed him with his eyes and shook his head in disdainful pity. "Calm down, it'll go fine," he repeated from time to time. Then they heard the doorbell.

It's her, the brother thought, horrified, and rushed to the bathroom.

Even in his hiding place, fuzzy sounds, footsteps, and muffled laughter reached him. He couldn't make sense of anything; he saw double, he had vertigo, he sat down on the ground. Food came up through his esophagus; he pushed it back with difficulty, swallowing saliva. He couldn't stop regurgitating his rebellious vomit, which filled his entire mouth a few times. Unable to resist anymore, he plunged his head into the toilet bowl and let it out. His brother the bastard, who'd had a weeklong bout of diarrhea, had forgotten to flush the toilet that day: a spray of half-digested stew with tomato sauce flew into the tranquil tide of runny, very mushy excrement, and splatters of shit hit him right in the face. He vomited again . . . Then someone knocked on the door, someone called him, but he didn't have the strength to respond.

After washing his face, he finally thought about leaving the bathroom but immediately remembered that outside, *she* was waiting to fuck him . . . How the hell would he get a hard-on? Surely she wouldn't be able to help but snicker at the sight of his flaccid penis. Better to run away . . . impossible . . . stay in the toilet . . . impossible . . . die . . . but how stupid . . . what then? And he could do nothing but prepare himself once again to leave. Like how a desperate man in a burning building throws himself out a window hoping to fly or be caught by the hand of God, he yanked the door open and ventured outside.

The memory of having lost his virginity in this low, little house on Assaad al-Assaad Street came back to haunt him in his old age—at this belated period in his life, sometimes it even seemed to him that he had been deflowered by his half-brother, the bastard.

This one procured some other women for him—not too many, but enough to shackle him.

8.

Though the legitimate son now fucked regularly, he wanted to fall in love. He couldn't, however, fall in love with one of his brother's offerings—those women seemed too soiled. He resolved therefore to find someone himself, and undertook some very discreet research in vain. It happened by chance that the first morning after the summer vacation, he noticed a new female student in his class. He thought for a moment about sitting with her, but the cascades of sweat that poured out of him at this idea helped him to quickly abandon this plan. For the entire first semester, he was content with simply observing her from afar. He finally dared to speak to her and, after saying hello, she responded with a hello back. Possessed by an amorous frenzy, he repeated the same move every morning, but at the end of a month and a half, he understood that he should try something else; so he managed to exchange first names with her, and that was all. In desperation, he confided his love to his brother; the bastard then knew what the origin of his own torment was.

Indeed, in recent months, the legitimate son had somewhat cooled toward him. Helpless, the bastard could only passively watch the gradual enfranchisement of his slave. He deigned to be much nicer to him, to praise him in front of their friends, to offer him more women, but the other one—so preoccupied by his secret— hardly noticed anything. To his great surprise, the bastard felt totally impotent and sometimes woke up in the middle of the night with terrible rages that he could only calm by banging his head against a wall. And why did it matter so much to him? This was the question that never ceased to torture him and for which he couldn't even find an initial response. Having tried everything, he resigned himself to it and fell into one of his usual deep melancholies, whose singular ridiculousness, so obvious to him in these circumstances, made it even more intolerable. He'd often thought of suicide before his brother finally came to find him, to confess his passion and ask his advice.

Keeping perfect control of himself and not showing any fragment of the anger that was devouring him internally, the bastard listened calmly right to the end. Then, after a brief moment of silence, he said to him in a way that he tried very hard to make sound as detached and nonchalant as possible, "Don't kid yourself; she's a bitch like the rest of them."

The other, outraged by these words, protested with a touching naïveté that she was as pure and chaste as one could be.

"Whether or not she's a virgin, I bet you I could fuck her in a couple of days!" the bastard cruelly threw out.

"No, no!" screamed the other before storming off, violently slamming the door behind him.

9.

The idea of fucking her then seized the bastard's entire being, to such an extent that putting it into practice became the central theme of his daydreams as well as his nighttime dreams. Was it simple vengeance or rather the hope of regaining his domination? He could hardly grant himself the opportunity to decide between these two alternatives, but, finding the idea still there one week later, he made a firm decision to put his plan into action. He first devoted himself to tedious and time-consuming speculation about how he might go about determining this girl's identity, something that seemed rather difficult, since his brother, with his excessively shy and discreet nature, was not at all the type to let his intimate inclinations show, even to an expert eye such as his. Base and cruel spying, a process he abhorred, would at the end of the day prove to be the only possible recourse.

So he found himself diligently lying in wait for any unusual movement on his brother's part—truly too infrequent to be of any use—peering through the windows of his classrooms, until he finally spotted his target. There was no doubt his brother had exquisite taste: she was an indescribable beauty. However, his hope for even the slightest connection with her would be no less than the incontrovertible proof of his total lack of experience in the world. He had to fuck her, to defile her: this would be the only remedy that would rescue his brother.

And one afternoon, putting on the seducer's face that suited him so well, he waited for her, leaning against the wall of a hallway that she usually crossed when leaving class. Spotting her from a distance, he pretended to be looking elsewhere, then, after she had overtaken him by several steps, he caught up with her in one leap and whispered quietly into her ear words that made the blood rush to her face and extracted an almost imperceptible smile from her lips. She spent that night with him, though she felt some reluctance about sleeping in this low, little house on Assaad al-Assad Street.

The next day, the bastard told his brother everything in minute detail. The legitimate son tried to punch him in the jaw but managed only to put himself in a hospital bed for two weeks.

10.

With a broken nose, a bloated face, and a small crack in his skull, he was in an extremely anxious state waiting for his father to arrive from the village. What would he tell him? How would he explain his relationship with his brother? There had never been an explicit prohibition on it, but many hints had already allowed him to guess that his father would find all dealings between him and the bastard repugnant. And indeed he was not mistaken: as soon as his father heard him say the name of his supposedly illegitimate son, he almost extended his son's hospital visit by a few weeks, but in the end managed to control himself.

A few clarifications are essential here: This old man in his seventies was a sort of leader of an ancient, powerful provincial family that still strictly observed certain tribal laws of its ancestors. Without dwelling too long on the details, suffice it to say that this family—made up of a number of branches—had for centuries subjugated all the other families in its village and lived according to a very strict code of honor. The changes wrought by this most recent era's radical social transformations had deprived the family of almost all of its privileges, but this only meant intensifying its commitment to the honor code, taking it to the point of fanaticism. Thus our patriarch compensated for the decrease in his external power with in-house tyranny; he literally had the power of life and death over the some two hundred members of his clan. It was not on his own initiative that the bastard had finally broken with his family; rather, he had been forced to do so by a decree from his father, whose authority he had seriously and continually damaged. This banishment—that many considered too magnanimous a punishment—had fixed him very well: his family despised him, and he detested them so intensely he hoped for no money, no help, nothing at all. However, there was a certain bitterness lodged in his throat, recalling past humiliations and reminding him that he still had accounts to settle. The fortuitous encounter with his brother leaving the bar was in this sense a marvelous occasion for him, which he couldn't help but fiercely hang on to with extended claws.

The old man thus refrained from breaking his big, knotted cane over the legitimate son's head and was content with simply throwing him extremely irate looks while nervously twiddling his fingers around his mustache, under which a terrible grin had frozen. The poor young man, lying in bed and suffocating with terror, searched in vain for a point on the wall to stare at in order to avoid his father's eyes. Finally, after lifting himself with difficulty off the armchair upon which he had been sitting and heading toward the door, the old man launched these words at him in a calm tone that nevertheless penetrated deep into the recesses of his soul and thwarted any retort in advance: "You will *never* see him again!"

11.

When he heard knocking at his door, the bastard immediately recognized his father's cane. Less surprised—he had been vaguely expecting it—than irritated, he roughly crushed his cigarette in the ashtray while lighting another and getting up to open the door; the next day, he was already abroad.

During this brief meeting, the old man proposed the following alternatives: either live in hell or leave the country for good with a certain sum of money. If no clarification followed the expression "live in hell," this was for the simple reason that there was no need for it: the bastard knew very well what his father was capable of.

12.

He liked Europe when he first settled there. But a few months later, a strange feeling started tormenting him. What at the beginning was merely a vague sense of some indefinable thing that he missed turned quickly into an unfounded rage. His bitterness deepened and he started drinking hard, with an unquenchable thirst. It was a frequently recurring dream—in which he saw himself sweating profusely under the shadow of his father's grin—that made him finally decide to once again tread upon the soil of his homeland, and then to rent his low, little house once more.

It took no time for the old man to learn of his son's return, though his warnings, delivered by messengers, had no effect. So he then took recourse in a far more efficient manner: a gang of five, armed with sticks, beat the bastard down. Some people living in the neighborhood found him near-dead in a dark corner on Assaad al-Assaad Street. His hospital stay was much longer than his brother's had been two years before. Handicapped for life, he left the hospital with a limp.

13.

It was months later.

After the old man left his legitimate son's room one afternoon, the latter, sitting all alone, found himself bewitched by the gun his father had placed on his bed. He stared at it with ardent, burning, voracious eyes—but from far away, very far away, as though in this way he were forestalling a dark temptation, which, if he approached even one step, would have been irresistible to him. And those terrible words seemed to still be ringing throughout his room, *Kill him, prove to me that I shouldn't regret my choice!*

After a while, he dared to take one step, a second, a third, and then another, and finally he found himself right next to his bed, his head slightly bent over the gun. He wanted to grab it but he merely mimed the gesture and started scrutinizing it again. His anxiety slightly quelled, his mind emptied of just about every thought, he felt himself gradually being devoured by numbing thoughts whose only focus was this weapon.

All of a sudden, the fact that his brother had been born on the same day he was—at almost the exact same time—seemed so strange that he was surprised that he'd never perceived it this way before. And then there was the question of the secret he had just learned about the illegitimate birth—that it had been attributed to the other one by the accident of an incidental gesture—which laid bare the contingent nature of his own fate, and through this even its absurdity. All of this caused a shiver of disgust and horror to convulse him as he thought about the 50 percent probability that it was he himself who was the bastard.

Contradictory ideas quickly passed through his head. As if to stop them, he grabbed the gun, shoved the barrel into his mouth, powerfully clamping it between his teeth and tasting it: unpleasant, cold, metallic. Somersaults of terror, mixed with a trace of pleasure, raced through his body each time he stroked the trigger. He finally made a decision and closed his eyes. But in the dark, small sparks behind his eyelids merged into one frame—first blurry, then little by little taking on more clarity. It was a face—perhaps his brother's, yes! Definitely his brother's face, sporting a majestic and disdainful attitude as always, with a broad ironic smile, proud and withering. Anger made him clamp down so hard on the barrel that he broke a tooth. He wanted to shoot, but as soon as he opened his eyes, the image faded away like a dream.

14.

The harassment of months of sleepless nights had led the bastard into a habit of hobbling around Assaad al-Assaad Street and the surrounding area an hour before dawn. Dirty roads accentuated the darkness of his gloomy ideas. However, his ruminations quickly took another path: he thought again about his father, their last meeting and the huge public insult he had committed against him, and the impossibility that the man would not take any action against him . . . But how would he take action, this father of his, he wondered while walking down his favorite road, the foulest one in the whole neighborhood. This long, thin, mud-filled alley sprawling out in front of him, in which only a tribe of rats elected to live, gave off an intense stench of sewer and decrepitude, strewn here and there with blackish puddles, torturously snaking through all kinds of garbage, rotten food surrounded by swarms of flies, dog and cat corpses devoured by vermin, charred car carcasses, disfigured, dismembered buildings, and other debris that had become unrecognizable with time. He cherished it, this alley. He nurtured a tender compassion for it; this all seemed to him a perfect reflection of his soul. He had never felt any kind of real sympathy before—for either a human or an animal; he couldn't remember any moment in his life in which he had.

The factors that prompted him to give his father a slap in the face in front of the whole family get-together last week remained obscure to him. He had gone there out of vengeance, an age-old desire to humiliate—at least, that's what he thought before the incident. But he felt something strange in seeing his father tumble to the ground under the powerful impact of the slap, it was something dark—soothing and dreadful at the same time—that when deciphered would eventually reveal his own fate to him. He only half succeeded in trying to revive this strange sensation. Looking to his right, he noticed a rotting dog, its belly gaping and *whence came forth dark battalions / of larvae that flowed out like a thick liquid.**

The thought, *He is going to have me killed,* passed through him like a sweet revelation. *He will never forgive, never forget. Even if he wants to, his position at the top of the family hierarchy will prevent him. He has to make an example of me—to preserve his honor, blood must flow.*

And thus he understood what had secretly motivated his slap.

He walked peacefully in this filthy alley when he felt something hard pressing on his spine and then climbing up his back, touching the nape of his neck, stopping right at the base of his skull. His fate had been sealed, he knew now; it was only the immediacy of this secretly-hoped-for outcome for which he was somewhat unprepared. Yet all his limbs trembled, he sweated like a pig, his terror was atrocious and indescribable. He had expected anything

---

*Baudelaire, *Les Fleurs du Mal,* "Une Charogne."

but this: instead of resigning himself to remaining impassive in the face of death as he had always delighted in imagining he would, he felt the warmth of urine flowing between his thighs. "Like dogs," he mumbled in a lucid moment, "we die just like dogs!"

In the depth of his desperation, a panting sound reached him, the sound of someone out of breath. He believed it was himself, that it was his own fear. But no, it was the other one. He turned sharply, but it took several seconds to recognize his brother. He seemed just as terrified as he, pale as a cadaver, barely managing to breathe, though strangely he wasn't shaking at all. In realizing that he was going to be felled by such a despicable and cowardly being, a savage rage possessed him. He wanted to pounce on his brother, bite his neck, rip out his veins, drink his blood and swim in it. It was a bit too late though. A bullet had already penetrated his skull.

Originally written in French.

MAYA ROSE

BY ZENA EL KHALIL

Ain el Mreisseh

I woke up unsure. I knew I felt something. Considerable. But wasn't very sure. As I squeezed my way out between my mama's legs, I knew it was already time to be somewhere else. Here in room 807 of the American University Hospital in Ain el Mreisseh, I began to let go of my life quite happily. The pounding heartbeat that connected me to my mama was slowly beginning to weaken, and everything was warm, oh so warm. I smiled and wrapped myself around our cord. I could hear the pushing and panting of my mama in the distance, and a drumming began in my head. Getting louder and louder. I wanted it like this, to go out with a bang. Here, within the pastel-green walls of the hospital where most Beirutis begin and end their lives. Cancer. War wounds. The flu. Silence. Silence is an illness that deeply affects my parents' generation. They are the ones who grew up with the bombs. They prefer alcohol to sobriety. And silence to reality. Who can blame them?

Nothing left to say. In silence, I would die. The quiet, the end. The birth of the universe was absolutely quiet, everything that came after was chaos, loud, the beginning of our death.

On the day I was born, the Great Wall fell. They say that I was born blue and without a heartbeat. My mother, Souraya, screamed in fear as the nurses tried everything to get me to breathe. They hit my back. Spanked my bottom. Flipped me up and down. Swayed me back and forth. I would say nothing. I would not cry, I would not breathe. I could see all of this as my soul rose away to begin its voyage into another life. A short overweight nurse with jet-black hair, in a sudden act of desperation, flew back against the radio that my mother had finely tuned to 96.2 FM, Radio Liban. My father, Rida, a local deejay, had planned to spin records for my birth. He would connect to my mother through song. He had chosen a mix of Al Green, Led Zeppelin, and Ziad Rahbani. Al, he believed, would help ease my way down my mother's birth canal, filling my heart with love and faith. Zeppelin would help me burst through her feminine folds and prepare me for life, giving me the motivation and courage to find beauty in a galaxy of pain. Ziad would be there as I took my first breath to help me accept all that was wrong and understand all that needed to be changed. Ziad would also provide me with the sense of humor and irony to laugh in the face of death, something we love to do here in Beirut. Death. Death, it seemed, is what I was destined for. I came out blue and neither Al nor Jimmy Page could help me. And Ziad . . . Ziad will be our last man standing in Beirut. He will survive all the wars, the civil wars, ideological wars, family wars . . . Ziad, even on the day the world ends, will still be here, cigarette hanging off his chapped lips, whiskey in hand, with something significant to say. As I twisted myself tighter around our cord, the final connection between me and my mama began to fade and Ziad's words were the last thing I ever heard. I died blue, with a smile on my face. And then I began to float up . . .

"*Ismaa', Ismaa' ya Rida . . .*"

My father, Rida, so self-absorbed in his ideas, failed to acknowledge that I might be born a woman. And that it could only be a woman's voice that would convince me to embrace this new lifetime. The nurse with jet-black hair—unable to control her tears, fears, anxiety, and bloated stomach of this morning's fermented yogurt breakfast—stumbled back and brushed against the small radio just as my father's voice was desperately announcing the next song. I could barely make out her name tag as I floated higher and higher. *Hello, my name is Rima*'s round and shapely ass hit the radio dial, disrupting the channel. My parents had spent weeks brainstorming about the music that would welcome me into this new world. Being the romantics that they are, they asked the doctor not to inform them of my gender. My aunt, an older woman who never married, was sure I was a boy. She claimed that boys made their mamas crave salt, while girls were sweet. Souraya only ate lemons during her pregnancy. She sprinkled them with salt and cumin. She put them in her water. Ate them with mangos. She preserved them in olive oil. Put them in her tea and in her lentil soup. Sour. Sour is what she craved. My mama had asked my father to play Ella, Nina, Patti, and Alanis. She believed they were all women of virtue who would bring me into a world with strength and courage. She was convinced that Patti Smith was the reincarnation of Asmahan, and Alanis was Oum Khalthoum. Therefore they bridged East and West, providing me with the best of both worlds.

I see them crying now and I just want to hold them and tell them everything is going to be all right. That they will have another chance, maybe. My mother, alone. My father, hunched over his vinyl. Who's going to tell him? He looks so small now. I want to hold him.

I leave the hospital and I fly over Ain el Mreisseh. I can see the Mediterranean Sea from here. It's absolutely blue and beautiful. I decide to take the big concrete steps that connect John Kennedy Street down to the sea. Recently, the steps have transformed into a graffiti haven. In the last few years, the youth of Beirut have taken to the walls for self-expression; everything from political slogans to gay rights paint the streets of this part of town. *Haifa for President! Freedom! Lesbians United!* On the left side of the stairs is the very end of the American University of Beirut campus, flanked by aging yellow bricks. On the right lays an abandoned plot of land ravaged by stray cats and out-of-control electricity wires, shrubs, and ivy. From here I can also see the hotel district, specifically the Holiday Inn. During the civil war, the militias fought to take control of these hotels because they were the tallest buildings in Beirut at the time. The hotels were strategic and from their rooftops anything and everyone could be shot down or thrown over. The Holiday Inn, towering above the city, is the only hotel still standing, and it's completely riddled with bullet holes. Large chunks of the facade were blown off by rocket-propelled grenades, tanks, and mortars. Completely hollowed out and with perfectly gridded balconies, this menacing piece of architecture is a tribute to the past, horribly scarred by artillery war wounds. A little to the right is the Murr Tower, which is even taller than the Holiday Inn. The Murr Tower was never finished and its dark and ominous skeletal structure rises above all of central Beirut like a ghostly sentinel. Neither building has been knocked down because, it is said, they are just too large and too difficult to remove. It would cost millions and no one is prepared for that sort of commitment. It makes me happy to see them among all the new glass-and-steel buildings. Physical proof of the atrocities we once committed. To me, they are beautiful memorials. We must never forget what we did to each other. They say that the world began in Beirut. They also say that the world will end in Beirut.

I pause for a minute and then glide down the concrete steps and run into Naila, struggling up. I assume she's on her way to see Souraya. Naila, now in her early forties, went through a divorce about ten years ago. Her husband couldn't stand being married to her and sent her packing after less than a year. She's still in love with him and has never been able to move on. To help pass the time, she regimentally paints her fingernails at Salon Sonia just down the street. Today she painted a rainbow—a different color for each nail; it's really "in" these days. Sometimes Sonia asks to experiment with glitter on top of color. On those days, Naila feels special, thinking she could be helping to advance fashion trends in Lebanon. Maybe one day her nails could appear in an ad or on the cover of a glamorous Beiruti society magazine. If only they weren't already so aged. She recently saw a billboard advertising a bank loan specifically for plastic surgery. Maybe she should finally get that nose job. Maybe, with the perfect nose, people would acknowledge her perfect nails. Maybe her ex would even consider taking her back. There is not a day that goes by without her thinking of him.

I linger for a moment and then dive into her. There is so much life here for someone who has suffered so much. True, she is lazy; loves to sleep in and hates cooking, but she is capable of so much love. I wrap myself around her heart and squeeze . . . sending signals rushing through her body. I want to tell her everything will be all right, but I know it won't. She is not going to find love again and her ankles will continue to swell. In a few years, she won't even be able to climb these stairs anymore. I squeeze tighter and she quickly sits down on a step, thinking she's having a heart attack. When I release, it sends her whole body shaking and she has the most incredible orgasm of her life. Right there on the steps, she hugs herself tight and screams in joy and fear. She will never experience anything like this again. And she will never be able to share this story with anyone. But she will always know how special she is and she will never give up on love. Until her ankles fail her, she will continue to walk up and down these stairs hoping for a replay of this afternoon.

I let go and fly up into the purple jacaranda tree above her, continuing my journey toward Graham Street. Beirut is most beautiful when the jacarandas are in bloom. For a moment I reflect on how these trees also exist in Havana and Islamabad, and it's beautiful to think about how we are all connected. Humans need passports to travel, but trees only need seeds. I leave Naila straddled on the stairs, smiling and sweating profusely. Naila is Rida's sister. It's just the two of them left now. Souraya will soon follow me in a horrible accident. On the day that our Speaker of the House of Parliament will be assassinated, Souraya will be walking by Uncle Deek Café along the Corniche at exactly 3:15 p.m. when explosives, the equivalent of two thousand kilograms of TNT, will detonate. They will not be able to find her body, as it will completely disintegrate. They will never know that she was pregnant again. What they will find, however, is her left shoe. The one with the pink insole. In Beirut, people blow people up like it's something casual.

I realize that I'm not ready to leave. I like it here . . . No, I love it. I want to stay, but I know I'm not supposed to be here now. The Great Wall has fallen and I'm supposed to be there soon. But I want to stay—in Beirut. They say that in Beirut, you live like there's no tomorrow. Every day is so intense. So extreme. Here, people work, argue, drive, dance, drink, and even make love as if it were their last day on earth. When you're constantly courting death, you learn how to appreciate life. You learn how to improvise dinners over candlelight because the electricity has just been cut again. You grow gardenias and jasmine to cover up bullet holes on your buildings. You become naturally creative because absolutely nothing is certain and no day is ever like the previous one.

I am halfway down Graham Street and I stop to watch the fishermen as they come into port. As they unload their small wooden boats with the night's catch of sardines and Sultan Ibrahim red snapper, I marvel on how this tiny port survived both the civil war as well as the monstrous rebuilding process. Prostitutes, fishermen, brand-new skyscrapers, and mimosa trees have all found a way to coexist here in Ain el Mreisseh. But there are also the Druze, a secretive monotheistic religious community who believe in reincarnation. Within the Druze faith, proselytism is not allowed and the Druze only marry other Druze. No one can join, no one can leave. This tight-knit community has held strong for centuries, withstanding occupations, wars, and even tsunamis. Rida and Naila were born Druze. Their family, the Assefs, are one of the oldest families in Ain el Mreisseh, along with the Oud, Ghawi, Sleit, Raouda, Hisshi, and Deek families. They say that the Druze moved to this part of Lebanon a century ago when the pious Sitt Mreisseh lived here. They surrounded her to protect her teachings and wisdom. When she died, they built her a shrine, which still survives today. *Ain el Mreisseh* literally means "the water spring of Mreisseh."

As a Muslim, Souraya was never fully accepted into Rida's family. The Assefs were practically one step away from disowning him, but upon the news that Souraya was pregnant, his uncles became a little more lenient. What will they think now? Naila will probably have to break the news to them. I turn around and see that she's still sitting on the steps. Her head rests on her arms, which are wound around her knees. It looks like she might be crying. The Druze claim their faith to be more than tens of thousands of years old. Recent DNA testing has found that Druze villages contain a striking range of high-frequency and high-diversity X haplogroup, a human mitochondrial DNA (mtDNA). The X haplogroup was prevalent in the genetic makeup of people living thirty thousand years ago. I want to leave this place now. Tradition is heavy here and it is because of tradition that Naila will never marry again. She will never meet her Druze prince and she will never have the strength to do what her brother did. I wonder if my death will be blamed on Souraya and Rida's unblessed union. I want to leave now. I really do.

I soar toward the east side of Ain el Mreisseh, to the hotels, bars, and bordellos. Just below the hotels is the infamous Zeitouni Street, now renamed Phoenicia Street, lined with nightclubs. Le Royale, Rock Inn, and Club 70 were all hot spots back in the sixties and seventies, but during the civil war they deteriorated into whorehouses. In Lebanon, prostitution is technically illegal, so pimps have come up with many creative ideas to profit from sex workers. The way it happens is by tricking the system: The prostitutes, mainly from Syria and Eastern Europe, enter the country with entertainment visas. They come in as "artists" or "dancers." They dance in "super nightclubs" like the Excellence here on this street, or the Excalibur or Cobra in Mameltain, just outside Beirut. Once inside, you buy yourself a bottle of whiskey or champagne that will cost around a hundred dollars. A girl will approach you and if you like her, you buy her a bottle too, another hundred dollars. You can spend the whole night talking with her and if she really likes you, she may allow you to kiss her and fool around a little. By five a.m. you have to exit the club. If the girl agrees to see you again, you can pick her up the next day around one p.m. and can spend the entire day with her in your apartment or a hotel. Since you don't go home with them the same night, the practice of "prostitution" is averted. Instead, because technically it's the next day, you're actually on a date. A paid date for around another hundred dollars.

I am in the East now, and I already feel lighter when a thought comes to mind: I want to find Club 70, where Rida and Souraya first met in the nineties during a brief period of postwar euphoria. I pause just before the Holiday Inn and a shiver passes through my body. So many people died here. I run my fingers across the facade of the twenty-second floor. There are still bloodstains inside this void of a structure. There is still graffiti on the walls, militia insignias and slogans. I smell burned flesh. I see bullet casings. Broken glass strewn across the floor. Stains. Excrement. Hair. I look down below and people are walking and driving, oblivious to the mess up here. It is strange to think that every day we look up at these buildings but never realize what remains inside. They are sleeping giants, and beasts lay stagnant in their bellies. I want to go down now. I see Phoenicia Street below. There it is, Club 70, just opposite Wash Me Car Wash. I perch on top of a small replica of a Fiat 500 that hangs just above the car wash entrance. Today Club 70 only attracts men, especially tourists, looking to get laid. But in the seventies, it was the "it" place. It wasn't as big as Cave de Roi or Le Grenier next door, where celebrities like Brigitte Bardot came from all around the world to party. Club 70 attracted a younger crowd who were discovering disco, bell-bottoms, hair spray, and polyester. During the civil war, Ain el Mreisseh became the dividing point between East and West Beirut and it was here that militias and prostitutes set up shop and began to thrive. After the civil war, Club 70 temporarily shut down, then reopened in the midnineties, hoping to bring back their golden era. It lasted a few years before falling back into old habits. It was during this short revival that Rida and Souraya met.

You would not believe me if I told you it was love at first sight. Rida was deejaying that night, and from the moment Souraya walked in through the door he knew they were going to spend the rest of their lives together. In the spirit of the glorious past of Club 70, Souraya wore a silver dress that glittered like a disco ball. Everywhere she turned, she was surrounded by light. Rida's friend Saa'deddine el Abyad (meaning "the white one") also took notice of her and immediately moved in for a dance. Saa'deddine was a bit of a lowlife who was wanted for numerous infractions of the law. He was called *el Abyad* because he always wore white linen and white snakeskin shoes, though his heart was far from it.

Rida knew that he had to move in quickly. He picked up his new Cypress Hill album and put on "Insane in the Brain." The crowd roared, started jumping up and down and headbanging. Souraya was thrown to the side and it was there and then that Rida reached his arm out to her and they locked eyes for the first time. As Souraya stood up, she hoped that Rida would not let her go. She hoped, in fact, that he would *never* let her go. He didn't. He pulled her up to his deejay stand and, for the rest of the night, they spun records together. By four a.m. they were completely in love with each other and it was so obvious that even Saa'deddine accepted it. There they were, the three of them throwing back shot after shot of vodka, lemon juice, and Tabasco.

Anything seemed possible that night. Hope. Freedom. Rebirth. Immortality. A great warmth fills my heart. It's so hard to accept how we can be so generous, but also so violent with each other. Club 70 is a microcosmic representation of this city. These walls have seen everything from love to blood. During lulls in the war or periods of relative calm, dancing is what has always brought people together here. With music, differences and religions are forgotten. Bodies brush past bodies and become flesh without cruel histories. And now I too believe that anything is possible.

Today the Great Wall fell and I'm late. I should already be there by now. Today, a new era begins in this part of the world. Today, the Great Wall that the Israelis built in the heart of the Holy Land fell. No one knows how and why. The Apartheid Wall separating the West Bank and Gaza from Israel, seven hundred kilometers in length and eight meters in height, just disappeared. The largest concrete protest banner in the world, covered in layers of writing and graffiti, no longer exists. There is nothing left to protest about. The fences are gone too. So are the roadblocks, checkpoints, and security towers. The news is only just beginning to spread. Some people are panicking, others are rejoicing. Most are calling it an intervention from God, some an alien invasion. Souraya never had a chance to meet me because I am on my way to Mount Carmel. I am to be part of the new generation of Palestinians and Israelis who will find each other and make peace once and for all. I feel so content to feel so needed.

As I climb up into the sky, I begin to summon the dead all around me. The dead who never received proper funerals during the wars. Whose bodies were left to rot. Whose souls were doomed to roam streets, confused, angry, and bitter. I call upon those in the mass graves here as well as in Syria and Iraq. I am building my army of forgotten innocence. It is our time now. It is time for a new way of life. It will not come easily, but it will happen. No more assassinations. No more bombs. No more borders. Resources will be plenty. Land will be shared.

I hover on the blue metal railings of the Corniche, facing the sea one last time. Souraya is absolutely devastated and Rida has now heard the news. He's rushing to her through impossible Beiruti traffic, honking his horn incessantly. Traffic that is not moving. He leaves his car in the middle of Hamra Street and starts to run, weaving his way through narrow roads lined with frail mimosa trees. They will be okay. They will get better. For a while, at least. Until the shit hits the fan again. But that is life, I guess. At least life in Lebanon. One bomb after the other. Life bombs. Love bombs. And bomb bombs. But we are resilient. Because we want to believe in second chances. And it may have very well just arrived.

I turn around and way goodbye to Ain el Mreisseh and the generations of my family who lived there. I take a moment, and from nowhere I hear Rida's voice. *"If I ever walked into a building and didn't know which way to turn, I would always go left. If I were lost in a forest and found myself at a crossroad I'd go left. Left. Left is always the answer. Left is always a good choice."*

Left seems like a good idea now. I stretch my arms out and hug the Corniche. I turn left and make my way south along the coast of the spectacular Mediterranean. Today, borders all around the world will cease to exist. My new army is guided by love. And nothing can stop love. So nothing can stop me. I can almost see Jerusalem from here.

Originally written in English.

PIZZA DELIVERY

BY BANA BEYDOUN

Manara

"Is that even possible? That a person's arm would remain stretched out, reaching up toward the sky after death . . . Or am I making that up?" she asked her friend Mark, the doctor.

He said that medically it's impossible, but added that there's always a chance that things deviate from their scientifically expected path. But he also added that it's so rare as to be quasi-hypothetical, and he couldn't take it any more seriously than the possibility of being struck by lightning as you're crossing the street. What was the name of that book that she kept borrowing from the school library, *Strange and Wonderful Things from Around the World* . . . or something like that? In one of the volumes there was a picture of a person who was burned, or "turned to charcoal," as the book put it, immediately after being struck by lightning while sitting on the balcony of his house. Reading about this left her completely lost in thought for quite a while. She wasn't able to say exactly if this was believable or not, and this doubt threw her into a state of intense disarray, for it had been very important for her—especially at that age—that there be clear and precise answers to everything.

Perhaps was a difficult word for her, even a painful one, and remains so today. *Perhaps* means that anything, or its opposite, might happen. For her, *perhaps* was like a big zero that might explode in her face at any moment, like a giant egg that might contain an enormous, savage dinosaur—or that might simply be empty. She couldn't contemplate which possibility was worse. Ultimately, even proven scientific facts were unbelievable at times. She remembered when her math teacher told her that if a minus sign precedes a negative number, it makes it into a positive number. She never believed this. How could two negatives produce a positive? When she tried to ask the teacher about it that day, she said, "Because that's how it is." In the end, she was grudgingly forced to accept this ridiculous fact, if only in order not to flunk. But after this, she went back to the equation every time she wasn't able to find a convincing reason to explain her own stupidity. For example, this equation might be the perfect explanation for her love for Khalid, even though he'd brought her nothing but trouble—no doubt all of his negatives must have engendered something positive in her heart.

Coming back to the question preoccupying her: Is it possible that the little girl at the Qana massacre died with her arm stretched out to the sky—as she imagined she'd seen it on television? What was she was pointing to . . . ? To something that caught her attention in the sky, perhaps the very same airplane that dropped the bomb on her? Or is this detail her own imagination's strange addition to the true scene of the massacre? Once she'd read that sometimes your imagination can recreate reality according to your own image of it. For example, if we see a child at a distance, most of the time we presume he's smiling at us, even if we can't really distinguish his facial features. But that's only because in our imaginations we see children as always smiling and, of course, always alive.

Maya startled awake from her inner monologue to a pair of black eyes staring at her and she screamed in fear, jumping back. The young man with the black eyes didn't move but looked at her with clear discomfort for a short time, then turned and walked on. It took her a moment to get herself together and continue on her stoll. It wasn't the first time this had happened to her; she was used to daydreaming and getting lost in her thoughts while walking. Sometimes people passing by would inadvertently bump into her and she'd jump with fright. It would then take her some time to recover, as if she needed to plant herself again in the geographic space where she was.

She continued on her way, daydreaming and pondering the mechanics of daydreaming itself—how the body can continue moving on its own as if completely detached from its owner. In bars, she would sometimes be jolted from a waking dream by some man sitting across the table smiling at her, thinking that she was looking at him. She was definitely better at seduction while daydreaming than when awake. This thought amused her, and she smiled and bent down to pick one of the purple flowers growing around the sidewalk next to Sanayeh Park, which she always walked alongside on her way to Abu Wadih's bar in Hamra, where she'd gotten used to spending her evenings recently.

The purple flowers seemed dark gray that evening in the shadow of darkness that covered Beirut after Israeli jets, as usual, had bombed the Électricité du Liban power plant. She remembered that time, during the last Israeli attack on Lebanon before this one, when she was forced to crouch alone in the darkness for the whole night. At the time, she was only fourteen years old and couldn't close her eyes until morning came, until she could see all of her body parts and be sure that they were all there . . . There in the dark she gradually lost all feeling in her extremities. Every so often, she patted herself to be sure that everything was in its usual place, but with only her two hands it was impossible to touch every part of her body. Even when she curled up into a ball there was always some extremity escaping from her to roam around in the darkness and slowly transform into a strange shape. Her hand suddenly became a snail, another time it stretched out like a ruler, then floated down like soft cotton. It wasn't just the sounds of bombs continuing all night long that made her anxious, but the thought of death while still imprisoned in the body of darkness, before the light could come to separate their two bodies, her body and the body of darkness. Light had always been her best friend, ever since childhood. Silent and warm, for some reason she always felt it loved her, still loves her, and that it alone could see what lives in her. She set the purple flower free, like always, and carried on walking; she didn't know why it was so difficult for her to hold on to things.

Had she forgotten about the flower in her hand, she knew it would slowly be strangled there, gnawing at her extremities, squeezed and crushed until it completely lost its color. She'd do this unintentionally, preoccupied by some idea in her head, then suddenly realize what she'd done and get sad like a small child. This situation wasn't limited to flowers but to almost everything, no matter if it was trivial or important. After this digression, she remembered the ring that Khalid had given her before his trip. She examined her finger, looking for the ring but not finding it there. She must have forgotten it at home on the sink again, though she didn't really have to keep taking it off since it was gold, and soap and water wouldn't damage it, as her girlfriend had informed her. She kept doing it, however, because she kept imagining that there was something stuck to it. She didn't want this ring to get lost—like the other gifts people had given her over the years—even Khalid didn't know the effort she expended every day to hold on to this gift, which she sometimes felt was a trust or heavy burden. Khalid wasn't like her, he held on to everything, even the smallest, most insignificant thing. His house was a strange museum, a collection of memories of every person who had passed through his life. One day she opened a small drawer next to his bed and found things that were hers, things that even she had forgotten about—a small red hair band, a soft leather bracelet, a flyer for a play she directed a long time ago, and small pieces of paper with some of her scribbles and incomprehensible words written on them. She really didn't understand why he kept all of these things, and when she asked him, his answer only increased her bewilderment:

Maya: Khalid, what's all this stuff?

Khalid: It's all yours, the hair band you forgot in the wash the first time you slept over at my place, the poster from the first time we met, you were hanging it on a wall in Hamra and I helped you, remember?

Maya: Yeah. The poster, yeah . . . the hair band, no. I thought it was the second time, when I came over to fight with you.

Khalid: You know . . . I've saved all our Facebook chats in a special file on my computer, along with all our phone messages from the time we met until now.

Maya: Why?

Khalid: I'm scared of my phone being lost or stolen, I don't know . . .

She remembered that she'd felt happy at the time. But she was also embarrassed that she couldn't recall all these details and wondered if this meant that she didn't love him enough. Her happiness didn't last long, however, because a few days later she opened another drawer by chance and in it she found that he'd kept mementos of his old girlfriend, Nisrine, arranged with the same enthusiasm and care as her things.

She stopped for a moment to try to listen to the sounds from Sanayeh Park, inside the white tents put up by the internally displaced people, fleeing Israeli bombings in the south and southern suburbs. She remembered her friend Majd, who'd said jokingly that morning that Xanax and condoms topped the IDPs' wish list. She didn't know why she didn't find this funny, but hurtful. It reminded her of a recurrent nightmare in which she found herself in the middle of the street wearing her pajamas, or the one where she's jolted awake among a bunch of strangers in her bedroom—that terrifying feeling that your private life has become public. She responded to Majd by asking him if he'd stopped having sex since the beginning of the war. He seemed embarrassed by her question, and replied in the negative.

One night, when she was still studying for her baccalaureate, she snuck over the park's walls with her friend Rami. She remembered how happy she'd felt to stretch out on the damp lawn, and how much happier she would have been if Rami, who she didn't like all that much, had not tried to hit on her the whole time. She wasn't attracted to him, she'd only gone with him for the thrill of sneaking in. It occurred to her that she should sneak into the garden now, go into a random tent, and lie down there. Anywhere would be better than going back home, where she wouldn't find Khalid. She didn't know why she always felt peace of mind everywhere but her own house. Perhaps all the problems in her relationship with Khalid started when he moved into her house. She didn't stop him; she was always living as though she were a guest in her own house anyway. Why did he do that to her? He planted himself in all the little details of her life and distanced her from everything related to his. He gave up his life to live her life, and then he gave up both her life and his and left to have a different one.

Throughout that time he'd had a dream that he'd just leave everything and travel abroad aimlessly. She didn't know why she didn't understand this dream of his—perhaps it was because her feeling of belonging didn't weigh on her the same way it did on him. Perhaps because she was fundamentally lost; this is likely why she was able to explore the same places again and again without getting exhausted or bored. She remembered that she'd read somewhere that fish lose their memory every five minutes, and that's why they can swim happily around a little pond. They forget where they are every five minutes and go back to swimming around in circles to discover the same place anew. Until now she hadn't found a better theory to explain her tremendous love for moving around in the same empty circles.

As usual, the voice of the policeman stationed in front of the barrier outside of the Ministry of the Interior across from Sanayeh Park woke her from her thoughts. He was flirting with her like always: "Bonsoir, mademoiselle." And as usual, she didn't respond and kept walking toward Hamra while listening to him chat with his colleague. This cop's behavior didn't really bother her; in some ways it was reassuring. The idiotic repetition made her feel as though life goes on despite the war and state of emergency that were so alive in her head. She did wish, however, that she understood what kind of pleasure he felt when he spoke to her, because he seemed really satisfied with himself every time. Perhaps it was the simple pleasure of repetition and anticipation based on what's come before—he knows that she won't answer and she knows that he'll always say the same thing. It's like the pleasure we feel when we watch a scene in a film we've seen before . . . that prescribed feeling of simple-minded control, like we're predicting something.

She stopped to listen to the sounds of the bombing; the rhythm had remained the same for the past two hours—strange how people can get used to any sound if they're forced to. The southern suburbs, which had been bombed throughout the assault, were no more than quarter of an hour's drive from where she was—but they seemed very far at the moment, like Khalid did. She remembered her first telephone conversation with him after he reached Canada. He told her about so many things that he'd seen: the strange man who'd stopped him in the train station to ask if he could spend the night at his place because space aliens had taken over his house; and the beauty of the snow that was falling that morning. But she wasn't really paying attention to all this. She was listening to another sound, the little sound between the words, like that little silence between the bombs now falling on the southern suburbs.

They announce the number of deaths on the news but they won't say how many were killed between one silence and another. Strange how in this specific moment she felt as though she really belonged to this country. Even stranger how Khalid's leaving co-incided with the beginning of the outbreak of the war. She slept that night wishing that the world would end and she woke the next morning and the world really was being destroyed. Since then she'd felt a strange guilt, as though she were making these things happen.

"Pssssssssssssssssst." She'd arrived at the midway point on the way down to Abu Wadih's bar when she heard a voice that she recognized right away. She was surprised—could it be the same man again?

"*Pssssssssssssssssssst.*" The second "*pssst*" left no doubt in her mind that this was the "*pssst*" she knew so well and was determined never to answer. But this one time only, she turned her head to confirm her doubts. Yes, it was the same man, the one who liked to flash her. He was always hidden in the same spot, behind some car, halfway down to Abu Wadih's bar, waiting for any young woman to walk by so he could call out to her, "*Pssssssssssssssssssst,*" and as soon as she turned, he'd pull down his pants.

She turned back around quickly and kept walking, drowning in laughter. She didn't expect to see him that evening, but it seemed that even war could not prevent this man from continuing his incomprehensible habit of showing his penis to passersby.

She remembered Myriam's hysterical reaction when she was with her and the man "*pssstpssst*"-ed the two of them, exposing himself as usual. She didn't know why this guy didn't frighten but, rather, amused her. Perhaps madness is a more appropriate reaction to life; rational people are the ones who frighten her the most, like Khalid with his well-mannered upbringing. She'd never seen him do anything wrong or behave in an improper way; even when he was drinking, he'd stay completely in control of his social consciousness. Honestly, only when he was drunk was he like her when she was fully alert.

She arrived at Abu Wadih's and the place was empty except for the bartender, Alaa, and one other customer, a hunchbacked man sitting at the side of the bar. For some reason this customer made her feel really nosy—she wasn't able to tell if he was actually hunchbacked or if it was just how he was sitting. He seemed very heavy in his body, as if at any second he might fall on the table or into his glass. She remembered the strange conversation that she and Khalid once had about Kundera's *The Unbearable Lightness of Being,* the very first time they met, and how he burst out laughing when she told him her interpretation of the stations of people's sadness and their meanings, according to the law of gravity. There's no doubt that gravity affects some people more than others, and because of this they continually experience feelings of heaviness that they associate with sadness and grief, while gravity weighs lighter on others and then they are lighter, and therefore happier, than the rest. The two of them had this conversation sitting at the table she'd passed by a moment ago. She ran her hand slowly over the wooden table as if to confirm it was still sturdy. Often when pain accosted her she liked to touch the things around her. For a while, whenever she woke up in the morning and was seized by the bitter awareness that Khalid had left, she'd place her hand against the cold wall and leave it there for a while. For some reason this reassured her.

She ordered an Almaza beer and went to sit by herself at a small table at the end of the room. She didn't recall ever sitting at this table with Khalid. She didn't usually like to sit in the corner; she hated looking at the wall. But since Khalid had gone, she felt that her relationship with walls had improved.

The day before she'd had a strange dream. Its protagonist was a sofa. The sofa was inside a house, she didn't know where. She saw a gray sofa at the end of a living room and believed that it was the same one in pictures of her old childhood home. She rushed into the sitting room, searching for a mirror to examine herself in, and the gray sofa took her back to the distant past before her parents separated, when her father moved with her brother to another city. After they left, her mother bought a new sofa because her father had taken the gray one with him to his new house.

In the logic of the dream, finding the sofa meant that she'd returned to her childhood. But she didn't find a mirror in the sitting room. She was disappointed; she'd really longed to see her face as a girl. She went back to the living room again and couldn't find the gray sofa either. In its place, there was a black leather sofa. She recognized it right away and was overcome by annoyance. This sofa was from Khalid's old living room. She walked over to it cautiously, touched it, and her hand felt something damp, like sweat. She tried to pull her hand away but it was stuck on the leather. She started wriggling it around to separate her skin from the leather, but it was no use and she started screaming.

She woke up, her neck wet with sweat, her hair stuck to it, and felt the same irritation she'd felt in her dream when touching the sofa. While recalling the dream, she wondered why her father chose to take the gray sofa but nothing else. The only time she cried after her parents separated was the day when she woke up in the morning, went into the living room, and didn't find the sofa there. She sat on the ground in the empty spot where it had been, leaned her head into her hands, and burst into tears. When her mother saw her, she didn't ask why she was crying, but simply sat down next to her, tears flowing from her eyes too. They didn't talk about it, but the following morning her mother bought a new sofa with all of the colors known to the world—and those unknown up until then too. Visitors gave them strange looks when they glimpsed their unusual sofa. But she and her mother were really happy with their beautiful, colorful sofa, which didn't remind them of anything at all. It was just completely amazing.

She finished her beer and went over to the bar to order a whiskey. This time, when she looked at the hunchbacked man sitting at the bar, she felt that his face was familiar, but she wasn't really able to tell if she actually knew him. He smiled at her and that's when she was sure she'd seen him before, but somewhere other than at Abu Wadih's bar. It was hard to forget a person who looked so peculiar: two small round eyes that she couldn't read any clear expression in—she saw in them right away familiarity mixed with a bit of dullness, which seemed somewhat deliberate, perhaps seeking out the kindness of others or concealing something else—a strangely deformed nose, and teeth that were no less curvy. In short, it was as though a hurricane had struck his face. Despite this, it was difficult to describe him as *ugly* . . . not because he was handsome, but because he was so completely out of the ordinary, as if he were created by a powerful and turbulent imagination. She smiled at him guardedly as she went back to her seat, but he turned around and seemed to stare at her. She concentrated her gaze on the wall in front of her in order to ignore him.

She looked at the large clock hanging on the wall behind the bar; it had just turned nine o'clock and the bar was starting to fill up as usual with new arrivals. She had never bought a watch in her whole life and all the watches that people had given her over the years in their lame attempts to force her to commit to her appointments with them were useless. The strange thing was that the watches themselves would sometimes stop working on their own once she put them on her wrist. She always rationalized this as time itself refusing to be known by her. Surely that was the sole logical explanation for this strange phenomenon.

She was about to light a cigarette when she saw Walid walking toward her. This surprised her because they hadn't talked in a long while, other than saying hello in passing from time to time. Walid approached her and smiled slowly as he always did.

Walid: Hey there, how're you?

Maya: Good, you?

Walid: I'm gonna order a drink and come back. What do you want, your usual whiskey?

Maya: I haven't finished my first one yet.

He didn't respond and went toward the bar. She thought it strange that he would say *your usual,* as though three years hadn't passed since they'd been together. She remembered one time she was here with Khalid, and Walid was sitting at the table across from them with his English girlfriend. Though she hadn't even said hi to him, Khalid asked her right away if they'd had a relationship in the past. She was weirded out how Khalid could have surmised that on his own. He told her that he knew immediately from the way Walid had looked at her.

Maya: What do you mean, how he looks at me?

Khalid: He looks at you like you're his.

Maya: But so much time has passed and now he has a partner, I don't think he even remembers—

Khalid: That doesn't matter. You don't know how men think. You know . . . if a man has seen a woman naked once, every time he sees her he imagines her like that. That's it . . . the picture never leaves his head.

At the time she puzzled over whether all men were really like that, or if it was just Khalid's jealousy that pushed him to these kinds of fantasies, even though he always said that her previous relationships with other men in no way bothered him. And it seemed clear at that moment that he didn't really accept the idea that a man other than him could ever have seen her naked. But perhaps she was also wrong . . . He'd proven to her many times that he'd been able to understand her previous lovers better than she could.

Walid handed her another whiskey and sat across from her at the table.

Walid: So it seems you're alone?

Maya: Yeah, you too.

She resorted to that inexplicable sarcasm she took refuge in when she couldn't find what she wanted to say. They both laughed together for no clear reason. After this, she understood that Walid's girlfriend had gone to England and he was getting ready to follow her there. Walid hadn't really had a deep impact on her life and she didn't remember suffering all that much when they broke up . . . his entering and then leaving her life happened with a strange calm. She wished that things could go like that with Khalid too.

Suddenly she found herself grateful to Walid for not staying too long in her life. Their relationship had not lasted more than two months when it ended with a stupid misunderstanding that neither one of them could be bothered to fix. Those relationships that finish before they've really started feel painful in the moment, like an abortion. But with time it becomes clear that this is the only kind of relationship that can preserve its beauty, like a movie star who commits suicide at the height of her brilliance. Despite the fact that it doesn't mean a lot to us, it's the only thing we can remember without real pain, as if it isn't really ours, but stolen from someone else's memory.

She remembered Khalid's words . . . is Walid imagining her naked right now? This thought amused her, but in any case, even if he were not visualizing her naked at that very moment, from the way he was talking, it seemed clear that he was determined to see her that way again.

Walid: So what are you doing later?

Maya: Going home. Why?

Walid: Do you wanna come over to my place?

His question surprised her, a clear and direct offer, with no preamble. Things had definitely changed since she was single and living alone in the city—that is to say, three years ago when she'd met Khalid. Normally it would take more than a drink and ten minutes of passing chitchat for two people to reach this stage. Or perhaps he believed he was within his bounds to proposition her with no preamble because the two of them had already been together. But that was a long time ago and she didn't feel any real connection between the man who she'd known and the one who was sitting beside her now. In fact, she hadn't found a way to deal with the past yet, except to completely repudiate it. She didn't have true feelings, either about her life now or about the years that had led up to now. Every morning she would wake up and think that she'd just been born all of a sudden, but she never really had that refreshing sense of rebirth. In reality, every morning she feels like she's worse off than the day before. She felt like all the time that had passed—twenty-five years—had been spent trying to be reborn as a being who wouldn't ever be complete; that's just her.

His voice roused her.

Walid: It's really crowded here, let's go have a drink on the veranda and listen to some good music, what do you say? Afterward, my place is close by.

She smiled at him as though congratulating him for the effort he expended trying to convince her.

Maya: I dunno.

Walid: Okay, I'm getting another drink and coming back.

She observed him carefully while he was moving away. He had a funny walk that was sort of like a caveman. He thrust his legs out and held his shoulders back in such an exaggerated way it seemed artificial, as if to display his virility to the whole world. She remembered the first time she had sex with him; she was sitting on his lap and suddenly he carried her from the living room into the bedroom and threw her on the bed. From that moment on, she started secretly calling him Caveman. But in what followed, it became clear that Caveman was totally preoccupied with his health, to an obsessive-compulsive degree. He was perpetually afraid of a potential heart attack. After they'd made love the first time and were lying together on the bed, he took her hand and put it on his heart.

Walid: It's beating really fast, isn't it?

Maya: No, it's normal.

Walid: If I died right now, what would you do?

She didn't know what to answer at that moment, but as usual when she couldn't find the appropriate response; her answer was harshly sarcastic without her meaning it to be.

Maya: I'd get out of there, of course, in case they suspected me of something.

She glanced at the bar and found the hunchbacked man staring at her. He smiled at her again and then she turned away, perhaps flinching a little. There was something strange about this man. She took her pack of cigarettes and went out to smoke and get some air. Walid was also there talking on the phone to his English girlfriend. She was far away but she could still hear some of what he was saying since he was talking in a loud voice. It seemed that the English girlfriend was checking on her plants and her cat; he was reassuring her that he was watering the plants and giving the cat her medicine every day . . . that the cat was still suffering from diarrhea but had improved a little bit. She imagined Caveman watering the plants and wiping up cat shit so she wasn't able to keep herself from bursting out laughing when he walked over to her.

Walid: What's up?

Maya: Nothing—I saw something that made me laugh.

Clearly he didn't understand, but he smiled at her anyway. As they started to go back inside, her cell phone rang. She looked at the screen and it was a number from outside Lebanon—Khalid, of course—so she quickly moved away from Walid and answered.

Khalid: Hey, what's up? Sounds like it's noisy where you are—you out?

Maya: Yeah, I'm at Abu Wadih's.

Khalid: I just got back home. I'm frozen, the temperature was -5 when I was coming back.

Maya: Whoa. Warm yourself up, habibi.

Khalid: Yeah, I will, I'm sitting under a blanket now, I can't move it's so cold. Are you going to stay out late? I can wait up so we can talk on Skype.

Maya: No, not late. I'll leave in a bit. But if you're tired, sleep, habibi, no problem.

Khalid: Who are you hanging out with?

Maya: Miriam and Lina.

Khalid: Listen, habibti, take a taxi if you want to go back home by yourself—don't take a servees.

Maya: Okay, fine, habibi, yellah, bye.

She hung up the phone, surprised at Khalid's insistence that she take a taxi home. She really wanted to believe that this was a sign that he cared about her, but this kind of care for her safety and security had only appeared after he left the country. When they were together in Lebanon he didn't care about things like that. Many times when she'd left his house alone at night he wouldn't offer to go with her. Why was he so worried about her now? Isn't he the one who'd left her alone here?

She went back inside and noticed that the hunchbacked man was no longer staring at her. For a second she thought she'd figured out who he was, but she bumped into someone passing by and the thought escaped her. She wanted to get back to the table and gather her stuff fast, since after Khalid's phone call she felt that something was constricting her breathing—she needed to leave . . . and quickly. She didn't find Walid. She sighed deeply, grabbed her purse, and rushed outside.

No doubt she'd been walking aimlessly for ten minutes or more before stopping. As soon as she did, her breathing started to even out. She felt cold and realized that she'd forgotten her coat at Abu Wadih's. But she had absolutely no desire to go back there this evening. She wrapped her shawl around her shoulders and observed the Hbeish guard station in front of her. Strange that her legs had brought her right here. She felt her phone vibrating in her bag; she'd gotten a new message. She thought that it would be from Khalid but when she looked at it, it was from Walid: *What happened? Where'd you disappear to?*

She considered responding, *You'd better get up and go home and water your plants, it's the right thing to do.* Of course she didn't do that, but she thought it was strange that he still had her number. She wondered what would happen if she decided to change her number without telling Khalid. What if she completely disappeared? Would he come search for her, or would he stay over there in Canada waiting for her on Skype? Probably the latter. She already feels it's another woman Khalid is waiting for on Skype, a ghost woman coming home every night to repeat the same electronic expressions so he could be reassured that everything was under control in the virtual love nest he built for her after he left her. What if she programmed Skype to speak to Khalid instead of her, would he even notice the difference?

She decided to keep going toward the lighthouse, though it felt a little reckless—or actually *a lot* reckless, especially at this time of night when no one went to the Corniche except a very select group chosen from the elite of the most hopeless social-welfare cases in Beirut and lovers who weren't lucky enough to find any other place to be alone. But this was exactly what she needed right now. She remembered the first night she slept over at Khalid's place in his old apartment, in Ain el Mreisseh near the sea, and how restorative that next morning was, when they sat together on a wooden bench on the Corniche. The mere sight of an empty boat in the middle of the sea frightened her and she asked Khalid about it. He told her that it must belong to a fisherman who was taking a swim nearby. Then he said that when he died he hoped they'd put him in a boat like that and set it on fire. He said that he'd seen that in a film. He spoke about his death with a strange passion and romance, adding that he was imagining that they'd grow old together. When they died they'd have both of their corpses put on the same boat and pushed out to sea, toward the unknown. She didn't have any clearly formulated reaction to this conversation. Should she be happy that he wanted to spend the rest of his life with her? But no, that isn't what he'd actually said. He didn't mention anything about their lives together, only about their death . . .

The sound of a motorbike interrupted her meditations and she quickly moved on, afraid. She feared that the person driving the motorbike was the hunchbacked man from Abu Wadih's, but he quickly disappeared into the darkness of the street before she could be sure. She kept walking cautiously for a few steps and then the motorbike came back toward her, really fast, as if it were going to run her over. This time she looked at the driver's face to confirm her doubts, retreating. It *was* the hunchbacked man. And he stopped his motorbike suddenly. She screamed so loudly that she even frightened herself, but the man didn't appear to have heard anything.

Maya: What do you want?

He kept staring at her with the same expression he'd had a little

while before at Abu Wadih's. She couldn't make out any emotion
on his face—he didn't seem perturbed but rather eerily calm. A
moment passed before she had the expected reaction to this kind
of situation, which is to try to escape quickly. She was more skilled
at running away from herself. Facing actual danger at that moment,
it took her a relatively long time to comprehend that it was real
and didn't just spring out of her imagination. Despite this late realization, she finally obeyed the urge to escape, running surprisingly
quickly given her small legs and her lungs destroyed by cigarettes.
The only problem was that she ran the wrong way and darkness was
advancing along with her. She wasn't completely aware of where
she was going, she could only hear the roar of the motorbike ringing
in her ears as it got closer and closer. It seemed as though her defeat
was imminent . . .

She didn't know how it happened. Did she fall on her own or
crash into the motorbike? But she found herself kneeling on the
ground and the hunchbacked man standing across from her staring
at her in the same way. She tried to get up but her knees wouldn't
support her. She felt that they were injured but she didn't look at
them and instead kept trying to stand. Suddenly the man lurched
from where he was, grabbed her, and helped her get up, but then
held firmly onto her arm, preventing her from moving. She couldn't
think of escaping this time, she was staring at the old building in
front of her, not believing that she'd arrived here. She was standing in front of Khalid's old building, all locked up and drowning in
the darkness of the street. She remembered how sad she was when
Khalid told her they would tear it down soon. Then she remembered the drawer where he used to keep her forgotten things. No
doubt he'd made her another drawer in Canada and was reflecting
on it with love and care at this very moment while she was here in
the grip of this demented man. In this completely deserted neighborhood, no one would hear her if she screamed.

"You don't recognize me," the hunchbacked man said in a low, embarrassed-sounding voice. She examined him, baffled; his features seemed to have changed, slowly coming into focus, though he maintained his grip on her arm while he kept on talking.

"I'm Mahmoud, I used to deliver pizza to you from the place at the end of the street when you lived here."

Why didn't she recognize him before? Perhaps because she saw him at Abu Wadih's in another context than the one she was used to. Or perhaps she'd erased him from her memory with all of the other memories she had of this place, in this house where she'd lived with Khalid. It was strange how her journey of escape had ended here of all places. Was it her legs that brought her here unconsciously? Or did he force her to take this particular road? She couldn't understand anything anymore. She, like everything, was in a totally surreal dream and the best solution would to be to surrender to the logic of the dream until it ended and she woke up . . .

"Of course I recognize you, but let go of my arm!" She tried to free herself from his grip, but his strong arms held her in place. She didn't do anything to resist. She merely tried to get some control over her rapid breathing. She didn't want him to know how afraid she was. She thought that if he smelled fear he would become more ferocious. She read somewhere that dogs could identify criminals by the scent of fear on them and therefore would attack them. From that time on she had a dog phobia. Whenever she saw a dog on the road she imagined it would swoop down on her, not because she was a criminal but because it would smell the fear and guilt oozing from her skin. But she could usually control herself, so she went ahead calmly, thinking that she would trick the dog and divert its nose from the passing gust of fear. Yet this didn't seem to be of any use with Mahmoud. She screamed without even being aware she was screaming: "Leave me alone, let me go! Are you listening? Leave me alone!"

She noticed that his left eye was twitching slowly and his mouth was twisted downward as if he were trying to pick up a smile that kept falling off.

Suddenly a rattle-like voice emerged from within him: "I love you." He said this looking at her as if he were waiting for her to say, *And I love you too.* It seemed clear that for him what was happening was not assault, as she was experiencing it, but an act of true love.

She forced herself to speak as calmly as she could: "Mahmoud, I have to go because my family is waiting for me at home. Let me go and I'll see you tomorrow. I'll give you my number. But right now I really have to go."

He didn't seem to have heard her and was finishing the conversation by himself. He seemed totally absent but he wouldn't let her go. Instead he pulled her violently toward him and grabbed her neck from behind. "I know I don't have money and I'm not educated but I'm gonna make a lot of money and buy a car and get my teeth fixed too—they're gonna look nice, like the guys you are with. And I'll order you pizza too but I won't let you open the door to anyone—I'm very jealous."

She was quiet for a moment and then something happened that she didn't expect. He let her go, turned around, and moved away from her, shouting while peering upward as though he were speaking with someone in the sky: "Mahmoud the Monster, Mahmoud the Monster! Listen to me, the Monster is speaking to you, listen to the Monster!"

She remained frozen in place, completely stunned, and watched him move farther and farther away. She didn't budge until she saw him turn toward his motorbike. Then she started running again, even though her knees were hurting. She heard the roar of the motorbike again and ran even faster, though after a while she realized that the sound was still the same distance away from her, it wasn't getting any nearer. She stopped and turned to see if he was following her. She saw him in the distance driving his motorbike toward a streetlight and then crashing into it. He reversed and then once again aimed at the light and crashed into it . . .

After walking for a quarter of an hour down the dark street alone, she finally got back to the Corniche. Dawn was breaking. She bent over the rail and stared at the empty boat, still in its usual place in the sea. She noticed that the sounds of the bombing continued, despite the cease-fire the Israelis had agreed to the day before. No doubt they'll exploit every second before sunrise to bomb whatever they can. They probably hope that this dawn will last forever, while the people who live in the southern suburbs are praying for the sun to rise again.

Her mind was fixated on a dawn from another time, stuck in her throat—like the empty boat, bobbing in the waves slowly—making it hard for her to breathe.

Originally written in Arabic.

UNDER THE TREE
OF MELANCHOLY

BY NAJWA BARAKAT

Gemmayzeh

I am Mr. Kaaaaaaa. And I am no one.

I lost my organs, one after the other, and I didn't do so voluntarily or because of disease or an explosion or an accident of any kind. Now that I've atrophied, been pruned and abbreviated into only one of my senses, I wonder regretfully if organ donation wouldn't have been the perfect choice for someone like me. If I had done it, my organs wouldn't have gone to waste. Had they all been intact and working together regularly, they would have enjoyed the flattery that the old Armenian doctor would have inundated me with, when I would have brought my organs to him. He would have come to receive them joyfully, repeating in a kind of coughing fit, which changed the Arabic letters *ha* and *ayn* to *kha* in his throat: "*Akhlan akhlan wa sakhlan*, greetings to the *orkhans* of Mr. K."

Nothing is left in my whole body except an eye, which I feel is a hole. I didn't say "my" eye, since nothing should be granted to me when I don't exist anymore. What is incomplete has no identity. What has no identity becomes common property, belonging to a genus and not to an individual. It becomes an unperson. Just like nouns when an article isn't there to aid them. I lost my own article. It happened one day. It really takes a huge effort to concentrate and remember the date. Perhaps it wasn't a day, but a divergent, motley mix of units of time that are impossible to measure. All I know is that after the language of people had shut me out, I started speaking a language that I called the language of *ayn* (meaning both *letter* and *eye*).

I expanded a tiny hole and glimpsed through it heads and voices, buildings and roads. As I was peering into it, all I had to do was grab hold of its edges, breathe deeply, then make one push upward to emerge with a giant, complete body, wearing a hat and coat and carrying suitcases and umbrellas.

Now I open the eye wide—more than an eye is able to be open—because I know that my continuity is dependent on it, and that when I close it, I will die and everything will disappear. I keep it open, alert, not so I can stay alive but so I can look after the tree of melancholy—to see it sending its seeds out onto the ground and growing with the passing seasons. I testify and I narrate; the language of *ayn* will disappear with me and won't be the language of anyone else after me. A faithful partner will depart, untouched by the tongue of any other man. We will die together like an animal whose species was made extinct, after it threw itself into the abyss of nothingness with joy and indifference. Two, three things at the most, I narrate. I utter this world's breath and I stop. A flicker. A fleck. Then nothing. Thanks, farewell, peace.

I settle down in whiteness, conscious that I am shaped like a cloud that will fade away later. I sit in doubtful blackness, with the eye closed. My body that no longer exists remains tattooed in me, like life on a dead face that departed without it realizing. I succeed in summoning my organs from the tissue of my garbled memory and they rise, knotted up, intermittently and uncoordinated. Or they come together, incomplete, in a chaos lacking logic or meaning. I sometimes feel myself a cubical board, broken into pieces, scattered around, having no beginning or clear destination. I must gather myself together cell by cell to be heavy enough that I can rise up again, a seemingly complete person, with my particularities and my weaknesses, even if disabled, diseased, or afflicted by the scourge.

My body—which is no longer separate from me, keeping me outside of it—is unprotected, with no claws or a back; I'm a worm, naked and slimy. It ejects me like bodies eject refuse through their excrement, because it's become too much for them and has consumed them. Often my own body grows large. Its survival, despite its absence, is the reason for my confusion, since sometimes it flourishes and I don't know if I've passed out or I'm sleeping or if I'm a dream that thinks itself awake.

Tumescent cities spread out within the folds of the miniature red veins which embroider the eye; half-flawed cities, whose buildings all around me are crumbling one wall at a time. Who could say if this rubble was a window to yesterday? Strange-tasting, bloated cities launch a metallic wail that cuts the veins of the eye and relegate its vision to blackness. Bathing in destruction. Penetrating a handful of sand. Darkness, complacency, and silence. Speechless stars. Extinguished explosions that don't shatter or fly away, but come together. They shrink. They atrophy. They decay. Black holes floating in the darkness of the universe. That is me. Or in this way I imagine myself, trivialized, so I can find a way to understand. If not, where do I imagine I am right now, and what does the person speaking inside me purport to say?

I am Mr. Kaaaaaaa and I am an eye.

Only a few things sit with me in the first level of my field of vision. If I rub it, moving the pupil from all the way on the right to all the way on the left, I see a ceramic vase my wife made in one of the strange educational classes she took following my return from "the years of my absence," as she used to refer to that period. Killing time, I think. Developing her true talent, she thinks, and professes openly. A ceramic vase of a confused shape, which is still in the process of maturing. It remained the color of clay, decorated with a yellow chrysanthemum. The comment on its yellowness did not appeal to its creator, leading to her face turning yellow and her right ear red—indicating a fit of anger. This is in contrast to her left ear, whose redness alerts me that I must make love with her right then, immediately.

That's what my wife is like—or what she *was* like—she would erupt for the most trivial of reasons. She's like a child. She has short black hair, wide honey-colored gazelle eyes, and a full mouth, which hides two front teeth that make her look like an aristocratic rabbit with lipstick whenever she laughs. Beautiful Jamilah excited attention with her full, taut body and its perfect proportions. Her unrelenting elegance and her mysterious femininity mobilized battalions of bottles, perfumes, and powders, filling drawers and tables if not cabinets and warehouses. Such a feminine woman is like a prairie—you think it is open and relaxed, hiding no surprises, danger, or deception, and then there you are in the middle of the outdoors, captivated, surrounded, closed in. But sometimes I wonder if she wasn't right, if the yellow color wasn't actually that of a chrysanthemum and if she didn't actually possess a true, unappreciated talent, which she never realized because of her bad luck marrying me.

Like a ball in a game whose name I can no longer recall, it's not enough for the earth to be grassy and buoyant, full of holes and flags, it needs a favorable wind, flexible arms, and an eye able to estimate distances. One tiny straw and the ball would deviate from its path, away from the holes. Since I lost my limbs and turned into a seeing eye, I became the stumbling block to my wife's talent that designed, drew, painted, embroidered, and stitched; her marvelous small hands cultivated yellow chrysanthemums on paintings, curtains, cloth, utensils, small tables, and dishes.

"You put different elements in conversation with each other and harmonize them!" she commented proudly while pondering the decor of the corner where she decided to put me. I didn't understand in the beginning if this was revenge—though that was the furthest thing from her sensitive, delicate temperament, which would generate streams of tears at the least emotion—or if it was a sign that she now saw me as flaccid, fragile, and weak like a chrysanthemum, yellow and waxlike.

My wife put me in front of the television the vast majority of the time. Sometimes she put me in the bedroom when she had guests over. When they came, she didn't like them to see me as a wide-open eye—a wandering, brazen, exhausted, sunken eye—forced into being a proxy, playing roles it can't handle in the absence of its fellow senses. In the end, she started not having people over, preferring to go out. This was less taxing on her and I didn't care one way or the other. But I wondered what compelled my wife to put me in these particular spots so I would be visible from every corner of the house, even from the outside and the balconies across from us and next to us, lying on the old red sofa, the lone remnant from all her late parents' furniture.

"The two of them died, one a few hours after the other," she would say, staring at me grave-faced. I see her look at me like she did her father who'd been half paralyzed, unable to speak or move. I'm sure he was behind her kindness toward me, her sympathy for me, and her accepting my presence in the house that she inherited and furnished, fully and completely, so that I didn't have even the least contribution to make to it. I believe she chose this corner for me thinking, gratefully, that I was an eye needing vision exercises. So she put me across from things with different dimensions to look at, thinking that I had a narrow sight line only a few steps from the balcony adjoining the neighbors' balcony and part of their washroom, adding on a respectable amount of the street. This street was shaded by two cinchona trees, the last of their kind, I believe, in all of Gemmayzeh, if not in all the surrounding areas too, indeed perhaps even in all Beirut. And not-negligible patches of the blue sky penetrated their greenness, certainly enough to activate the muscles of this last organ which remained alive and raging in me.

A fly announced its entrance into my field of vision, buzzing at my left side. It circled around a little, confused, before leaving quickly. I heard my wife moving behind me. She was wearing her red shoes with the high heels that she keeps in a cloth bag and only takes out for special occasions. The clock on the wall indicated ten minutes past four o'clock. This isn't the usual time for parties. The fly returned once more, on my right side this time, before landing on one of the yellow chrysanthemums. A random idea came to me:

Do bees recognize the taste of all different flowers, or do they just hap-hazardly taste the ones where they land?

My wife moved around the house with a nervousness not appropriate to the mood of half past four in the afternoon. The fly too was dismayed to discover that the field of chrysanthemums tasted like cloth and cold glass. My wife then appeared in my range of vision. She calmed down after taking off her shoes with the noisy heels. She came over and kissed the eye. I could only see the space between her breasts and the embroidery on her red bra. They're color-coordinated. The bra and the shoes.

My wife picked up the eye and dragged it to the bathroom. She put it in the bathtub and started rubbing it with soap and water. She rinsed it with warm water and then did the same again. She said that its smell has become a stench. The eye could only smell expensive perfume mixed with the sweat between her breasts. My wife took off her dress and kept on her camisole. The heat—flames of hot water and the fire of her movements—was making her feel suffocated. Her red bra rose up and made her quavering breasts dangle before they calmed down and stared at the eye.

My wife helped me, using a loofa saturated with soapy foam to reach its back. Her erect nipple approached the eye as though challenging it. Her breast touched the eye gently, perhaps it was tickling the nipple, and perhaps the eye woke and responded. But no. The eye can't touch the breast—it is fully aware and cognizant of the fact that it isn't a hand, mouth, or tongue. My wife was angry at the eye and pushed it under the water, leaving it there for a few seconds. The eye thought that its moment of salvation had finally arrived and rejoiced. My wife pushed the eye with her foot after she herself entered the bathwater naked and stretched it out onto its back. The eye relished the feel of her soft skin, but didn't blink. Her warm belly moved, rising and falling, coming and going, with soap bubbles tickling, breathless and quivering.

The phone rang and my wife picked it up, saying fuzzy words into it, including *shoes* and *four o'clock* and *useless appointments* and something about the importance or the disease of forgetfulness. Meanwhile, the eye submissively waited naked on the towel atop the cold tiles. My wife stopped talking, hung up the phone, and noticed that I'd turned blue, so she held me up to rub me, dry me off, and put on my underclothes while humming a tune, expressing her tender mood of joy. She took me up to the bedroom, swaddled me in my clothes, and asked me if I'd enjoy stretching out on the bed. The eye answered, "No," so she returned me to my throne on the red sofa.

Our neighbor was standing on the balcony. His face was twitchy as he gazed at our balcony and from there to the street. My wife went out onto the balcony but didn't raise her glance at him. There was something different in her gait and posture. She picked up the hose and watered the potted plants. She watered them the day before too, the eye thought. Their roots will be worn out if she keeps on like this. Had she perhaps forgotten? Or was something disturbing her and preoccupying her mind? What a question. How could she not be preoccupied when she was feeling the loss of her husband who she loved, cared for, and was devoted to?

Certain words, images, and ideas are mixed up for me, as if I've come across them at the very moment they are changing or taking shape. I can discern only one specific detail without an essence from a voice, color, or form. It's as if a giant hand cast a veneer of whiteness over the world with barely recognizable things looming behind its tiny holes.

Therefore I feel I should name and enumerate. Anything. Everything. What falls within my range of vision and what I guess or imagine in its surroundings. And I can make a list: leaves, clouds, footsteps, cubed tiles, birds—individually and in flocks—jets of rain, electricity wires, yellow chrysanthemums, the people living in the little screen, curtain rings, electric switches, passersby, lines, spots, dots, cars, electricity poles, voices, potted plants, colors . . . everything. Anything.

I list them so I don't forget, so I don't grow too distant from a world whose mayhem still reaches me and whose chaos still confuses me. I still have to reside here, even if only for a while. I rely on my exercises to pass time, chewing on a language as if I'd never learned it, as if it had suckled me, turned on me like a serpent, to bite off words whose taste had died long ago and whose return continues to hover within my range, like the whispering of water. Capturing the wind. A memory that wobbles on the edge of the tongue. A city hidden by sand where a fragment of a vase finally revealed a thread linking it to the urban fabric. I am the specter of a language swaddled by the wind.

I hear: "*Alif, ba, ta, tha*'" ("A, B, C, D") . . . I see letters themselves repeating. I see them passing against a black background, like train carriages, hand in hand, and I wait patiently for one letter after another to cross my optical screen. But only emptiness, silence, and silly letters start forming themselves again in combinations not organized by meaning or name. Thus passed "the years of my absence," as my wife liked to call the period when I was away from her. The expression makes me laugh and I pity her when I remember her saying it, her tongue faltering breathlessly, scared someone might clarify it or a rude guest might correct her.

During "the years of my absence," I used to sit in the darkness of my soul and count. Counting relaxed me and it still does. It circulates through me like drugs. Numbers penetrate deeply, then begin to bubble up from inside like soap. They bubble up, ossify, and increase until they fill me, scraping the sticky viscous muck and everything that hurts, disturbs, and sickens. Places with no light, sound, or breeze whatsoever help me concentrate. I don't complain about staying in places that can barely accommodate my feet if I stretch them out. I can stay squashed up on top of myself, eye closed, absorbed in numbers until passing out, not sleeping, after which I start trying to keep track of how long I was out.

When they took me out of the "hole," as they called it, I kept cheating, starting fights, and quibbling until I gave them an excuse to put me back there, my bloody body swollen with bruises and cuts. Neither severe beatings nor humiliation, nor other types of physical pain made me cry. Only my memory, my anguish, and my regret for what I thought was love and kindness, but at the end of the day was worse than evil.

My brother—he had no name except "my brother," since he only answered when I called him that—didn't like names. One sound sufficed for him, as in when he chose only one letter from my name—*Kaf*—and started calling me that, stretching it out, as he did when he started calling my parents "Maaaaaa" and "Paaaaaaaa." They forced him to count and, unlike me, counting tasted like a kind of torture to him. Addition and subtraction required him to use his fingers and other things. That was until I found him the solution in an imaginary bag, which we sketched out together in his mind, into which he put every number that he had previously kept in his hand, waiting to complete the computation process.

He'd scream "Kaaaa!" then bang his head against the ground if he didn't find me next to him. When I'd come, he'd gurgle like a fountain, hugging the tree as he would a human—living beings and inanimate objects weren't different to him. My mother's female relatives said, "God bless the Creator of two brothers who don't resemble each other at all—either in looks or temperament. Praise be to Him, the one who beats you with one hand and supports you with the other" . . . I started thinking about the one they called "Praise be to Him." The one who supported my mother when she was giving birth to me and beat her when she gave birth to my brother, as he fell from her belly onto the ground and hit his head on the tiles, rolling onto his face, his eyes shrunken, his limbs diminished. Fearing this "Praise be to Him" would direct another blow at him, perhaps as revenge, my brother didn't want to grow up as other children do.

Despite this, for some reason I don't understand—and contrary to the comments of everyone who spun around in our orbit, including our parents—I started to feel we were twins: as if he were the night and I the day, he the white and I the black, he the letter and I the dot. I remained amazed and astonished, not understanding how people didn't see the resemblance between us, to the point where I put all the blame for this on "Praise be to Him," who confused people. He put a soul in me which had my brother's body shape, and he instilled in my brother a soul that matched my own looks. So my soul lived as a stranger, having nowhere to settle down, in exile in a place it didn't know, where it didn't fit in, harboring a desire to leave and go where its twin was hidden, locked up in shackles and dirt.

They pitied him and I envied him. Lying in bed, I wished he were the one about whom people said, "Beautiful features and a good head on his shoulders," and I were the one about whom they said, "Poor thing, deranged looks and a deficient mind." Because of my jealousy I started acting like he did while holding his hand, walking together to school: I would take my hand from his, making sure no one was watching, and then I'd start to cover everything with wet kisses. I'd open up my schoolbag and eat my snack before the bell rang, marking the arrival of the ten o'clock break, or I'd throw it to a homeless dog or stray cat, or I'd put it in a hole in a tree stump, and on top of all that I'd kiss it because . . . because it was there, on the side of the road. I'd take off my school uniform and throw out the coins in my pockets. If my shoes were too tight or a pebble got into them, I would take them off too and walk barefoot, not feeling pain, cold, or shame. My brother's laughter would accompany me, rising up behind me and causing a huge bevy of leaves to fall from the trees onto us.

My brother was the only one who missed me after what befell me. In any case, he is the only one I missed too. Others would pass by the eye and not linger or tarry. Passersby, people in transit, visitors. Capturing the wind. I don't remember any of their features, and they don't leave any trace on me. The faces which come back to me are themselves few, wild, and don't tolerate any intimacy.

Sometimes I can put names to them, when the waters of memories explode within me; I'm not aware of them flowing down in my lower regions.

This is how "Ta" came in disguise, hiding behind memories that weren't his, despite all my miserable attempts to make him go away. Ta, who I fell in love with when we were still children. Because he stopped to watch me play with my brother. He didn't laugh. He didn't ridicule. Because he approached us trying to be friendly, begging us to include him in our clique. Because I didn't understand at the beginning and didn't believe. Because I prevented my brother from hugging him and kissing him like he did with every other stranger. Because I started noticing him every day following us from a distance. Like a dog. And because I saw him one day playing with my brother, when he didn't see me; he picked my brother up off the ground, wiped his runny nose, straightened his clothes, and kissed his head. And because when I approached, he stopped silently and asked, "What's his name?" I said, "My brother, he doesn't have another name." He said, "Then he's my brother too!"

AAAAAAAAH . . .

My wife rushes over to me, alarmed. My eyes are bulging, fluids streaming out of them, which she catches with her hands so they won't soil her red sofa. She asks me what's wrong, repeating, "Do you want me to call the doctor?"

What doctor? And what use are all the doctors in the world to me if I can't turn back the wheel of time even a few seconds? A few seconds, not more, to push my life to the junction, which would deviate from a hell whose fires only subside to crane up its neck anew. A few seconds, my God, and I would rewind parts of the tape. I would see Ta walking with my brother and playing with him, not noticing me after he lifted him from the ground, straightened his clothes, and wiped his nose. I would go over to them and remain silent, not uttering a sound, until he asked me what his name was. I would answer, "My brother. You aren't related to him and if you come near him again, I'll bust your nose and even God won't be able to fix it" . . . So Ta, who was cowardly by nature, would have walked away frightened, head bowed, leaving my brother and me alone, never to return.

But I didn't rebuke him, I didn't make him walk away, and Ta got closer and closer to us until he started haunting us. On the way to school, in school, and on the way home. We were almost like relatives—even the family on both sides followed us. In any case, they didn't have a choice. As we grew older his infatuation with and devotion to us increased, as did our trust and devotion to him. I even started relying on him and leaving him alone with my brother, whenever desire called me. I was at the age of discovering desire in all its forms and I would forget my brother or to wonder about Ta's devotion to him. I would forget to think about how strange it was that he wasn't passionate about life like I was. So I'd push any doubts about him or rebukes to my own conscience right to the back of my mind.

When I discovered what was happening, they were together in the garage where my parents had set up a place for us to play when we were little. As we got older, they transformed it into a kind of space to hang out where we could have our forbidden dreams, secret conversations, and crazy music in private. My brother would rejoice when we'd take him there and he loved spending time there with us, since he could feel that perhaps he was like us, equal to us, far from the eyes of the family. We would enter, and he would explode like a volcano because it didn't matter if we threw our things around in a mess or if havoc was wreaked on the place. We'd stand idly watching him playing our drums, strumming the strings of instruments very dear to our hearts, or ripping up pages of magazines we'd bought. The garage remained our oasis for many years. When I grew up and fell in love with my aristocratic rabbit and she was determined that we get married or break up, Ta convinced me to accept a compromise. He would stay with "our brother" and take over his care and protection so my parents—hardworking govern-

ment employees who only came back home late in the evening—
wouldn't send him where disabled people like him were sent . . .

I heard a moan and rattle of the throat, so I looked through the
keyhole and saw Ta there, standing with his trousers scrunched up
around his knees, his naked bum convulsing. I thought, *He's having
an intimate moment, I won't disturb him,* so I took a couple of steps
back. But just then I heard my brother's voice, weak and strangled
as though a large hand were covering his mouth. Could Ta be having sex with a girl when my brother is there watching him? I wondered if he'd offered to stay with my brother and watch over him
just so it would be possible to make love in secret? Who is this girl
he's hiding from me? Why the need for all these secrets?

The voice got louder, so I bent down again and this time I saw
Ta standing to the side, stroking his erect member, putting strawberry
cream on it—the kind my brother was so fond of—and showing
it off, adorned with sweets, to a person who the keyhole wouldn't
allow me to discern until Ta moved backward and my brother's
distorted, wretched face appeared before me, soiled with a mix of
cream and semen.

I don't know how I got the door open and reached him, faster
than an untamed wind, stronger than an earthquake, and started
hitting, punching, kicking, and beating him. Until what was underneath me was just a mess of features covered in blood and urine. I
didn't regain consciousness from my waking coma until my brother
took my hand and pulled me—us—out of the garage. I didn't want
to go with him, as though I intuited from that moment that I'd lost
the right to be outside, anywhere outside. He sat me on the doorstep of our house and, perching down next to me, put his head on
my shoulder like he used to when he was sleepy. He cried a little
and then fell asleep. When he woke up, it was already evening and
my family came, with Ta's family behind them, bringing the police,
who took us away—me to jail, Ta to the cemetery, and my brother
to one of those centers they call "special."

During "my absence," I learned that my brother had lost his appetite and that he used to ask for me from morning to night, while banging his head on the wall, repeating, "Kaaaaaa." Even looking at him makes your heart bleed, that's what my wife told me on one of her visits, after I entrusted her with his care. Whenever he saw her he would get more agitated and angry until the nurses would remove him, restraining his arms and legs and gagging him. Finally, she asked my permission to stop visiting him since every time he expected to see me and not her. My family stopped their visits to him too. But every time I asked about him, they'd all reassure me that he wanted for nothing, that he was in good hands, and that specialists were caring for him. I thought that prison came as a mercy to my parents, since it delivered them of me, because had I remained outside I wouldn't have let them do this to him and I would have inevitably committed two more crimes without batting an eyelid.

The eye knows that my brother died because of his loss—that he withered and decayed, oppressed and wanting, missing both me and Ta.

What I can't stand to think about is the certainty that he was—despite all that happened to him for so many years—still attached to Ta and loved him, unable to feel hatred or malice. When I think about that, it ignites remorse and defeat in me. I feel a burning fire inside myself, spreading through every inch of my insides, not leaving a trace on what originally were destruction and ruins.

Years have passed since this incident and the end of my sentence, which elapsed after five years since they determined mine was a "crime of passion," as the lawyer told me. As though it was somehow dictated by my passion. My passion for whom? My passion for my brother? My passion for Ta? Or my passion for our small family, made up of the three of us, motivated by the fact that our families were busy and not looking after us. This led to a desire within us to find that missing care by providing it to others. So I didn't search for an explanation for what happened, though it was the image of myself, scattered around like a doll whose limbs had been torn off, organs removed, and features smashed—that's what worried me. That's how my bodily functions and senses were all disrupted—my heart died, my intestines were squashed, my liver ripped out, and all that was left was an eye.

I am Mr. Kaaaa and I am nothing.

I sit down on the earth beneath the tree of melancholy, the lone tree, the last tree, my back against its trunk, my legs and feet sunken deeply into the grass and dirt. The plain lays out flat in front of me on a gentle slope, empty of anything that might hinder the coming of the wind. Not a pebble. Not a wisp of straw. Not a stick of wood. Leaves rustle above me and I know that I am about to expel my last breath. The eye looks up to the sky. A single cloud is passing by. A small cloud that doesn't disturb the tyranny of the sun. I hear a crackle of laughter moving among the branches, a gentle breeze drops fresh buds on my face and head. I hear it prancing about frivolously, whispering before looking over on me from within the lacy leaves with two small eyes and a half-open mouth full of saliva. The eye trembles, delighted, quivering, tearing up, and fluttering before opening its mouth, filled with a voice tumbling down on the plain, touching the grass.

"Khaaa . . ."

Then a blink. And a dot. And disconnect . . .

Originally written in Arabic.

ETERNITY AND THE HOURGLASS

BY HYAM YARED

Trabaud Street

"Time doesn't exist. In fact, it never existed," Hanane mumbles aloud while waiting her turn. It's been nineteen years now that she's waiting her turn in the cramped room on the second floor of the G Building on rue Trabaud, a narrow street on the East Side of Beirut.

While climbing the stairs two by two, she met the old lady who lives on the third floor. She pretended not to see her. Since she regained the use of her feet, she only takes the stairs. Upon reaching the landing, she looked at her watch. The hands showed 11:45. *And we've reduced nothingness to this*—she said to herself—*to stupid hands on a watch. Time is nothing but an invention, an illusion. It's not time that contains us*—she tells herself—*it's we who perceive it. Time is emptiness that our consciousness makes measurable.*

She wanted to share her discovery with her shrink. The prospect of talking about it makes her feverish. It was already 11:46 when she crossed the doorstep into the waiting room. She sat down, like always, on the armchair next to a coffee table, buckling under the weight of newspapers placed there to kill time.

The decor hasn't changed in nineteen years. She bears a grudge against the patient before her who is encroaching on her time. Forty-five minutes of consultation. Not one minute more. She knows her shrink is inflexible, but today she'll tell him—even if this means going over her allotted time.

She even wrote down the date of her discovery. January 20,

2011. She wrote it down right at the bottom of another list of other 20th of Januaries, noted in black marker. She finds it surprising that her discovery coincides with her list of 20th of Januaries. The sentence came to her while sleeping. *Time doesn't exist.* Upon waking, she jumped out of bed, seized her list, scribbled *January 20, 2011*, adding alongside it: *Time doesn't exist.* The fact that the nonexistence of time can be written down as a date and time—specifically a January 20—made her smile. She wanted to mark this event in pencil at the bottom of her list. That way, she could unseat time at will, she could wring its neck. She counts them. That's the number: nineteen 20th of Januaries. From the date of her discovery, nothing will ever be the same. Suffering. Pain. In order not to live these things, she'll now be able to think about how atemporal they are.

As soon as the door opens, she jumps up, puts her scrap of paper in her pocket, and smiles. The smell of his pipe wafting through the room comforts her. She knows it's her turn. Every Wednesday she waits for her shrink to appear in the doorway. Waving his hand, he motions to her to come in. She gets up and walks through hurriedly. As soon as the door shuts on them, Hanane is more fearless than ever.

"There is no time, doctor, there's just a hole. My body is an hourglass. The moment copulates in my blood over and over again. Each second is a woman giving birth. I give birth to time ad infinitum. Do you understand? I am time. Today we are January 20, 2011—that is to say *nowhere*. Time doesn't exist."

Hanane almost jumps out of her chair while speaking. Of all of this man's patients, she's the one who intrigues him the most. And exasperates him the most too. In nineteen years, even if her motor skills are in the process of being normalized, she nonetheless seems hopelessly stuck in mental lethargy. He experiences a feeling of powerlessness that he drowns out by puffing on his pipe. This morning, Hanane watches him preparing his tobacco like he always does at the beginning of a session. While filling up his pipe, he observes his patient's hands. Sometimes it seems to Hanane that he doesn't even see her. That he looks past her. She wiggles impatiently and continues on:

"We all have it all wrong. It isn't us who are captives of time, but the reverse. I live this space, therefore time is. Its measure is our consciousness. I'm telling you that in reality my body contains blood. Of the past. Of the future. Everything is an illusion. Atemporal, time is its own contradiction. It simply takes revenge and makes death flow through us. Do you hear me? Time is envious of the full power of our imagination through which it was born. It's unbearable to be a captive. Do you remember the hourglass that my father gave us? He was proud of his purchase: an eighteenth-century hourglass that he bought for next to nothing from an antique dealer at the Basta flea market. Of all the many objects he bought while antiquing there, he only exhibited this one—putting it right in the middle of the living room on the mantelpiece above the fireplace. Now it has been nineteen years that this object of measurement sits proudly, uselessly, in the same place. We, too, remain in the same place. The sand does nothing. Neither does time. Vanity lies in how space is organized."

And then she stopped talking.

Of course he remembers the hourglass. Whenever she called for extra sessions, it would inevitably be because she'd been in contact with the object on the very same day. Merely seeing the hourglass would trigger a crisis in her. This conical object, its sand enclosed by two glass vials and connected by a hole, anguished her. At first, she remained planted for hours in front of the door to the formal living room where the object could be found. She never crossed the room with her eyes open. Whenever she approached the hourglass, she tensed up, squinted, and breathed deeply before continuing on her way.

Despite the shrink's advice, her mother refused to move the object. Nonetheless, nineteen years earlier, it was she who had brought her daughter for a consultation, on the advice of a friend.

She followed her friend's directions to reach the clinic. After arriving at the top of the street, they passed by an old lady with disheveled hair and too much makeup who was pacing back and forth on the sidewalk. Her comings and goings gave off the smell of cheap perfume.

"If you pass a crazy lady standing on the sidewalk," her mother's friend said, "that means you're there. She rents a flat on the third floor; she's a nymphomaniac at the end of her career who picks up clients on the street. She's ugly and she stinks. Since no one wants her, she offers her body—for a fee—to construction workers to jump on after work. From time to time she finds clients who are in greater distress than she is who are interested in her decrepitude." Then, her mother's friend added seamlessly, "Avoid the crazy lady, bypass her, and ring for the second floor at the large gate just behind where she is."

Her mother did as she was told. She pushed her daughter's wheelchair, climbed up onto the sidewalk, and rang the building's intercom behind the old lady. The man on the second floor who opened the door to them was charming. A tall man, he had a carefully tended mustache jutting out below severe, dark eyes. A certain intensity radiated from his profile. Hanane remained indifferent to men's charm. She stared at her feet. The shrink motioned to them to come into the room in which there was a chaise lounge and two armchairs facing a desk, sitting behind which he seemed mostly to be protecting himself against the world. When he invited them to speak, Hanane said nothing.

"Doctor," her mother said, "for three months my daughter has found it pointless to move, walk, or eat. She remains stuck in the same position—sitting, her eyes staring at her legs. She froze, all of a sudden, on the very same day that my husband bought an hourglass. As soon as he took it out of its package, my daughter stiffened up. At the beginning, she was still walking normally—though more slowly—but nothing foreshadowed her refusal to move at all. It happened suddenly, shortly after the hourglass was bought. In fact, she stopped walking completely when her father died. She abhors her feet. She accuses them of wanting to make her move ahead. The idea of putting one foot in front of the other terrorizes her. She even refused to take part in the funeral procession. We visited practically every doctor in the city and did all the tests you can do. Physiologically, they detected nothing abnormal. She still stares at her legs, repeating endlessly that it's pointless to insist; she won't move forward. Sometimes she attacks them, swears at them, and accuses them of wanting to betray her. She screams at them, tells them that she's going die anyway, that she's already dead. Other times, she says she's going to be born later. I don't understand her delusions at all. Her father's death made her go mad . . . Even to sit her down on a wheelchair I had to twist her around . . ."

The shrink listened to the mother's speech, his eyes riveted on the barely pubescent girl who gave no sign of life. And what if delusions consist of misunderstanding delusions themselves? He nodded his head before interrupting the mother and proposing that she take a forty-five-minute walk without her daughter. When she came back, he took her aside.

"Ma'am, your daughter suffers from an inversion of time and an inability to adjust her perception of time to its usual standards of measurement. For her, moving ahead is regressing into the past. She moves ahead by going back toward yesterday. In other words, her future has already happened. She speaks of an hourglass sitting on a mantelpiece. It seems that this object is the trigger for this inversion. The sand moving through the vial terrorizes her. For her, it would need to slide from bottom to top. She's devastated by the idea that time moves forward."

Her mother understood nothing about this explanation—a future mixed with an inversion of measurements that advance backward toward tomorrow from bottom to top—and even less about the link between the hourglass and her daughter's illness. Until then, she had connected her daughter's illness to her father's death, on January 20th, 1992, a few days after the purchase of the hourglass. Seeing the object was when the troubles with her motor skills became apparent, but her paralysis didn't declare itself until the funeral. Just a little before, Hanane had struggled to even walk past the hourglass. Each time she came near it her breathing became constricted. Sometimes nausea followed her dizziness. Violent headaches took hold of her. She felt she was being sucked into a hole. Sometimes she'd scream, "No, not inside! Not into the hole! I refuse to move, the past is dead!"

Her father would lecture her: "Have you finished your tantrum? Move on."

Hanane would stagger forward.

A few hours before he died, on that January 20th of 1992, Hanane struggled really hard to brave the living room door and walk toward the fireplace. Coming right up to the object, she took a deep breath, quickly grabbed it, and put it away in the dresser drawer next to the wall.

When her father came back home, he took off his shoes as usual, breathing a long, satisfied sigh. Then, sprawled in his armchair—one hand on the armrest and the other fingering his rosary—he looked at the fireplace. Seeing the flat surface of the mantelpiece, as empty as it was smooth, his breathing slowed and, without any sound at all escaping from his mouth, a pain in his chest pinned him down right where he was. If it hadn't been for the sound of the rosary falling onto the marble-tiled floor, her mother wouldn't have realized that he died. When she saw her husband's body spread out, his head tilted backward, she moved quickly: she phoned the doctor, called her daughter, phoned the doctor again. Powerless, she'd witnessed the first heart attack in a series that her husband would eventually succumb to that very night.

Hanane observed the scene with equanimity. It was from that day on that she started making preposterous statements, accompanied by reverse body movements her mother couldn't recognize. It was now impossible to make her put one foot in front of the other. As soon as the period of receiving condolences was over, her mother did two things that to her mind were urgent: she took her daughter to a shrink, and she put the hourglass back in the same spot where her husband had placed it before his death. Superstitious, she associated it with his death and feared that removing it would mean that long years of unhappiness would befall her and her daughter. The shrink indeed had to concede on this point, finding it wise that his patient should stay in contact with some kind of object that measured time, despite the symptoms from which she was suffering.

"Births, I hate births. Out of birthing spasms, my father was born, right before my eyes." This is how Hanane told the story of her father's death to her shrink the next day. She pointed her finger behind her to indicate tomorrow and wrote down her next session on pages of her daily planner that had already passed. He stared at her, while her movements remained all entangled, disjointed. Even the war had no impact on how entrenched his patient was. The mounds of dead bodies on TV elicited no compassion in her whatsoever. She feared living much more than dying, and showed no response to destruction. The few times that she revealed any interest in life during these nineteen years were in an effort to not upset her mother. She knew very well that her illness was making her mother sad. She would have really liked to take her in her arms, to tell her to stop calling upon "the Lord's help in this curse."

Hanane couldn't bear to see her mother selling her soul to an eternal being in this way. Eternity is only nothingness, she told her. "She prays to God, do you realize that?" she told the shrink. "She prays to an eternal being who depends on her."

Hanane didn't plan anything. At the age of thirty-five, after nineteen years of therapy, things erupted inside her abruptly. She could launch into endless monologues and then right in the middle of a sentence sink into a silence heavier than a ton of leaden weights, then not move anymore, not speak anymore. At times, she would extract her little scrap of paper from her pocket and would pass the rest of the session feverishly scrunching it up. Eventually the shrink knew exactly when Hanane would take out this crumpled scrap of paper that she carried with her everywhere. Since she'd been in therapy, she was never separated from it.

It was the therapist who had, at first, introduced the concept to her, inviting her to write down everything that crossed her mind. He had hoped in this way to make her regain contact with a chronological perception of time. "This is part of the game," he told her at the beginning of a session, putting a sheet of A4-sized paper down in front of her. On that day, the forty-five minutes elapsed like that. Hanane didn't say one word and was content to stare at the paper without moving. She had the impression that the page's emptiness had spread throughout the room, devouring the shrink, his pipe, and the smell of tobacco. She shook her head a few times. Aside from several televised newsflashes, she didn't think of anything that she could write down.

Just before the end of the session, she grabbed a black pen resting on the desk and wrote diligently: *January 20, 1992 = the death of my father = the arrival of the hourglass*. Then, without warning, as though she'd never simply just stopped walking, she got up out of the wheelchair, betraying no sigh of surprise, and left.

When she saw her daughter walking, the mother had to restrain herself from raving. The shrink had directed her not to show any signs of keen interest in anything in front of her daughter, for fear that too overt an allusion to her illness might block her anew. In any case, for him, victory resided above all in his client's regaining her perception of time.

For the first time, Hanane connected an object of time measurement to facts and dates. From this day on, she started writing down all events related to January 20 that came after the arrival of the hourglass. In her eyes, no other date in the year deserved to be identified. For nineteen years she only marked down 20th of Januaries. The shrink tried in vain to try to transform this exercise into a daily ritual, telling her that there were 365 days in the year, but nothing worked. Hanane only played this game on the

20th of January each year. This date was marked by different events between 1992 and 2010. Audrey Hepburn died January 20, 1993; Barack Obama was inaugurated president of the United States in 2009; George W. Bush was inaugurated eight years earlier; Arafat's victory after the first Palestinian general elections in 1996; the former Argentinian dictator Reynaldo Bignone was arrested in 1999 . . . She even found it useful to compile an inventory of deaths caused by the avian flu epidemic on January 20, 2007.

Hanane is feverish. The shrink fills his pipe. Their silence is interrupted by the sighs that rise in a crescendo. Hanane knows that the neighbor on the third floor has found a client. "Orgasms are a noisy hobby. And useless." The shrink is surprised that she says this . . . she who is so focused whenever he appeals to her sense of perception. She even refuses to confirm the existence of her own body, each time that he tries to draw attention to the fact that she herself has aged since she started coming to him. Hanane would prefer to be outside of time and of her body. The sighs continue to reach them. She has to speak or plug her ears. She can't stand the upstairs neighbor's small cries. She has to cover them up. She twiddles her fingers and starts talking. He doesn't like it when she speaks in bursts. He doesn't like her fingers either.

"My mother keeps forbidding me to put the hourglass away. She says that she needs to have it there on the mantelpiece to remember my father. I still see him, sitting on his armchair. Just as the sand flowed through it, his head nodded from side to side. The problem is measurement. The neighbor's screams are also a measurement. And then his head fell, soft like death. But life is also soft. I want to be so steep that nothing can move across me. Not your eyes, not your thoughts. I want to be steeper than time. This morning I passed by the hourglass and felt nothing for the first time. Do you know why? Because I discovered that time doesn't exist. I should have thought about this earlier. I am my own free will. Only I, and I alone, can put an end to everything. God, time, eternity. I crush them. Like insects. It is enough just to think about it. Time doesn't exist. Exit, time. Exit. Pshhht."

"So what did you write down today other than that time doesn't exist? After all, today is the 20th of January."

"Nothing. Didn't feel like it." Then she corrects herself: "Oh yes, I wrote down that Kalthoum Sarrai died."

"Don't know her."

"She played the part of Super Nanny in the French version of a show by that same name. She died of cancer. Like me. I died of that too."

Her shrink frowns. He doesn't like it when she starts using the past tense to speak about the future. He is quick to follow up: "What do you know about your own death?"

"Everything."

"What do you mean, *everything*?"

"Just that."

"And what about joy? Won't you ever list that?"

"Joy is flat."

"What do you mean?"

"Just that. Flat. As flat as the Beqaa Valley." She pantomimes a flat surface with her hands.

"But at the end of the day, all you mark down on your list are disasters, dictatorships, epidemics, and cancers. History has also known happy occasions . . . And friends? Don't you have any that bring you joy?"

"Sure I do, but they're all flat too."

When her responses become incomprehensible, he knows it's pointless to press on. But he always tries nonetheless. He wants to understand why Hanane persists in never listing events before 1992, the year her father died. Every time he has pursued this question with her, she has retreated into herself. Her retreat starts with her eyes. Her ability to talk follows, it becomes confused and then she's silent. He tries in vain to tell her that she can't mourn for so many years, but she absolutely refuses to touch the 20th of Januaries before the ones already on her list. Yet it's his responsibility. Before the end of each session, he always mentions it. This time he grasps at a straw.

"But if time doesn't exist, you could add the nonexistence of events before 1992 to your list."

"It isn't necessary to predict everything," she answers tersely. Ever since she first deciphered his methods of diversion, she's found it ludicrous to sidle up to madness.

The young woman's closed expression makes him understand that a locked world has descended upon her. Her sense of urgency from the beginning of the session is now nothing but a memory. She doesn't even take her crumpled list out of her pocket, as she always does when she wants to drown the silence with frantic movements. She will freeze, stand up, and, for the first time since she's been coming to him, approach his desk. She doesn't tell him that she finds him cowardly. Instead, she stares at him and with a sharp motion, thrusts out her hand to him.

Hanane has never yet shown any desire for physical contact whatsoever. Disconcerted, he holds his hand out to her in return. Her eyes focus on him, but she doesn't make any another movement. Nervously, he leans slightly toward her. When their fingers touch, Hanane's hand is as cold as a cadaver's.

The next Wednesday Hanane doesn't come, though she hadn't canceled her appointment. Opening his office door, the shrink finds Hanane's mother sitting in her daughter's usual place. He motions for her to enter. The mother shakes her head and hands him a piece of paper. He immediately recognizes Hanane's list of her life's 20th of Januaries. This scrap of paper no longer looks like anything. He smoothes it out. A single date has been added to the list. A date before 1992. A January 20th in the year 1985. Next to the year he can read:

Strange body penetrated my body. This isn't about time, God, or eternity. It is about my father's dick. When his penis entered my body, time left. That hurt, and then nothing. "A trickle of blood doesn't matter," my father said. When I saw victims of the war on TV, that also didn't matter. Pain is immobile. So are we. Chronos isn't time. Time isn't time. Where I am, time is. I kill myself because metastasis is imminent. Cancer is lucidity. Everything hates us. The past. The future. They hate each other. Chronology is nothing but an illusion. We are victims of the compression of nothingness into a notion called time . . . it's pain that makes eternity, not time.

Her mother found the scrap of paper next to her daughter's lifeless body on the day after January 20, 2011. Next to her in bloodred was written: *Time doesn't exist. I cut off its head.*

Originally written in French.

PART II

PANORAMA OF THE SOUL

BEIRUT APPLES

BY LEILA EID

Bourj Hammoud

O ctober 10. The tenth day of the tenth month. Hah, oh my God.

10/10 . . . it's my birthday . . . What if they came back? Just like that, and walked through this door right now at their real, young ages. Amer, my father; Farah, my mother (I used to joke and tease her when she'd get angry at me and cry, reminding her that her name meant *joy*); Amir, Rustum, and Zeina, my siblings—they are bringing me little gifts and a big birthday cake. Would they know me now that I'm older than them? I'd perhaps be a more appropriate father to them now than a brother, even though I was the eldest child. As for Amer and Farah, I'm nearly their age and we've become close friends. Who knows, perhaps we'd sit together and reminisce about our childhood and adolescence.

But how would they know my address? And if they knew it, would I even see them? Can the dead come back to life? What if they hadn't died, and I'd merely imagined this—what if they were alive and remembering me? Do I really want to see them? Do I really want to see anyone? Me—who's walking terrified, pressed up against every wall on the ship, as if I were a shadow, trying to hide from the apparition of a human, cat, or even a mouse, seeking shelter in the closest container or near a broken lamppost. I wait, trembling and shivering like someone touched by madness.

I didn't sleep after I heard Amer saying that night, "Farah, Farah, we can't stay here much longer . . . Listen to me . . . we've become nothing but live offerings, ready victims, even if they haven't announced it openly . . . As soon as one person is killed or kidnapped in the capital, we'll be the first revenge, the surrogate for unknown blood spilled in a dark and unjust dispute. They killed Samer that night. No one could protect him . . . They said that five masked men abducted him from his house after they raped his wife in front of him. They showed mercy to his children when they shoved them into the bathroom, threatening to pour cold water on them if they so much as made a single sound. His eldest son was not so lucky, his arm was broken—his siblings heard it crack—when he attempted to scream, calling for help, trying to defend his parents. They were stricken by what seemed like a mute stupor . . . They executed Samer right there behind the olive press. Jihad, Rameh, and I saw a wet explosion, red splattered on the wall . . .

"When Nael and his fiancée suddenly disappeared, everyone said they left to elope, they ran off to get married far away because Nael is the neighborhood strongman and the handsome fellow didn't have the means to pay for the wedding. That's how he presented Nawal's parents with a fait accompli. Some people snickered, saying that it all happened with Nawal's father's agreement, because he was known for his extreme stinginess—this way he'd be able to escape from the financial burdens of a wedding and the related hospitality . . . Then the village—though I can no longer say the whole village—was stunned, because it became clear to me and everyone else that the people being killed were all the same kind of people, when the corpses of the couple who'd eloped were found on the way out of Tell al-Qasa'yin, where no son of Adam—and not even the jackals—dared to pass because of the savageness of the place, its thick, wild plant growth and the poisonous snakes. Then, when Fares was found dead in his orchard under the walnut tree, a labneh sandwich in one hand and a flask of village 'araq in the other, they said he killed himself, the growing season is sparse this year. Fares couldn't bear the brunt of his debt and all this loss so he killed himself . . . His pruning clamp was leaning cold and sad against the tree trunk, wishing it could utter a testimony of truth for its old friend . . . It was also said that Hani drowned in the lake, he wasn't good at swimming, he's been afraid of water since his childhood. He used to get a beating and then he'd go take a bath, according to what his mother said . . . His comrades weren't able to rescue him, the boat was getting farther away and then gave out when they tried to return to help him . . . Who can utter a tale different from all the others, which rationalizes the tragic departure of these souls?

"What secret word, my Farah, is being spread through the alleys, houses, gardens, pools of water, and winds, preventing everyone from having funerals, reporting, and making complaints? Need I spell things out for you, telling you more stories of their mysterious disappearance? Their disappearance drenched with the mercilessness of a forcible death, their torture and execution, only because they belong to a particular sect, to a sect and its presumed thought, a kind of classification as it becomes a strange new identity, no longer having the right to exist here among a different majority group. How do they appoint themselves the gods of the new era, controlling the destiny of innocent people and ending their lives in this way, tearing them up by their roots and throwing them away like the weeds that grow around the edges of ancient balconies? By what right . . . by what right . . . ? Should I tell you more? Should I recite to you the mythical conversation I had with the ghosts of these corpses? How they visit me in dreams when I'm sleeping and then I can't sleep anymore . . . We have to leave, I can't tolerate the thought of any kind of harm coming to you and the children, I can't stand the thought of our family ending like this . . . We must leave as soon as possible. Tomorrow is better than later . . . Tomorrow we'll leave for Beirut . . ."

"Oh Amer, the war is at its fiercest over there. That's what we see and hear on the news every evening. It shows guns, bombs, destruction, and murder everywhere," I heard Farah saying in a low voice.

But Amer cut her off before she could continue: "If we die over there they'll know us, give us a funeral, and bury us—not throw our corpses to the monsters without even saying a prayer."

"*What harms the sheep after it's flayed?* Isn't that what you said once . . . ? If we die we're dead. Isn't that true, Dad?" But of course Amer didn't hear me.

W-e w-i-l-l l-e-a-v-e for B-e-i-r-u-u-u-u-u-u-t . . . We will leave for Beirut . . . W-e w-i-l-l l-e-a-v-e . . . B-e-i-r-u-t . . . The sentence rang in my ears and my head like the loud, irritating howl of a car horn . . . Exactly like the horn of Bahjat's car, he's the most famous show-off in our village. *We will leave for Beirut.* How, when I am a son of the plains and natural springs? I am a child of the hills and the little valley, I truly delight in being a shepherd, taking care of goats, cows, and sheep. To whom will I leave the sky here, as I'm the guardian of the dust-covered mountain, whose color is that of our newly born foal? In my heart, I carry the secrets of the clouds and the melting snow on the peaks. I entrusted to the river a song that would make every grain of wheat—and every pomegranate and fig tree—grow, a song for the orphaned walnut tree on the roof of our house and for the grapevines.

Where are you taking us, Dad? To Beirut, what is this Beirut . . . where is it located? Is it frightening? Why did Harut burst into tears when his father told him, "We are going back to Beirut"? Is there enough space over there for me to travel with my kite that I handle like a helmsman, all of whose dreams are contained on his ship? Will there be a mukhtar there whom I will force to buy a new tarboush every week because I stole his and hid it in the cellar where I had a dozen or more, into which I crammed my childhood treasures: the biggest egg, the biggest turtle, the biggest heart-shaped stone, the biggest fossilized shell, Miss Noura's glasses, my friend Rendala's hairband, my colored marbles, the first lira you gave me, and a beautiful picture of you between my grandfather and grandmother . . . Will they call us over there to help shovel the snow from the roof of the school? We'll rush over, running like soldiers to the most important battle. Our heads will swivel around, ultrasurprised and buoyant, when we arrive and see our classrooms converted into a warm shelter for bobwhites, owls, and some stray cats and dogs, even jackals. The cold made them all forget their antipathy toward each other and they shared our school's roofs with mutual empathy.

Oh Dad, what else can I say? I have a lot of questions, the most important is how can I pack up, right now in one night, all of my things and memories, what place can contain them . . . can Beirut contain them?

We were stuffed into Amer's Honda with all the bags we could find and the things Farah considered necessary . . . I didn't know where my siblings got the song they kept repeating throughout the journey, "*Toot toot, to Beirut . . . Daddy take us on a trip . . .*" It compelled my father to shout, ordering them to calm down the first time, and to yell, "Silence!" the second . . . But then he smiled at Zeina, looking at me in the mirror when she asked him, "Daddy, can we pick olives and grapes there like Rustom and Amir said, or only red apples like Majd told me?"

Did Beirut appear, in the way I saw it from the windows of the car, *high*? That is to say, *in ecstasy*? (This is a word that I hadn't heard before and that I'm not good at using. Remembering it now, it seems really appropriate, after learning its meaning and having experienced it when I smoked hashish for the first time with Harut and our friends.) Lying back innocently, permitting her beautiful naked body to be torn apart by guests, visitors, and her own people, Beirut—accustomed to many invasions, of foreigners, greedy people, earthquakes, and tremors—always came back even more beautiful and glorious than before, that's what we learned in our history books. What does it feel today when its people are dividing up its meat and leaving only the bones? Do cities go mad due to their excess beauty, and unable to stand their own perfection, consume themselves? Will they come back again more beautiful than before? Will their splendor be further restored? Who will inform them that one day they may be disfigured?

Getting together with Abu Harut and his family was warm and intimate. They received us with love and friendship. Umm Harut didn't stop talking, explaining, describing, kissing and hugging me on one side while hugging and kissing my siblings on the other, until we felt safe and at home. With the same impulse, she didn't hesitate to push us off her lap if she heard bullets whizzing by or the thundering of a faraway explosion. She would rush over to the window, pointing with her hand, saying loudly in her heavy Armenian accent: "Aman, my Lord Aman, how can he say one day there is a cease-fire? . . . Aman, this radio lies and the television does too, anyway . . . far . . . far, let's go, Umm Majd, come up to the kitchen with me. I am making lahmajoun for you all, the boy must be hungry . . ."

Not long after that day, it became clear how relationships would be in the future: my father + Abu Harut, my mother + Umm Harut, these people would be our only relatives. Harut and I took over a corner of the living room and started talking like old friends, monitoring our parents with wide smiles and watching how our siblings played together in harmony. I had seen his little brother Kevork before, but for a while I couldn't stop looking at Tamara's face. Tamara is his sister, about whom I almost called out to my father the very first moment I saw her, "This is the gazelle, it's her. Why don't you believe me when I tell you that I saw her jumping in front of me, soft, redheaded, and luminous, in Marjat al-Zaarour? She stopped for a moment once and stared right into my eyes before disappearing in a fog like a thick cloud of incense."

I remember very well the day I saw Harut for the first time in our village, together with his father who used to come to our farm regularly—sometimes for work and other times to drink a glass of 'araq with my father. Because of his work, Abu Harut used to know the livestock traders in our area as well as the owners of the farms. That day, Harut told me that they owned a butcher's shop in Bourj Hammoud and were among the most famous makers of basterma—a traditional Armenian dish of cured meat with a mix of spices—which I hadn't heard of before. It later became one of my favorite dishes, along with patsha, sujouk, and other delicious Armenian foods that my mother began cooking as a consequence. Harut didn't inform me at the time that I would see my gazelle again many years later at their house.

I don't know why Abu Harut preferred always dealing with my father, since he owned such a small herd. He remained a loyal friend, visiting us whenever the opportunity arose, sometimes bringing Harut with him, even after my father had to sell his little herd to Abu Jawwad, who devoured everything and everybody, totally destroying the livelihoods of the smallholders.

My father didn't belong to a party and I'd never felt that he paid attention to politics or anything other than fulfilling our requests, preserving the stability of our family life, and securing everything we needed. We were the world to him, our mother and us. I contemplated his face while he was drinking coffee with Abu Harut, neither of them pausing their conversation at all except to drink what was in their cups. At the time, a naive hunch made me guess that my father didn't want to either blend in on the East Side of the city, or to melt into the West Side (that's what the two halves of divided Beirut were called at that time). It was perhaps for this reason that he rang his Armenian friend asking for help.

I remember what he whispered to my mother after Abu Harut left: "In Lebanon, there are nearly a hundred thousand Armenians, scattered all throughout its different regions. Many live in Bourj Hammoud, Anjar, and Antelias and have gotten Lebanese citizenship. They have a number of representatives in the parliament distributed between three main parties: Tashnag, Henchag, and Ramgavar. Armenians have played an important role in Lebanese society for a long time, holding a certain weight in political life. Today they keep the same distance from all of the sects that the Lebanese people belong to. They haven't retreated from these ethical principles and they are liked and respected by everyone. That's why their area of Beirut has remained safer than others."

Amer continued: "Abu Harut, like all Armenians, will always remember what happened to his ancestors: the great massacre that began on April 24, 1915. On that day, the Turkish forces imprisoned six hundred Armenian leaders in Istanbul and proceeded to liquidate them, killing all their boys and men. Every soldier in the Turkish army of Armenian origin was discharged, sent to do hard labor, and then killed. The Armenians in Eastern Anatolia were given a notice to evacuate their houses within twenty-four hours or else be killed. When they left their villages, the liquidation of all the healthy men was complete, and only the women, children, and old people were allowed to flee, walking hundreds of kilometers on foot without food or medicine."

Every time he tells it to me, the story makes him cry, as though he doesn't want to forget how on that road women were raped, others were tortured, until almost all of them perished in one way or another. Or how the Kurdish and Turkoman tribes joined the Ottoman soldiers in torturing the Armenians. So that in roughly a year, no less than a million Armenians were killed—that is to say, half of the Armenians living in the shadow of the Ottoman Empire. Abu Harut would tell me that the Turks, despite the abomination of this tragedy, didn't recognize the murder of more than three hundred thousand people and refused to admit that this operation had been planned, intentionally and resolutely.

In any case, arranging a place for us to live was not difficult for Abu Harut. My father had money and some savings, enough for us to not need support from anyone else, and moreover he could get a license to use the Honda as a taxi.

No shape before me was clear, everything seemed like a mirage, an unreal world covered by a thick blue fog, which I carried with me from my village between the mountains and the plains. At this time, the houses in Beirut would empty and fill with people in strange ways, sometimes without good reason. Areas had not yet become definitively entrenched or their sectarian identities absolutely clear. But the singularity of Bourj Hammoud—where Abu

Harut and his family had lived from the time his father had come to Lebanon, and whose landmarks are preserved in my memory and my heart—was reflected in its houses, alleys, and markets, populated by large families, most of whom the war couldn't budge from the property they owned, despite all of the displacement happening in Lebanon. Shops and pharmacies were spread throughout their neighborhoods, carrying the names of their home regions in Armenia in two languages—Armenian and Arabic—reflecting their attachment to their mother tongue and an identity that had not faded away in its owners' souls, despite the passage of time. What was notable was that the people of Bourj Hammoud's refused to be grouped within a special segregated "ghetto," off-limits to others. I heard Abu Harut speak disapprovingly about this, stressing, "We will never form a closed society, this region of ours reflects a model of coexistence between different sects, and this naming—*ghetto*—advances political goals. Look, Abu Majd, look next door to the Armenian shops and you'll find Muhammad's shop, Joseph's shop, or Sacco's . . ."

That area has its own special scent; I can still almost smell the fragrant mix of hot spices which flavored their delicious food, and hear Harut's voice in my ear saying cheerfully, "There are many kinds of food which we brought to the Lebanese that they like—sujouk and basterma—just as we took tabbouleh, kibbe, and stuffed vine leaves from them." He saw a kind of fusion and reciprocity in this. He followed up, imitating his father: "We took hospitality and generosity from you, baba, and you took from us many kinds of arts and crafts, like jewelry and shoemaking . . . and don't forget fixing watches, baba, ha ha ha!"

But the Armenians are so distinguished by their "broken" Arabic that this became a general way for Lebanese people to refer to Armenians, since most of the elderly people from Armenia would masculinize the feminine and feminize the masculine, and squeeze the word *baba* into their speech, a sign of affection perhaps.

After visiting many apartments, my father chose one in a building that was modern, relative to the other houses and buildings nearby. It wasn't located in Bourj Hammoud or deep inside it—on the al-Nabaa side, for example. It wasn't even in Doura, an area bordering it and stretching out from the coast to the Northern Metn. It was along the big highway from which we could see Karantina and, in the blink of an eye, the "West Side" of the capital at the time. So were we really on the "East Side"? I don't know because on the right side there was a little old mosque which worshippers frequented all the time, as well as that modest church with its round domes on the north side. The building was located right between them and even the news reports—from radio or television stations, which we started to follow when bombardments on our area intensified—weren't able to determine once and for all which area this building that Amer chose as the location for our new home belonged to.

I couldn't count the number of explosions that had gone off and bombs that had fallen, either on people or on buildings, when we found ourselves on the threshold of our alleged youth. That's how we used to measure our lives in Beirut, not in years at all. Some of us, when we wanted to remember happy or sad things, started to connect them to an endless, bloody series: the War of the Souqs, Tel al-Zaatar, the Battle of the Hotels, the murder of Bachir Gemayel, the entry of the Deterrent Force, the Hundred-Day War on Ashrafieh by the Syrian army, the Mountain War, the War of the Camps, the Israeli invasion . . . Sabra and Shatila . . . There was no need to count the years here, as I said, our lives were made of gunfire, random bullets shot by depraved snipers.

However, our days were not free from periods when there were truces, long ones sometimes, and then we would forget that this multifaceted Lebanese War, which never held to a fixed stance on anything, hadn't yet finished and had itself forgotten that it hadn't yet come to an end. This perhaps goes back to the fact that from our childhood it was a reality that peace had merely become a word—always tenuous and elusive—and if it were able to prevail here one day, it would seem artificial. Despite this, I didn't neglect my studies. Indeed, I was actually working hard and Harut nicknamed me "The Genius." But on summer vacation I would fulfill my violent desire to discover everything. Entertainment began in the cinemas and Harut and I would move around between the Sevan, Carminique, Arax, Florida, and Canar (theaters with the names of Armenian towns and villages) to choose what suited our mood: westerns, documentaries, horror flicks, romantic comedies, and adventures. We wouldn't hesitate to leave a film at the beginning if we heard people whispering that another cinema was showing an exciting sex movie.

My talent in the subjects of science and mathematics became evident. My head worked like a little computer, absorbing information, memorizing numbers, and solving problems effortlessly. I used to help Harut with his lessons and he would repay me by letting me into the depths of his Armenian world, boasting about me in front of his comrades in "the Party"—that I was the only one able to disassemble a Kalashnikov and put it back together again in seconds, that I was also the only one who memorized the names of the explosives found in shells and bombs, like the back of my hand, and that I could make hundreds from it if I wanted to . . . I was his friend and his treasure and he was my only friend who I was proud of, so I didn't refuse when he asked me to join the party. This ensured I would stay with him and accompany him on the local neighborhood security patrols and surveillance in the area.

Before the war broke out there were Armenian leaders and strongmen too, who ruled streets and neighborhoods with a tight grip, just like the prominent Lebanese ones who became famous. However, the war dampened their fires, put an end to their roles and their near-mythical legends. New leaders and strongmen took their place, imposing a military reality under the influence of armed parties and militias.

The neighborhood, home to so many Armenians, remained for the most part distant from the thunder of bombs and exchange of incursions, which the combatants undertook to seize strategic buildings and areas beyond those already under their control. But no matter how it was contained, the sparks of the war would undoubtedly escape from time to time, afflicting many people's hearts with greed in the absence of both law and the authority of the state. But the Party, as Harut said, was ready and able to impose its will, with a kind of autonomous governance and stringent reverence, so that things wouldn't "get out of control," as was happening in other regions of Lebanon. Behind an old government building, Harut took me to see this one night; he showed me with my own eyes how the death penalty was implemented for hooligans, anyone tempted by heroics or who strayed from the will of the party and obedience to it.

Would my friendship with Harut and his love for me, my ability to understand the Armenian language, and my belonging to the Party (and this is a tricky if not impossible matter for a non-Armenian person, and perhaps what made my mother constantly repeat that my grandmother's late mother was Armenian) intercede on my behalf? Would all these factors intervene one day and enable Abu Harut to accept me as his son-in-law and allow me to marry his only daughter Tamara? Tamara, who was blossoming like magic with the beauty of a wild red rose and whose splendor and uniqueness Farah had been always proud of in the village. Tamara knew that I loved her and that I was sure I lived in her heart and her two sweet eyes . . . But Armenian fathers, in spite of everything, don't consent to marry their daughters to "sons of Arabs," except reluctantly. And yet I presumed there was still time, and that I would be able to add to the list of my good qualities later . . . so I thought.

The naked women at the Dixino nightclub no longer excited me as much as the poker machine at Paradisio, one of the many amusement centers that sprouted up like mushrooms during the war spreading all over. Perhaps I'm not being precise enough about describing my feelings: I spent an entire week in the embrace of

"Raquel," not leaving the room, obsessed with all the sexual pleasure that I discovered. However, it is possible to say that a different, fleeting exaltation possessed me when I entered this place, accompanied by Harut, out of curiosity. It was the same exaltation as the one that overwhelms a child who's entering an amusement park for the first time. Was the reason the lights, the music, or those intoxicating sights which deceived the eyes of the people occupied by their games, fixing their attention on the numbers and symbols cascading before them on those graceful machines, making us pass by right near them, invisible like ghosts? Was I enticed by the relief on their faces at the moment they won, knowing that I was not a money-collecting enthusiast? Or was it the direct challenge that my mind formulated at that moment to discover the secret of those machines' programs? What is the right time to start ejecting money after the pockets of so many people have been exhausted? Would I be able to decode the mystery and be the cleverest and luckiest player? Or is this the time in which I smelled it burning—like in our teen years—and which passes with a delightful slowness, here in this place that seemed outside of time, without thinking about the death lurking in the very molecules of air that we breathe in Beirut? I don't know what reason to give for my attraction, nor do I know what gripped me, but I do know that I was suddenly a child again and desperately wanted to play with that machine.

Only a short time passed before I got used to the place and started going there without Harut. This made me feel more relaxed. Something led me to Paradisio like I was bewitched. I didn't think about my future there, or my past in my village, or the shaky and unstable present in which I was living . . . as if I were on a swing.

I am the little plant uprooted from in front of the doorstep of our house. No longer planted in soil, my aerial roots extend upward, suspended in midair, not touching any land at all. Who am I? For a time I was not Majd the village kid, and of course I was not a city kid either. I wasn't Christian or Muslim; I wasn't Lebanese or Armenian. I tried hard to be something but I couldn't. Who am I?

When did I become a monster who didn't dare scare anyone but himself, because he was so distant from his fluid self, like a colorless liquid, a self whose truth he didn't show until he forgot it? I am merely what others want to see . . . When did I start taking on this role? How and why?

My anger at myself, Beirut, and Lebanon perhaps didn't stop at the Paradisio, but I eventually did calm down and forget the bitter taste filling my mouth for a little bit. The place game me distance from my questioning and my reality that made me homeless and without an identity in Lebanon, the distant Lebanon that still didn't know me and neither did I know it. Here alone did I dare to separate out the features of my face as I used to see them in the mirror every evening. Here alone I cast off my face, my age, my body, my sexual desires; I reconciled with my old age and accepted it, as befits my feeling that I don't belong. Exactly like the poker machine, which doesn't distinguish between one player and another. Thus I was there alone . . . free of Harut, my family, and my love for Tamara. Unrestrained by these chains, I didn't have to speak, think, or concentrate on anything. I used to lose money there with massive pleasure, as though I were spending a part of my life that I didn't want. I was donating it to the devil. To counterbalance this, I returned once again to give from my pocket what I had won yesterday and buy new clothing for the naked angel of my dreams.

I don't know how this happened, but one day I suddenly noticed I was totally immersed, to the point of being almost in a coma, in the body of this machine of fleeting death, this machine of the next life. This machine of dreams. Perhaps the four red hearts on the colored screen in front of me were my sure win in the carré ace game, the special prize dedicated to someone who got lucky that night. For moments the place returned to reality and the people had to wake up for a few minutes and everyone around me started to yell with joy or greed, cursing their luck, feeling deep jealousy, before returning to their previous state—that is to say, disconnected from reality. But none of this matters. Only one voice filled my ears and it didn't care about the amount that Avo, the owner of Para-disio, gave to me with his own hand.

I hadn't informed anyone where I was. Did my mother send him after me because it was my birthday and everyone wanted to surprise me because I always ran away from these kinds of occa-sions? Was it the sound of the explosion that thundered a bit earlier and shook up my heart for a minute but that I ignored? This wasn't the first time I stayed out very late during intensive bombardments. Was it because of the party's state of alert, fearing a surprise attack?

"Inch beses, Harut?"—What's up?—I asked in Armenian. He didn't answer but grabbed my hand and led me outside.

I don't know how much time passed with me over there driven into the ground like a nail. Did I die all of a sudden and arrive at the gates of hell with the tongue of the flames of hellfire charring my face? As we approached my apartment building, the sounds of little explosions, one after another, increased because of gas can-isters in people's apartments and cars parked both in front of the building and under it. These sounds brought me back to reality but I was not sure that I had really returned. It seemed to me as if I were observing the scene from above, or from behind a transpar-ent curtain. I saw the paramedics, Party and civilian ambulances, armed men belonging to the official security forces and the militias. Women and men in nightgowns and pajamas, party clothes and normal clothes. Babies and children and teenage boys and girls and old people. Toys were flying through the air, mixed with papers, arms and legs, and dreams. All of it seemed tenuous, light, and floating, hovering above land without gravity. Is this Resurrection Day? Have the dead risen?

Hurry, there are people alive, hurry, there are corpses, hurry, there's someone burning and he's alive, there's someone choking and he's alive, someone trying to lift a wall off his shattered skull, without hands . . . Hurry . . . hurry, there's the voice of a child.

"Hurry, they're alive . . . Majd, they are alive, hurry up!" Harut

called from the seventh hell or seventh heaven, I don't know . . .
I'd gotten separated from him when I saw the bloodied faces of my
family, their closed eyes, black dust obscuring their features and everything else. Were they sleeping, had they lost consciousness, were
they alive, or were they simply dead?

I didn't dare approach the ambulance and I didn't even have a
desire to accompany them. In reality, I couldn't. All I could do was
run—run or fly—toward the port with Harut's voice ringing in my
ears as though it were coming from another world: "Where are you
going? You have to come with me to the hospital, they may be alive
. . . Come back . . . come back . . ."

But I kept running like someone penetrating an endless, closed
in, red-hot fog. I couldn't feel any part of my body. I became an er-
rant, gelatinous mass of that angry air that Beirut breathed. I was a
screaming voice, weighed down by pain I couldn't bear. How could
Harut dare to call me to come back?

Did he not see the lock of incandescent fire from Tamara's red
hair silently fading into the blood flowing from Zeina's sliced open
cheek? Is it conceivable that I alone saw her translucent shoulders,
like my passionate desire for her, embracing like two stems of broken lilies, pinned down like a murdered dove among the bodies of
my family and the others?

I saw her hair, I saw her shoulders, and I saw my life extinguished
at that moment. Her red hair, which for so long had excited my passion, my dreams, and my hopes, was a volcano. Here it is now—like
everything else—smoldering in front of me, and sleeping . . .

Come back? Come back to whom?

On the tenth day of the tenth month that year, a little bit before midnight, I stole onto that unknown ship, which was carrying
boxes of red apples. The ship was ready to leave from the port of
Beirut. I never came back.

Originally written in Arabic.

BIRD NATION

BY RAWI HAGE

Corniche/Ashrafieh

I t is a contested fact that wheat is behind the current global obe-sity epidemic. Many new studies claim that newly genetically modified wheat is the decisive factor in, among other mental and physical complications, weight gain. Let us take, as a specimen, the Lebanese population and thoroughly scrutinize the subject, so that we might deduce whether wheat and its derivatives are, in fact, a grand contributor to the obesity of this small nation. We observe that obesity is most visible in the rulers, politicians, and, certainly, the clerical class.

The use of utensils at the Lebanese table is not essential. The fork and the spoon were originally absent, introduced only during French rule of the region. But there was no need for them at all because the Lebanese had found a way to use their thin bread as both a grabbing device and a scooping utensil. This practice, one must admit, is an ingenious way of preserving both autonomous and hygienic practice in a cuisine that encourages sharing and the communal consumption of food. Each person rips off a small piece of bread and uses it to handle the food and consume it. He or she will go on to take a new, freshly ripped piece of bread to scoop or grab again. In this manner, every bit of food is consumed, and every consumption uses a new and clean utensil.

There are exceptions, of course, such as when eating birds, which one eats with bare hands and without the use of bread. For such occasions, a word was invented, *nesh*, which means *eating without bread*.

Lebanon's renowned cuisine could well be one of the most diverse and healthy in the world. Well, without the wheat factor, of course. Wheat, or more precisely bread, is the country's misdemeanor, perhaps even its underappreciated tragedy, along with its unbearable rulers, noise, corruption, the constant threat of war, and its mad traffic.

Lebanese have a great affinity for the taste of birds. Birds are killed indiscriminately, hunted and plucked, opened and emptied of their entrails, and then grilled and served with pieces of lemon and a lot of salt. Small birds are often devoured with their bones. One takes a special pride in the cracking of a bone in one's mouth.

Before the devastating effects of the pesticide DDT, widely used and still in use in what little agricultural space is left in this small country, birds were found in abundance in Lebanon and Syria. However, hunters, much like birds, disregarded borders in the pursuit of killing. Between the devastating effect of chemicals and the hunt, the bird population was almost wiped out.

A cry of alarm went up from some environmental organizations and, ironically, from eager hunters—who in the absence of birds began turning their guns into imaginary flying goats—and the Lebanese government banned hunting in 1995.

The law was effective for a while; there was a small recovery and a comeback by the birds, but the politicians eventually turned a blind eye to their plight, the warlords found the law a bit amusing, and the clergy never challenged the beliefs that the earth belongs to man, nature is at the servitude of men, and God created the birds to be disposed of by man, etc.

Finally, in the absence of birds, the Lebanese went back to consuming the remaining varieties of food, their fingers tearing and waving many little pieces of bread.

The result of these habits was the nation's expansion—individual expansion, that is. A nation of round, fat midgets was seen squeezing themselves into their little old French-made cars, vehicles they had so dearly cherished through the decades. But their wheat bellies and humongous asses could no longer fit. One day, a merchant's wife was stuck in her own car for hours. Another day, a politician's car had to be dismantled in order to pull him out. The merchant husband decided to try to introduce bigger vehicles to this bread-and car-loving nation. Four-wheel drive, wider and more numerous seats, higher wheels and larger trunks, cars massive enough to fit a fresh kill, no matter how large or small its size. A special feature allowed the trunk to be transformed, metamorphosing into a small seat for the foreign maid who, mysteriously enough, never gained weight, always retaining her diminutive size, thereby fitting into the small seat and accompanying the family on their voyages.

One must mention here that, upon further study, it was observed that these maids stayed thin and fit because they stuck to their original diet of rice, vegetables, and spices.

Soon the country was filled with large cars. The popularity of these spacious cars triggered an existential crisis for politicians and warlords alike, for it had always been customary for this important strata of society to own the largest cars. Size, here as in many other places of the world, signaled importance and status. But with this democratization, largeness could no longer effectively distinguish the rulers from the common. The car merchants came upon an ingenious solution. Glass-tinted windows! Black glass that allowed the vehicle's occupants to see out while remaining veiled and un-recognizable inside. Within a matter of months, the entire ruling class had acquired tinted windows. A convoy of five large cars with darkened windows inspired reverence and indicated importance, if not danger.

This flock of cars was to be avoided at any cost. If one happened to get in the way, the risk of getting shot was elevated. The best thing to do was move out of the way and let the power machines pass.

With time, the tinted windows expanded beyond the class of politicians and warlords. Cars belonging to the family members of politicians were, by default, outfitted with tinted windows. The concubines and mistresses of warlords found it very convenient to pass, incognito, through residential neighborhoods. Later on, the favorite singers of warlords, as well as ministers' acquaintances and business partners, were also granted permission to acquire these dark shades.

Slowly, the license for invisibility was so widespread as to become banalized. The whole city drove veiled in glass and metal. People were no longer able to assess wealth, honor, and danger. All of a sudden, the city felt equal and the people lost their sense of self-worth. Invisibility had a devastating effect on suit merchants, hair gel suppliers, and the purveyors of haute couture, lipstick, and high-heeled shoes.

All was gloom until one day the clergy announced that the pope would visit the country in the month of April. The arrival of the popemobile liberated the Lebanese from their darkness and isolation.

After the failure of the tinted-window experiment, the popemobile was a revelation. Herds of popemobiles accumulated in Beirut, on streets that prided themselves on their taste, fashion, culture, and, certainly, on the availability of good food.

Wide cubes of transparent glass mounted onto the backs of small trucks dotted the traffic jams, crawled along the Corniche, through Ashrafieh, into the mountains, and beyond. Men drove with prideful smiles on their faces and women paraded their latest XXL dresses, lifting their thick ankles to model European heels. In the presence of the popemobile, one heard the Lebs sigh in awe, *There must be a god! After the visit of his holiness, look how all flourishes again and how the stores are suddenly full with enthusiastic shoppers!*

The blowing machines of the hairdressers never ceased their generation of money and winds, the streets glittered with stretches of painted nails and color-soaked toes. *Long live the pope and his transparent, protective, mobile shrine!* Christians, Muslims, and Druze were all heard say.

But summer came and the suffocating heat hit every glass

cube, sizzling every trunk and dashboard. Men blasted their air-conditioning to no avail. Inside the popemobile *automobile*, sweat condensed like fog on holy water. The merciless sun transformed every car into a spectacular beam of light. Men had to exit their cars. They were seen carrying their women on their backs. Water from plastic bottles was poured onto feeble faces. *Lebanon is burning again,* a man was heard to say. *If it is not the war, it is the sun.*

From the tops of buildings and from the cockpits of airplanes, Beirut glittered with the reflections of thousands of glass cubicles. *Oh, here it is, ladies and gentlemen,* one pilot announced to his passengers, *the Paris of the Middle East, the Jewel of the East . . .*

But, helas, brightness from afar is fire nearby. A whole nation was seen walking toward the beach in search of relief. Women divorced their most valuable shoes and dipped their painted, round, corpulent toes into the Mediterranean waters. Men rolled their large bellies and saggy breasts into the dirty sands as if they were bears, dogs, or stranded whales.

People ate and listened to their radios. In between songs, a news flash announced that a beam of light was seen continuously shining from Beirut. It was so bright that an Israeli jet plane that had been hovering over the city taking photographs was forced to land. *The pilot,* the news anchor said, *was blinded by the power of the light.*

Let's drink to that, the people said, *and let's eat as well! Let's forget about the cars! Let's sell them to the hunters in the villages for a reduced price! If these cars can bring down a plane, imagine what they can do to a bird!*

Afterward, the city was emptied of popemobiles, as well as signs and photographs welcoming His Holiness.

Meanwhile, the same merchant, while watching the news on CNN, saw a large, wide military car that struck him as the antidote to his past failures.

The HUMMER! he shouted. Yes, that American military car is spacious enough for a family, clear enough for every occupant to be seen, and its open top allows natural ventilation, meaning no man or women will ever be hot again.

The first Hummer that reached Beirut came straight from the desert of Iraq. After a thorough cleaning and a good coat of yellow paint, the merchant drove through town, blasting music by a kitsch singer with false teeth and, well, false everything. Two young Russian girls were hired to stand on the backseat in bikinis. They drank champagne and waved to the crowd.

Within the month, every household owned one or two Hummers. Businessmen, politicians, warlords, housewives, and mistresses drove these wide and spacious cars in the thousands. Lines of Hummers expanded into the streets of Beirut like bloated cadavers, getting stuck on sidewalks, between parked cars, and in the narrow alleys. In frustration, the politicians' bodyguards shot in the air to make space. But, helas, nothing moved. The traffic fell into a chronic stillness, a crippling traffic jam that lasted for weeks. Pedestrians were seen crawling beneath Hummers, trying to find passage. Small-car owners were seen ducking in fear from the bullets of the Hummer owners.

But then a supernatural phenomenon happened. Ordinary people were seen growing feathers on their backs. Their feathers thickened into wings, and with every flutter they started to slowly elevate until they were floating above the traffic and into the air. Flocks of people flapped their wings and learned to fly. Only the rulers and their entourages did not grow feathers. Only the rulers remained beneath this nation of colorful citizens flying over the city, and though they shouted and waved their hands to the flying people above, no one noticed them anymore. The sky was covered with clothes, shoes, falling hats, and wings.

And as the people started to move along, above, and away, a politician and his bodyguard were seen lifting their rifles and pointing them at the sky.

Originally written in English.

DIRTY TEETH

BY THE AMAZIN' SARDINE

Monot Street

22:56

Beirut was pulsating with life at night like a swarm of vermin in a warm grave. A panoramic stretch of dirty black and bloodred vertical patches. And there was an apparition of me.

I was strutting like an aristo dressed for the wedding of someone he would like to embarrass, swashbuckling real proper, with a promise of a night of stinking filth to be remembered by school cooks and tour guides for the ages to come.

The red patches.

I threw an eye through.

Hump, hump, hump. Vag incognita and cock incognito, ya akhi. Red red humping and black liquids drop dropped from the edges of the bed and Abdullah the client turned out to be a demon.

"Wlik kifak ya Sheikhna?" some solemnity asked me with obvious jubilation. I didn't bother to answer. There were sharmingas and lilylilhoes yameen shemal. And yameen shemal, they were eyeing around, searching this line of insignificant whores, lined on this patch of a black wall, menstruating black chunks from their souls, and bloodred marmaladed on their lips, and old cold black eyes searching, searching this line of insignificant whores, searching for some strutting wazwaz akhou sharmouta like me who had been blessed by the hard work and earnings of his forefathers.

"Yes. You are really hard to get by . . . you, you, you . . . mythical creatures, you. Biiiiiig slimy positions. You have been crawling upward since the dawn of time. Top fuckin' floors by now. But you don't come down here often. No, sniff sniff and the like, you don't come down here often. You must fuck a different breed of cunt, ya Sheikhna."

Really, ya surprisingly eloquent whore?

3anjad, truer words had not been barfed. I've fucked Eurotrash and whatnot, but nothing beats homegrown cultured cunt. Yeah, les femmes de mon pays can moan in at least three languages.

I exterminated the last remaining whiteness of my cigara with one hungry cruel drag. I flicked it when I was done to a far-faraway land. The cigara's eyes just flipped over and the trail it left behind cut the skies in two, faceup, like a kamikaze jet plane in a gravityless planet. It went smaller and smaller into the distance until it could be eyed no more. Then the skies became one once again. All blurry. I focused my eyes. I saw a sign. *Monot Street.* I smiled like the devil.

Monot Street, baby boys. It's three letters away from monotony, that part is true. But yalla, drunk as I was, I did not feel any difference. And a cunt here is like a cunt there, and since we're here, we might as well get it here.

I have to admit, I was beyond fucked really bloody, with a dwindling bag of heroin in my pocket and my Ka was rushing through my spine torrently. I looked around with half-closed eyes of disdain and everyone around me was also oh-so-very-fucked, I swear. And it felt nice to at least share something with the populace.

To say Beirut has a drug problem is inaccurate. Because it's not a problem. We are all in control and have been cutting down recently anyway.

But I did go clean once, I have to admit that, very bad idea, an awakening of conscience, blablabla, unwelcomed guest inside my craney, horrible misconception ya akhi, thought I'd clear up my blood for a while, concentrate on the madrassa and shit, aim really high in the Shia religious ladder of society, you know, but to be honest, I'm glad I did—as in, cutting off the supply for a while— because it hits fuckin' harder now.

So yeah, I went clean for a stretch and then I went back at it real nasty and bad, my dreams of preaching Islamically on a massive scale now down the drain: in exchange for wenches, liquor, and drugs, hundreds of grams on thousands of naked backs of lilylilhoes washed with millions of liters. I was as clean as a glass cup in a fancy restaurant, but now, now, my dear dearest brother, no really, you are, walla, we are at the bottom of the stinking stink of the sink, eyeing up and fighting for rancorous drops falling from above. Like rain in Arabia. Blessed blessed sick, falling at us, to wash us dirty.

00:34

Anyway. So when I came in to the bordello, I swear, a light blinded everyone's eyes as they went whatwhatwhat at me. They could all smell the wozz in me as I was passing by like a gust of testosterone in an abandoned harem, I swear.

"Wlik welcome ya Sheikhna!" said the Pimpette Superior, and then she went on excreting an abomination of peasant vocabulary phrased in the form of a question which I will rephrase to you now in decent English.

It went thusly.

She: "What wouldst thou do milord-sheikh? Shall we go at it drinkwards foremost before wenching our way through the wenches, or flipside?"

So I retorted with: "Drinkwards let it be then, drinkwards is bestwards as we speak, ya amar!" I notched the volume switch higher for the two catwalk-material sharmingas on my right to ear and think I am confident. They eyed me real proper from top to bottom and stopped halfway. Then halfway from left to right and stopped halfway.

Weeeeell, modesty is by far one of the many dashing traits in my sizzling personality, but if you really wish to divulge, yes, big package ya madamet, you bet I swear! It's not the pants, it's nasty Eri, Eeeeeeri, oink! Oh Eri, oink oink! Only known by a slew . . . he's a killer, the Circumcised Madrefûcker they call 'im on the street, frowning one-eyed Cyclops, regurgitator of green pustular sins and black sticky fire, the brimstone and the venereal baby boys, and demonic hordes of children project by the scores of gazillions, whole continents crowding behind the eye, a sacrifice of a peninsula, vanishing into the sea, forever waiting, waiting to shatter the gate to smithereens and drown the world.

"Wlik ya ahla bel sheikh! What we like tonight? Eh?"

"Crissycross Bloody fucking Mary!" I ordered as I crossed my chest. The bartender was all smiley smiley of course, sidi.

Oh, and *shikishikishikishiki* was their excuse for music.

A window. I threw an eye through.

A stretch of red in the black sky. I smiled. Bleeding rectums beckoned.

Bang slammed a door. I looked back.

Three belly dancers stormed out of their rooms laughing, the eastern gate blown to hell, thank God, the chador keys thrown away for Allah is away on business and nothing beats reporting to an absentee boss. These virgins of heaven were flashing me their bosoms as we spoke, giggling as they went from room to room.

A stallion and vixens I swear to god we are, we Oriental god-looking bastards. God made us out of His own disgusting spat image. Read your scriptures, Euro-trash! It's all there. We are as tempestuous and cruel and gorgeous as Yahweh. You too-whites, you too-blacks, you too-yellows are simply mutations of the image of the god of Genesis. You're like us, but you're a little fucked up. But it's nothing to be ashamed of, really. Weather and living conditions *do* take their toll.

Then . . . *splaf*! Glass under my nose, very fuckin' fast that was! I looked at him. He smiled at me with green teeth showing. "Come here, you. The Ayrton Senna of bartenders, I knight thee." And I put a ten-thousand-lira bill in his pocket.

"EuheuheuEuheuheuGeuheu!" he slyly remarked.

"You may go now," I told him.

I nosed the glass. Very rancid, of course. He made it in a second to impress me. I took a sip, tonguing it up and down, left and right, in my palate for testing. Oh fuck it, what am I doing? Al kohol is al kohol, and the tongue will just have to take it. No?

I say yes.

No?

I don't know, I think I'll go with yes.

Then a lilylilhoe, delightfully underage, freshly cropped, tallish, she came out of nowhere, I swear, she grabbeth my face and licketh my ear. Oh the nasty schlupka! Ayayay ya Allah, not the bloody ear! For you see, ya akhi, due to a horrific childhood collision injury I was smitten as a result with a G-spot there. The lilylilhoe must have had inside information for she went at it with knowledge.

So she laughed and of course she asked for a drink.

"Ya walad, give the lady what she wants."

She shrieked, "Yiiiiih! Shu mahdum! Lady! Hahaha!"

I smiled.

"Yiiiiih! Leish hek snenak? Your teeth are all black, mister! Pourquoi?"

"Later, ya amar," I said to her, and then after a wink, "Mesh in public, okay?"

"Hahahahaha!" she retorted.

It became clear I was just regularly spouting pearls of comedy because everything I said made her laugh. So I kept talking as she dreamily observed my mouth move and being moved like a leaf when deep sounds came out. Every inch of my skin was a map that she devised with care like Christopher when his sailors began to rebel. And every time I spoke she nodded, and it was Holy Scriptures that she wrote down on her little tabula rasa.

"Badde fuut 'al bathroom, okay?"

"Okay, ya amar."

She smiled and she swooshed away just like that, and her hair zebrafied the lightbulb, and I saw her squeezing between the jiggling, giggling fat bodies and the harharhars of her horrible friends.

"What's with ze rosy schlupka, eh? Shu? You like rosy schlup-kas? You don't like zis?"

I was still looking back, smiling like an autistic kid, when she came along.

I looked back once more and oh my goodness—we were under assault yet again! Mojo soldiers! Left flank, left flank! This time by a sharminga like no other, I swear. So I eyed her really proper to give a frank answer as to whether I want zis or not and, by Jove, cab-bie! Hooooold! For she was a yummy-yummy-swallow-every-drop kind of wench, ya cabbie! Her lips were warm and sanctified beyond perfection by the god-trampler Silicon. Her breasts seemed to gasp for air under her Victoria and Fatima's Secret. An oh-just-tear-me-apart soiree dress and really outlandish earrings. Perfect hourglass figure but time was running out. 36, I give her, 36 or 37, not more. She was staring at me right through the eyelobes, and then without prior warning, she looked down at Eri. Eri grumbled. A steady slow hum. She ran her heels underneath my sheikhly black dress and she woke up Eri who was in a deserving slumber. *Blitzkrieg Allah almighty!* I thought to myself.

"Shu ismik ya amar?" I asked.

"Esmeh Chastity," she answered.

Hahahaha, how bloody goddamn cute! Her name was fuckin' Chastity.

"And what's the name of the rosy schlupka bi sharafik?"

"Esmah Fidelity." She was getting jealous so she said that as if she just ate a whole pile of horseshit.

"Fidelity, is it?" I said with a huge grin.

2:11

So I followed the sharminga home and she felt suddenly motherly toward Fidelity so we were three. They discussed a price between themselves and then informed me of their findings, which I thought reasonable. We got downright nasty halfway through in the cab, and the cabbie was bearded and all, and was going apologies to Allah for us, and he dropped us in Bourj Hammoud after hurling us with some calligraphied insults. Aaaaaaaah Bourj Hammoud, the den of Armenian thieves and jewelry carvers.

So we entered the crummy tasteless apartment and we went at it, humping humping hohoho all night long, as if we were to die with the light of day, ya know, the John Donne's kind of hatred to the fucking sun, oh why dost thou thus through windows and through curtains call on us, ey? Why? Hurry hurry, one more fuck baby girls before the light shines us blind like the residents of Plato Hotel. One more kamikaze squadron of children projects missing Pearl Harbor by miles. Oh lonely egg thou art. On your backs, a genocide in your mouths, on your hair, on the curtains, watch out! I'm gonna spill an Africa on your fingers, in your mouth, I swear, an Asia plus two Chinas on your bosoms. Get the lifeboats, baby girls, for I am coming and my ancestral swine will sustain it until we are all dead. Oh how lonely thou art, oh you egg.

I got them bare like fallen vineless Eves and I served them real proper. The time of their lives, they told me.

And the wind blew in the room. Our long hair flew here and there, this way and that, slapping about, as a sol diez drowned the room with utter madness.

I wiped. I wore my pants and went out.

4:32

It was geese-bumping-in-walls kinda weather, really fuckin' cold, so I walked faster. Having felt no additional warmth whatsoever, I walked slowly again.

Bravo, boy. First fuck in ages. Paid for and billed. Romance at its utmost sickening point.

Chastity and Fidelity were looking real nasty in my craney now, I could only vision those snapshots where they were ugliest, where I felt they were most inauthentic, and I could remember distinctly and in a demonically distorted way every time they talked or smiled or winked at each other without me knowing why.

The nastiest snapshot of them all was when I gave them the liras. They snatched away at the cash like junkies and they quickly melted it in a blackened tired spoon and injected their veins with green. Fidelity's nostrils leaked green and I got frightened when I looked. She smiled stupidly and her teeth were deep green.

So I walked and I walked and Bourj Hammoud is what I left behind. I passed by Karantina. Oh good fuckin' God, what aroma! I inhaled gloriously. Hmmmm, oh the marvelous smell of the total surrender of the diseased and the deceased to come. Karantina, baby boys, all the fuckin' foreign niggers and yellows rotting in their foreign diseases, and seeping through the walls decades of Falestinian and Christian blood. Genocides leak for a good while, ya know? And the earth is ever-thirsty for more. A very charming place, walla. Top of the list for things to see if you're passing through.

The alleys are very narrow in Beirut so there is almost never a horizon. We can't eye the sky anymore, a web of electric wires shades the sun, and there was a little moonlight zebrafying the whole landscape.

Shit, I couldn't even feel my Eri.

Oh good God, it was almost day. Fuckin' lovely. Yalla, prepare ourselves: the soundtrack of Beirut in the morning we will ear in a while for it is dawn. Time for work and prayer, oh you little shits! Yalla, wake the fuck up!

I waited.

The first ziggurat chanter hit the first note. Envy stirred all the others and an amalgam of chanters shattered the cold morning sky, competing in volume and in a very Oriental way, constantly evading the right notes to praise the Allah. Oh yes, we prance around him, the Allah and his Prophet, ya know, that's why we can't draw them. They feed on vagueness, and they wither away if defined.

For you see, me broder, we play music and pray to God the same way we speak here, yamin shemal, left and right, nothing we say means what you think it means.

Westerners, they usually get to the point quite quickly. We in

Arab Bay insinuate everything we want and eventually, as a conse-quence, our musical notes as well. Might this be it? Or this or that? Who knows? And a sitar goes wild in the background to empha-size the existential disaster. *Tininini.* Who knows? *Tininininini. Wlik,* who knoooooows? And then we fall into the Tarab state, which is a typically Oriental state of musical mystical ecstasy, and we are thrown yamin shemal from one yalatifness to another, and we weep out of delight as we're flashbacking to memories of first kisses, pre-mature ejaculations, and warm milk from well-endowed mothers, and then, at last, after such a long, painful wait, when he, or she, hits that note, that fuckin' note we came to ear, we just flip back-ward, shiver and quiver while foaming on the floor, socially aware no longer, space and time coagulating into one, our teeth clicket-ing and clacketing. Yeah, we fall, ya akhi. Again, in a very clumsy Oriental kind of way.

As for the West, these Catholic Nazis, well, they hit a sol diez, stop at that, ponder, mutter a boring hmmm, and write it down on old parchment and dream of glory forever as they are devising the next note. Do you think such a culture, even if given all the time in the world, can devise something so repetitive and so pointless and yet so hypnotizing like swirling dervishes or belly dancers? Of course not, they don't have the total lack of discipline and the easi-ness of elation we have.

As for our Muslim chanters, oh they never stop chanting their monotonous chanting. Fugue after fugue after fugue. Fuguing and prancing here and there, bouhouhouing five times a day, and the swings of personnel are necessary, of course, because it is a very hard job to cry genuinely all the time.

And I've grown tired of prancing, to be honest, and I ache for a bit of Nazi in my soup really. Some order, some discipline, some straightforward speech, get to the fuckin' point, don't interrupt! I wish we were Germans, man, we would wait with anticipation for the verb. We Arabs, on the other hand, put the verb first then shit two hundred adjectives and go hahaha then bouhouhou all of a sudden and reminisce then reluctantly place a point while panting. And we are always shocked when we are interrupted.

From afar the ziggurat looks like a gigantic archaic razor. The real tangible filth can only be experienced once you get near. The whole thing triangular and black or straight-up sky-scratcher material, panoramic and black. It's always black anyway. All the temples of God are painted black now.

So many times have I wished to set all these goddamn temples on fire. Yes, I am a man of god (well, I was) and I crave to see all His temples razed to the ground, yes mortals, for the Lord He is offended by your edifices. Your temples are but abominations in the eyes of our Lord God. Aaaaaaah fuck this. Set them all on fire mygod, aaaaaaamen baby boys, my order first and then all the remaining ones, all of them. All of them, I pray to god. All of them, goddamn ignorant cunts looking up, always looking up and waiting, looking so unevolved and all, instead of looking in and laughing so much everything around us is so fuckin' hilarious.

The ruin might be heartbreaking, it's true (just like all ruins are). But the children will finally have the fuckin' space they need to play at ease. And whatever you were afraid of will be gone, and all the lilylilhoes will be virgins again, I swear. No harm done, Hymen. The betrothed of thee, Antigone, oh he will come back and save thee on time. Just you wait. Be patient. Be good. And kill the clergy every chance you get.

5:05

Khalas, it is known, I might be awful in every single way, but seriously, look at this place! Akh Ya Allah. Look at it. It is done. It can no longer last. Just look at it, ya akhi. The knees of this place are shaking under the weight.

I have to leave this hellhole of a godless, dripping-with-disease place before it blows in my fuckin' face.

No Ka in my spine, of course. My bones are hollow and the forty-seven winds of the East blow through them.

I craved to be clean so I could just walk safely home. I don't know why, but something felt very unright and not even getting home offered me consolation. Something in my belly was going crunchy crunch, and it was not butterflies. Nothing this sugary, I'm sure. I felt as if there were a satanic baby inside me, screeching and squealing with black horns and green ejaculations from every hole in its body, and eating avidly at my insides with fork and scissors.

05:36

He climbed the last flight of stairs, went toward the fronty-door, head facing hell, looked through his pockets, clickety clack, where for art thou keys, clickety clack click clack, where for art thou? Can't we simply barge into our own houses?

The door squeaked open.

"Dirty Teeth!" She paused. "Priest Renzīn akhiran decides to show up." She was waiting for me, in the dark, on the stairs, like a gargoyle from Notre Dame de la Faillite.

I was not startled. No, I just closed my eyes in an I-knew-it kinda way. I looked at her.

"What are you doing here?"

"Can I come in first?"

No.

No.

No.

Fuck no.

No fuckin' chance in fuckin' hell no.

"Sure."

Eesh went in first, her bag jingling jangling, and her hair pitch-blacking the little light there was. He followed her in and closed the door behind him. And as the door closed, his stomach churned the way it churned when he would lock himself outside without the keys, or worse, when you closed the door on a chunk of your gut.

"You don't seem too delighted to see me," she said, smiling as she put down her things, obviously planning to stay. Renegade locks were brought back to the original chignon and she resembled a predator when she did that.

I stared at her and didn't answer.

"I need a place to sleep, walla, c'est tout. Would you do that for me?" She got closer and looked me straight in the eyeball. Her nostrils quivered. Sniff . . . Hmmm . . . He smells of women . . . "Can you do that for me, ya habibi, ya Dirty Teeth?"

Yeah. This is what she calls me. *Dirty Teeth*. Because . . . well . . . because I never brush my teeth and they really look horrible, because the quality of your words and the intention behind every phrase you utter apparently affects your gum. There is a certain negativity that one spews as he cusses and badmouths, and it makes our teeth rot faster. So I eared anyway. In any case, you should take one eye at my teeth and you can immediately tell that I am not one to be trusted.

So yeah, Dirty Teeth. But then again, baby boys, what's in a name? No, really, what's in a name? That which we call a rose by any other name would smell as sweet, no?

"Fine. But I can't hang. I need sleepage. I'm fucked really bloody tonight. Sorry."

"Do you have any left?"

Oh good cunt almighty! It would have taken me two decades of shame and stuttering and finger civil wars to utter a request as such. Oh God, this intolerable boldness! This savage carpe diem dressed with the robe of total need.

I didn't answer. I took off my pants, searched my pockets, and took out the last remaining brown I had, leaving nothing for myself. Having drunk this much I won't be taking that tonight anyway, this goes without saying.

And she deserves the whole stash for the way she asked me for it.

And if you've gone in and out of brown, me broder, you surely know that giving your whole stash to someone can only mean one of two things: ONE, you want a specific something from the person you are giving your stash to, and he surely and of coursely knows what it is; or TWO, something that goes along this line: Here, take it, you have it, no please, take it all. Happy? Good! Now, I don't want to eye your fuckin' face ever again. The most vicious of gifts, a white Pandora's box grinded. Walla.

"Here, take it."

"I'll leave you some."

"No need to, Eesh. Really. No need to. Goodie nacht and the like."

"Goodie nacht, Dirty Teeth."

My knees gave in. And as I was crumbling I aimed at the mattress and collapsed on ground zero. Yes. Floor mattress. No bed. Takes too much space.

One fleeting thought, and then another, then I multiplied Z by a trillion and they spread in my room.

6:02

Go child. Go child, they said to me. So I went, naturally. You always do in dreams, there is no notion of good sense there, you just go anywhere you're told to go and nothing feels like it is your decision, so I did and I ended up walking on clouds and I realized at that point that clouds were naught but the white fingerprints of God as He tries to caress our world. And then I followed my Allah like a hunter hunting a haunted wounded deer in the desert. Then the deer turned mewards and swooshed just like that into a beautiful woman and swooshed again into a gigantic old man who just stared at me with loving hatred in his eyes. I was instantly burned like a Cathar in a spontaneous combustion, burned for all the mischief I had made and caused, and I accepted my punishment, ya akhi, though painless it was surely not. I was then redeemed for all I have done, and I was caressed by a figure in the heights which was bright as bright can be. It was probably the sun itself, can't really vision it now.

Then, out of nowhere, god savagely attacked me and filled my neck with love bites, and my neck was as mistreated as the necks of the likes of Moe, Jesus, Akhenaton, and such as, combined. I screamed: *Enough!* But all I wanted was: more, more, embrace my torso with your strong legs and squeeze the life out of me.

I knelt and I eared an eerie voice telling me: *Oh Renzin, ya Sheikh Renzin, you're forgiven.* And I fell down from heaven in slow-motion like a Prometheus on fire, burning like a gigantic zeppelin, and thousands and thousands of little ones were crying and going bouhouhou, I don't believe it, bouhouhou, Renzin is down, children, Sheikh Renzin is going down!

And all throughout, Eesh was looking at me squirm like a worm, all tattooed and riddled with wounds, skinny and hairy, revolting in everything and in every way, and she was crying. And who could possibly blame her? Look at me, what kind of father could I possibly be?

Originally written in English.

THE BOXES

BY Mazen Maarouf

Caracas

1.

When I was very young, twenty-one years before this moment, my name was Yamen. I loved little boxes and I know that they loved me too. We agreed that we were just the same. In everything. In our smells, our way of walking, how we closed our eyes, those things. I used to see boxes as six closed eyes connected to each other. I had only two eyes, like all people, animals, and birds. But I practiced closing them like boxes did. Completely vertical. And I still practice. I never manage it completely—when I close my eyes and touch my drooping eyelids, I find that they aren't completely vertical. How can I describe this to you all? I don't know. They just aren't vertical, they aren't straight like a ruler. And so I practice. And the boxes know that and wait for me to succeed so they can be happy like me. Because practice will make us resemble each other, even if it takes a number of years. The important thing is to get there. And this is what helps me to sleep better every night.

My mother doesn't wake me up because there's no reason to wake me up. Schools are closed because it's summer vacation. Or because the war is about to start. Or both. The important thing is that I'm sleeping more and that even while asleep I am practicing tightening my eyelids so that they come down completely vertical.

But I also practice another thing. Each and every day, I practice rolling like a box. On the carpet. I bend my knees and ball myself up so that my arms are at a right angle to my chest. I then try to push myself up. This exercise is also difficult. Especially the stage when you have to turn yourself upside down and balance on just your head and knees. If our house were positioned on a slope like our building is, then this would surely be much easier. I wouldn't have minded rolling myself down the slope had there not been so many cars there, as well as the residents of our building and the building next to ours who greeted passersby, even strangers, by throwing things at them—potatoes, empty cans of sardines, bottle tops, balloons filled with dirty water, and other things.

I came to an agreement with the boxes I made that we'd change every day. And they accepted it. In reality, that's because I wasn't able to make boxes of the same size every day. Indeed, what I made weren't exactly boxes, but rather forms very much like boxes, so much so that if you saw them you couldn't call them anything other than boxes, unless you were a math professor or a carpenter. But the boxes didn't think about all this. All they cared about was being closed on all sides. And empty. I valued that a lot because everything around me was getting bigger, increasing in size. Even the cities being destroyed had something in them that was expanding and filling them up. I don't know what to call it, but when I look in a history book at two pictures of this city before the war and during the war, a feeling inside me tells me that something in the city had grown and expanded in the second picture.

My intense love for boxes made me want to visit a number of places around the world with them. When I thought about all the countries of the world, I thought about the amusement parks in those countries. And I decided to not take the boxes there. No doubt, like me they would see many children flying toward giant, colorful rides—swinging and flying and crawling and bouncing around—and not one of them would be interested in what a small box could do. In those foreign countries I wouldn't allow myself to wander around among the children whose languages I couldn't even speak, to convince them of the power of a small box to carry the whole world around in parts and move it to other places.

For the sake of these boxes alone, not for my own sake, I wanted to copy myself like you copy a piece of paper in a photocopy machine. Then I would put each copy of myself into a small box. Afterward, I would become closed and empty like them. And I would leave the boxes in places far away from each other. Nothing would bring them together. One of the places would perhaps be a cave. Perhaps the second place would be some fancy, decorated trunk at the bottom of the sea. Perhaps the third place would be a hill of debris made of old telephones in a village very far from here.

2.

That was all I wanted to know about the power of small wooden boxes before I got close to Nazmi. I became his good friend when he started to help me collect wood. He used to steal it from the shop at the bottom of the slope, where he worked. But this shouldn't lead anyone to believe that he was one of those bad boys in the neighborhood. As for me, when I learned the wood was stolen I didn't get angry with him. I didn't care about the circumstances that brought the wood to my house. Indeed, I urged him to bring more. I would use all the expressions that meant *bring me* when I talked to him. But I didn't ever once utter the word *steal*.

It's important to remember the first time we had a conversation about the usefulness of wood. I realized that he was a simple man and that is all anyone knew about him. My realization was not because of my great insight. No boy of eleven is able to use *insightful* as word to describe himself. I believe in order to be insightful you shouldn't ever sleep. You should constantly observe everything around you. Like someone spying on everything—no matter whether moving or still—in order to live some additional days. I can't be insightful. I don't want to warn anyone about anything. It's as if I need to sleep and practice closing my eyelids vertically, and I still can't manage to do it. I can't speak about the paths of the planets, or about people's lives either, because I haven't delved into these things. I don't mind becoming a part of any life that others might suggest for me in the future; however, I'm busy right now. I don't have time. My preoccupations are deep and confined to the boxes. Raising them higher. I don't know how.

In addition to the question of the eyelids, I also have to practice rolling on the rug, as I mentioned before. Then there's my interest in Nazmi's story. Now. Telling it with no additions or deletions. Because he was simple and his life didn't require any explanations, excess letters, or doctors. In the beginning of our friendship he assigned me the nickname "Eraser." The name embarrassed me. It embarrassed me a lot and I was afraid it would stick to me. But then I added up the weight of his daily misery—carrying heavy gas cylinders on his shoulder, from the foot of the hill all the way up to the top, to the top floor of the tallest building, so he could install it with the help of a heavy screwdriver—"the wrench," as we used to call it. Sometimes he had to go back down the hill again to the street and search for it because it had slipped out of the back pocket of his loose trousers without him noticing. When I thought about all this, I felt that Eraser was a nice compensation. And that he wouldn't call me this name were he not convinced of my ability to erase his daily misery in minutes, those very same minutes we spend at night on the roof of the building throwing wooden boxes in the air.

"Up! Up! To the top of the hill! To the top floor!" he shouted, shutting his eyes tight. He closed them as if they were extraneous things on his face.

So I corrected him: "The sky isn't the beginning of the incline, and it isn't the top floor at the beginning of the incline. The sky is farther away. A lot farther than that. Farther than the top of a column or the horn of a truck."

He asked me, "When will we get there?"

He often asked questions like this. Difficult ones that I didn't know anything about. I felt that these questions were very serious. More serious than me and all my thoughts. They used to spoil my woodworking projects for a moment. But I started to love him like someone who loves a burden. A burden of small boxes. Indeed, I felt that I was responsible for him, so I shared my secret with him about the relationship of boxes to space, and particularly the stars. He hadn't seen stars before. That's what he told me. I got frustrated a lot. And I blamed him. But he'd be perplexed and tell me that this wasn't a fault of his whole body, but a fault of his head alone, in fact a very small part of his head, the part that hadn't ever thought of looking at the sky at night . . .

But from the time he first found out about the existence of stars, he started carrying gas canisters to houses along the incline all day long—up Beirut's Caracas Hill—while staring at the sky. He would stare and wonder if the stars were really there. *Are all these stars merely a trick of the night?* I am sure he meant an evil trick. I expended all my energy trying to convince him that the stars were actually there, but I couldn't. I didn't care. Until one evening when I told him, "We'll throw wooden boxes up toward space."

And he followed up enthusiastically, "Stars?"

But I carried on, ignoring what he was saying because I had started to get irritated. "The boxes will come back to us bringing us things that no one has read about before. Special kinds of signs. Small, secret signs, lost long ago, which will ride in the boxes. Because they have been waiting for the boxes for a long time. Someday, you and I will get all these boxes after they come back. We will catch things much more valuable than stars. We will catch a dictionary."

I told him this in a serious tone. But after that I tried at home to speculate as to what these signs that I'd mentioned could mean to him. I needed only one sign, one clear and obvious sign easy for a young boy like me to explain to someone. To Nazmi. To convince him of it and its relevance to all things in existence. His imagination was weak. He felt that his head lived on its own, although the two of them—him and his head—were attached. Like a medicine capsule. I used to notice that his head was really oval shaped. He laughed and I laughed along with him. He said, "My head lives above me. It sees everything it wants, it doesn't care, I have nothing to do with it. As for me, I live underneath it. I have two eyes that I can't see without. I see with them and I only think things that come to me through them."

For a moment I was convinced that Nazmi wasn't just a simple child. But all that disappeared when I realized that I needed a sign. A special sign that he'd seen before and through which he could be convinced of my secret about the relationship of boxes to space.

I recalled all the conversations that we'd had. The next day, I resolved to emerge from this battle victorious. I told him, "You know, in olden times, there were people like us. But this incline wasn't here. Where was it? Scattered all around somewhere else. It's merely 'things' collected from faraway places that were brought here. They came here and became an incline. But someone collected these things. Perhaps it was a boy. Merely a boy like us. He used wooden boxes or perhaps he had a different way. The important thing is that he collected them, guided by signs. Special signs. Every 'thing' has a special mark, distinguishing it from any other 'thing.' Everything becomes old and rots. Like bread. It crumbles. Even if you do everything you can to prevent it. Even if you go now and use all the strength in your arms to set up the incline in reverse, it would rot and everything in it would also rot after a while."

But he seemed not to understand anything I said. I remembered what he told me about his head and his eyes. And I gathered that his head perhaps understood my words but his eyes, no.

To make matters easier and not just for his eyes, for myself also, I simplified the story: "Let's start with the shop. You see it every day. It will be taken apart. The display. The stuff in it. The shelves. The refrigerators. The magazine displays. The cash register. The scale for vegetables and fruit. The storage room at the back. The bathroom. The basement filled with rats and mice. Everything in it will decompose into small pieces and wait. What we will have at the bottom of the street won't be a shop but a mound of these pieces mixed up all together. But gathering together all these pieces and returning them to what they were isn't difficult. Because each of them has a special sign. And the boxes that we will send up into space will leave. That's for sure. But they'll come back to us one day with special signs for everything as a whole. We will compile a big dictionary of all these signs. The biggest dictionary of life. Of everything in life."

He asked me, "Does every star in the sky have a special sign for it too?"

"Of course," I answered fervently, and then added, "I heard that gathering all these pieces together will fall on our shoulders. This is what older people always do with younger people. We have to be prepared. The wooden boxes are my plan. What I told you about the shop will also happen to the incline, the football stadium, the Ferris wheel at the amusement park, the Rawda coffee shop, the pool, every building, shop, closet, washing machine, television, window, metal . . . everything. We'll move this entire incline somewhere else and it will become ours. We could even set it up differently than it is now. We could, for example, return it to what it used to be. To years past. If we seize the signs, the incline will be ours. Yours and mine."

But he was silent. He showed no interest whatsoever in the question of owning the incline. But he asked me, "If everything disintegrates into fragments, what will we do when the small wooden boxes also decompose into fragments? Yes. How do you know they won't decompose before coming back to us?"

I was struck dumb.

Then he asked, "Has your tongue decomposed, Eraser?"

I stuck out my tongue at him to show him that it was still there. Then we started laughing very hard. I was sure that when I laughed with Nazmi, a thick, cool, white foam was intensifying, taking on the form of birds near a wooden bench for strange people who we don't know. The people feed seeds to that foam, thinking that it's really birds, and when they feed it, it increases and thickens further and we can no longer stop laughing.

3.

I'm not a clever box maker. Especially small boxes. I use the wood that Nazmi brings to me, cutting it with a blade. Though it's fine wood and possible to break by hand, or by foot, I used to cut it with a knife. By hand or foot, splinters fall from it that I then have to snap with my fingers.

Once, while I was passing the blade over a wooden board, it left a dark line that wasn't lead but looked like it. I deduced that I had to use a lead pencil to mark the wood before cutting it. I started putting it behind my ear like carpenters do when walking down the street. Because I was afraid that the blade had done that in order to join the lead pencil to it, while I was away at work. The next day I brought the blade a home, a broken case. After work, I inserted a screw into the blade's open belly and twisted it a little so it couldn't come out of the case and injure anyone. Because it wasn't designed to cut wood, I avoided putting pressure on it during work so it wouldn't get stuck inside the wood or harm its blade. This would have required me to pass over the same line again, and this is what explains my long-term obsession with constructing boxes. People used to call this "respect." But it caused my fingertips to swell. Though I didn't cry. I didn't cry even once, especially not in front of the boxes.

I also had nails, thread, pipe, glue, and adhesive tape. I didn't use the nails but saved them until I could buy a hammer. Sometimes I cut the thread with my teeth and sometimes that hurt. Once I lost a milk tooth when the thread got stuck around it when I was pulling on it. Right afterward, mothers in the building started to use string to pull out their children's loose teeth.

In the evening, I used to tuck the small boxes into my schoolbag. I would refuse to let my mother sell the bag at the end of the summer like she did at the beginning of every school year. But I didn't completely fill the bag with boxes. I had to leave some space. A space the size of the sleeve of a sweater. I'm not talking about the sleeve of *my* sweater, but the sleeve of Nazmi's sweater. Nazmi, who was perhaps my friend and perhaps not. What I do know is that Nazmi was three or four years older than me, and after I tucked the boxes in the bag, I was sure that the empty space left was the size of his hand. Every day, I kept saying to myself, *Today. Today I will let him take the first box from the bag.*

But I didn't follow through on my decision after all. I didn't trust Nazmi's ability to control his strength, especially when he was excited. What if his hand broke the box while removing it from the bag? Shattered it into fragments? We would fight. Nazmi would be angry and feel sorry for me, and he would kneel in front of the building's entrance and hit his head against the edge of the cement until it bled. As usual, children his own age would circle around him and make fun of him. I was really afraid of the sight of blood. Even before the war came down onto our street overlooking the sea. It dates back to the time I saw Zuhayr, the son of the vegetable seller, covered in blood after he fell from the chains of the spinning electric swing in the amusement park. Nazmi didn't apologize. Because no one taught him that when we make a mistake we apologize. But we knew it. Everyone in the neighborhood knew it. When he made a mistake, he would do everything he could to convince us that it wouldn't happen again. So the next time Nazmi would insist on taking the first box out of the bag, but I was sure that he—like the time before—would crush it in his strong hand like a cookie. Because I really loved him, I didn't want Nazmi to hit his head on the cement and cry. I really did love him. But I feared for the boxes. I couldn't show him my love because I feared for the boxes. Because Nazmi didn't only get attached to people quickly, but also their things.

One Tuesday evening, I put all the small wooden boxes in my bag. I climbed up to the roof of the building. The sky was clear and smooth. I smiled, saying to myself, *There's no mucus tonight.* We used to consider the clouds a collection of strips of mucus. So I thought: *We can choose an endless number of stars so that we can leave some for the next day*. I waited for Nazmi. But after many hours, the stars started getting bigger, inflating, swelling up. They became faces. They moved from one side of the sky to the other. I was no longer able to follow how they flowed through the sky. They used to bump into each other like marbles. Giant marbles. And they emitted terrible sounds. They split open the edge of the roof and the flimsy aluminum antennas, which we used to bend on purpose as revenge against the neighbors who treated Nazmi badly when he delivered gas canisters to them. Indeed, even the Ferris wheel at the amusement park started shaking to the right and left like a giant coin. It was lit up. But I didn't leave. I opened the bag and looked at the boxes. Then I looked again at the stars. I measured them. Lengthwise and then crosswise. From where I was standing on the rooftop. I only used two fingers. That was the latest method I'd discovered to measure the size of the stars.

If Nazmi had been here he would have learned it easily. If he'd been able to hear me, I would have said to him, "It isn't difficult at all. We do it just like this. It's like when we close our eyes, like usual. But for this we close only one eye, and the other one we don't use . . . We keep it open." I made a distance between the first finger on my hand—the first thick, short finger—and the second one that we use to point out new places to people. Then I unzipped the bag. I opened my two fingers to the size of a star and the space between them seemed bigger than all the small boxes. I closed the bag right away. I sat on the flimsy edge of the roof. But it wasn't going to collapse, otherwise I wouldn't sit there. I started getting sleepy. I dozed off a bit. Then I woke up. The floor where Nazmi lived, in the fifth building on the way down the incline, was not lit up. I kept looking at the half of the apartment where he lived with his family. I could perhaps notice some movement in the kitchen, behind the giant glass doors and the clothesline. I threw a look from where I was to the entrance of the building, but I got dizzy and was afraid to lose my balance and fall. I took out the halawa sandwich that Nazmi and I were supposed to share and devoured it. It was stale.

I believed it would help me not to faint. I didn't leave him even a bite.

The stars were still crashing into each other. And the sound was loud. So much so that people left their houses. They were carrying their belongings and bringing their children out. The police were waiting under the building to be sure everyone left. After a little while my father came, angrily. He slapped me and took me by the hand and emptied the boxes onto the roof. No, it's not good for my reputation that I accuse my father of that. I'm the one who emptied the boxes. I left the building with him, we left the building together. Me and my father and my mother. My mother was crying too and threatening that she'd make me pay for this later in our new house. I saw a lot of people leaving, emptying their apartments, evicting themselves from the building. They shook hands quickly, then jumped in their cars, revved their motors, and took off without looking back.

There was a car waiting for us as well. I sat next to the window. From my spot, I couldn't see the half of the apartment Nazmi and his family lived in. I saw the people from the other family who lived in the other half of the apartment. All of them were on the balcony. I wanted to speak to them, I waved at them, but no one saw me. My hand was small and it was dark. Everyone was screaming—the policemen, children, women, the men in the pickup trucks. Everyone. I thought about doing something clever. So clever that no one around us—me, my mother, and my father—could guess. I lifted my head and looked at the stars. They had stopped quarreling. They went back to their natural size. I measured them again with the same new method. And I grew sad. Sad for the small wooden boxes left there. My feeling of sadness soon faded, however. Quickly. With the speed of a star which crashed into its sister. Just as quickly my sadness faded at the thought that Nazmi would come up to the roof after leaving all the people and the police, and he would complete what we had started together. I only hoped that he would close his eyes tight.

4.

After our departure from the building, a rumor started that the police hadn't come because of the noise of the stars crashing into each other. But rather because of the colonel who lived in the building across the street. People used to hate him and the police who gathered by his house. He was always grouchy. But I doubted this rumor. I'd never seen the colonel harm anyone and I used to sometimes defend him to Nazmi on the roof. I would say, "He probably saw something bad today and he's grouchy because he's sad."

I defended him even though I didn't need to, and Nazmi would interrupt me, saying, "Why don't we start throwing boxes?"

Perhaps I said that because I thought I loved his daughter Dalia and thought she'd love me when she grew up. In the morning I would stand behind the window, holding a big mug of hot milk. But I wouldn't start drinking from it until I saw her come and stand in the window of her own house, across from me. She wasn't standing behind the window for my sake. But to watch the street, the cars, and the military jeeps waiting for her father down below. She used to watch every idea, person, and cat on the incline except me. Like me, she carried a mug that I always convinced myself also had milk in it. Perhaps this mug had special maramiya herbal tea to treat diarrhea or mint tea to stop her vomiting or some other drink to improve her breath. But I always believed that there was milk in her mug. On the days when Dalia didn't stand behind the window, I poured my milk out into the potted plants. Their lactose increased daily until they'd become so much lighter you could no longer say that they were green.

I imagined that Dalia lived in a palace. A palace squeezed onto the first floor of the building across the street. Our house was also on the first floor but she never once looked in my direction. In the beginning I thought it was because of the wide street separating our two buildings. I said surely our house is very, very far from the building across the street. I concluded from this that Dalia was younger than me, much younger. That the people, like me, who can cross the street from our building to the one facing it easily take giant footsteps. If you didn't take giant footsteps you couldn't see faraway places, like Dalia's house. Dalia couldn't see me because of her tiny footsteps and her youth. In order for me to help her realize that she lived near us, in our space with us, the children older than her, I wanted to rename Caracas Hill the Colonel's Hill.

I asked Nazmi to promote the new name. But he was afraid and warned me, "Perhaps the colonel will get angry, shoot the wooden boxes, and knock them down from above." Later I learned that Dalia had been sent abroad to a a faraway country with a forest to receive some kind of treatment.

5.

The letter reached me. From Nazmi. It was written on the back of an invoice from the shop. On the back there were a lot of numbers and on the front, words. Two groups. Numbers also have a long life, which we don't understand at all. Numbers have been breeding and giving birth to other numbers for hundreds of years, though all we do is count them; we believe that when we cross them out, they're gone. But actually they nest in invoices and walls, heads and files. Most of them are found inside our stores of phenomenal forgetfulness. These stores of forgetfulness fill up every day with new numbers. And the numbers there get to know their relatives that have also been divided for generations. But before they get to these stores they walk close by us most of the time, though we only feel them when they are written down on paper. They decrease when we die and increase if the opposite happens. We also know nothing about their feelings. Or their voices. But then they appear as long as electricity cables, and connect cities and people together. Sometimes they connect two boys. Like Nazmi and me, for example. Even if one of them is lying on his back in a hospital and the other is lying on his back at home. And for this to happen, these two boys lying on their backs must think about the same secret. Even this secret is merely a handful of stars in the sky, where they never saw a wooden box arrive.

"I won't be able to meet you on the roof of the building after today. I hope this doesn't upset you. I have a room now. In a faraway hospital with a big warm bed. It's well lit. It has lamps in it that you can't find in the shops. If I improve my behavior they may put in a television for me. Perhaps a small television, perhaps not. Sometimes I entertain myself by looking at the fluid dripping through the IV tube but that gets boring fast. The sound of these drops is muffled. I have gotten to know all the little sounds without being forced to hear them. But all the muffled sounds are distant at the end of the day. Even the drops of medicine, which scramble around inside the veins in my arm, seem very distant because they are muffled. They are not as close as they seem or very close at all. I feel like they aren't mine. I dream that I'm pushing a long train with my hands, a train carrying all the stars in the sky in coal carts. It's true that I've never seen a train except on a chewing gum wrapper in the shop, but I've dreamed of a train. It was also yellow and pink. The stars were dusty and my hands were big. Bigger than they should be, and thicker too. Because of this my back is bowed and you see me hunched over toward the ground. When I woke up I was thinking about the locust. I don't know where the train has arrived. The locust we found on the roof, do you have any news about it? I urged you that day to open one of the boxes and put it inside. You had to do it. We put the locust inside, we resealed the box and threw it with the other boxes. I closed my eyes with all my strength. Sometimes I think that this locust is eating a little piece of the moon, that it tricked us and didn't reach the stars. I hope I'm mistaken, but after my mother falls asleep in the chair, I go up to the roof of the hospital and look at the moon. Sometimes it seems to me that its color has changed on one of its sides. I fear that the locust is eating it. Are you sure the moon is so big that it can keep rising above people's houses even after we did this? Can you send it some gauze? In boxes? The gauze could fill in the missing, eaten part and no one will notice. In the hospital no one asks me where I'm going. I leave my room and steal down the stairs. I can't take the bag of medicine out of my arm but I drag it with me on a metal pole. On the roof I'm completely alone. I close my eyes as tightly as I can like I always used to do when I was with you. And I lift my head up. Toward the sky. It seems to me that when I close my eyes, the color of the sky suddenly changes and becomes the color of the little strap around a gas canister. That thing we put between the screw-top and the tube so that gas wouldn't leak. I think that perhaps the night is this layer of artificial leather that prevents our dreams from leaking out of us and rising. Up above the sky. To what is above the night. Did you ever wonder what we could find sitting up above the night? But after I close my eyes, I totally know when to open them. Yes. At the very moment you stop throwing boxes on the roof of the building, I open my eyes here on the hospital roof, holding onto the medicine pole with both hands because I'm exhausted. I won't open my eyes except when you ask me to."

6.

I wanted to tell Nazmi more of the secrets connected to the boxes. When we threw them in the air, they rose, slithering along invisible tracks. Tracks like the chains of the only swing at the amusement park. Every box takes a different sinuous route from every other box (and to make it easier, I would have to ask Nazmi to imagine the pipes of the sink instead of imagining the amusement park chains on a winding frame). With distance, feverish boxes grow hotter and open the moment they arrive at the star. No box pays attention to its right or left. It doesn't look at any other box, nor at the passengers who wave at it from the airplane, nor at high-flying birds, nor even at the boats in the sea or the beams from the black-and-white-striped lighthouse on the street parallel to ours. It doesn't pay attention to anything, but instead passes on its way, concentrating on how to not waste energy for nothing and to not be delayed in arriving at its desired star.

But Nazmi went to hospital the day before we left the building. My parents had decided to leave and hadn't informed me of this ahead of time. This surprised me, so I was forced to leave with them at the last minute. Were it not for that I would have stayed. I would have hidden in the electricity room that gave off the stench of urine soaked into the land under the building. I would have lived inside it and finished preparing all the boxes there. We left because the war began. But the war at that time was still small. Like children. It wasn't more than sounds that came and went. Personally, I didn't see the war at all. I didn't see anything, therefore I can't tell you anything about it. They started to talk about it on the radio at the time and stopped talking about anything else. But the sound of the war wasn't like the sound of the radio. Its sound wasn't like any spoken word. It wasn't like Nazmi's voice or even the sounds of the boxes after they are thrown. The colonel also left for the mountains. Nazmi didn't come to the roof of the building the night before or the night we left. When I finally read his letter, it was after he'd already died of leukemia, blood cancer, more than three years earlier. I wished that I hadn't ever gotten close to the gas-canister boy. I felt kind of jealous of him because he died. Nazmi became this precious piece of paper that I folded in the small wooden boxes. Without him, I couldn't unfold this paper anymore or even see the boxes as I saw them before.

When I entered the shop to get some wooden vegetable crates that first time, Nazmi asked me what I was going to do with them. I said, "Boxes." Because I didn't want to tell him what I thought about the desultory things in the world, I added the word *stars* to the word *boxes*. So it became, "Boxes for stars." Then I finished, "Small boxes, I throw them in the sky when it's dark outside."

"What do you mean by *stars*?"

"They are small bodies that shine in the sky at night. Like little crumbs of bread."

"I never thought about looking at the sky before. I spend my days moving things, canisters of gas, for the people who live on this street. Everything is heavy. I hate all heavy things and avoid looking at them when I can. Therefore I don't look at the sky. Because the sky is itself a heavy thing. Don't you think? At school, don't you study how heavy the sky is?"

Nazmi refused to give me any crates that day. But the next afternoon he knocked on the door of our house and had three crates with him. He said excitedly, "These wooden crates are for you. Can I come with you when you throw the boxes at the sky? How many boxes can you complete by tomorrow?"

"I don't know, I will try as hard as I can," I answered him, bewildered.

"I can bring you string, glue, and nails—yes, even gas-canister wrenches. I will tell the owner of the shop that they fell out of my pocket. He will punish me but his punishment won't last for more than one day. Could a wrench be helpful in preparing boxes?"

Nazmi brought me string, glue, and nails. I don't know where he got them. As for the wrench, I refused to accept it because it was too heavy for me.

The next day I found Nazmi standing in front of me. He asked, "Can I go with you? I won't look at the star you are looking at. I will look at another star."

But I stipulated that he should close his eyes and I would throw the boxes. Like him, I closed my eyes. Because the boxes won't get anywhere if an eye can see them. The pupil of the eye is small and if we look at the box with it, the box will be inside it. And in that case it won't be able to get out. Instead, it would plunge into the depths of his eye, inside his head, and from there would sink toward his chest, stomach, and intestines. There are no stars in the intestines. It will generate a pain in the teeth when its muscles start pushing the box slowly, from the belly on up, to leave our mouths when we're sleeping. Not all muscles do that, only children's muscles. What I said to Nazmi was true, so I also used to be afraid to look at the boxes while I was throwing them. After doing this, I left the roof immediately.

Like all people, Nazmi had two rows of teeth. But when he closed his mouth they didn't line up on top of each other evenly. I used to always see a space between them. For that reason Nazmi was unable to pronounce some letters: *tha'*, *jeem*, *dhal*, *zay*, *seen*, and *sahd*. All of these letters used to come out of his mouth the same, like a combination of the sounds for *sheen* and *sahd*. Once on the roof of the building I tried to teach him correct pronunciation. But he started to cry, and I asked him why he was crying, acting like I was angry, trying to stop myself from bursting into tears like him. But he didn't tell me why he was crying. He didn't tell me anything. He calmed down and asked me not to try to teach him pronunciation again. He had to hear himself pronounce the names of things wrong, but knowing at the same time that he couldn't correct them. He wanted these things, which belonged to life, to be disturbed when hearing their names pronounced by people incorrectly.

"No doubt, everything in the world has gotten used to hearing its name like this for a long time now," he would say.

I used to answer him, "I believe that. In class, the teacher said that sky, sun, clouds, pebble, purple, evil, box, rainbow, star, and others are things that didn't change their names for hundreds and hundreds of years."

Then he asked, "But these things, have their forms not dwindled since this time called 'hundreds and hundreds of years ago'? Is it possible that some form fades away but its name stays the same?"

I didn't answer these complex questions of his but I felt that they'd sprouted up in his mind because of the shape of his two big hands.

The roof of the building wasn't pretty and it wasn't clean. Rusted, broken antennas, the rubble of rocks, a broken clothesline, and water tanks were strewn around on it. But from atop we used to be able to see Beirut's lighthouse. It was a column, standing on a hill, shining at night. The lighthouse might have seemed very tall to someone looking at it but it wasn't. It was short and thick. What was actually raised up was the hill underneath it. We also used to see the water. The entire sea, right to its very end. At the end of the sea there was a horizontal blue line that had a starting point and an ending point. These two points seemed sturdy, as if nothing could move them, and the mainland shrunk with every dot as if a clamp was holding it fixed in place. We used to see a lot of swimming pools. Three or perhaps four. One of them used to stay lit at night because it was for the soldiers and secret police. There were always elderly divers swimming extremely slowly and carrying fishing nets on their shoulders. We used to distinguish them by the gleam of the flashlight that they carried in their hands. Then on the back side we used to be able to look out over the al-Aoud family's big garden in which many kinds of trees grew, like pomegranates, guava, and bitter oranges, where both distant and nearby birds used to come and sometimes chirp at night. But that didn't concern us. Similarly, we used to look over two tennis courts at the sports club called "Escape" in English. Then there was, in a distant area far from the sea, a football stadium for some professional team. Nazmi and I concluded that this stadium was miles longer and wider than the corridor of our building. There was a Ferris wheel in Beirut's amusement park which never stopped turning; in the winter the wind would come to the sea to play with it and make it turn around to the left and right.

From atop the roof, the wooden boxes were thrown up with the greatest possible force. I threw them. Before he closed his eyes, Nazmi was looking at me, repeating that same question he always did: "Can I throw just one box? Just one? I want to throw one box to the stars."

"No, you're not ready for this yet."

"But I'm older than you. I asked my sister and she said that I'm older than you."

I didn't want to risk it though. For fear that his big hands, powerful like his questions, would crush one of them. The most important thing for me was that he keep his eyes closed while I threw them in the air.

"Be careful not to open your eye, even a little crack. If the boxes know that you're looking at them, they will change course and come back to us. After that we won't be able to send any other boxes up."

Then he took my hand and put it over his eyes. His face was large and his bones very prominent. Because of this I preferred not to touch his face. "Squeeze your hand over both my eyes. Or on the eye you think I will open. Throw all the boxes, except one, let me throw one box. Just one box." But I kept refusing. I always refused. I refused and was afraid. I was afraid that he'd get angry. That I'd get angry. That he'd come down to the building entrance and bash his head against the wall.

The small wooden boxes would sometimes settle on the balcony of one of the building's apartments after I sent it up. One time, Nazmi and I were listening to the sound of them colliding before opening our eyes and he asked, "What's that sound?"

"Perhaps it's the box we threw colliding with a distant star," I answered.

"But the sound is very close. Does the sound of the stars resemble the sound of the banisters?"

"Exactly, especially if it's colliding with a small wooden box. That's because of its shape."

"Its shape? What's the shape of a star? Is it like a cube of white cheese?"

"Exactly. Bulgarian cheese with anise. Intensely white. You can see it in my geography book. But stars don't have sharp corners, all of their edges are curved and smooth."

"How can you ensure that the box will reach the star that you want it to? What if another one lured it?"

"It's possible. The sun can lure a box or birds or even clouds.

Once I threw a box but some white birds grabbed it at a great height and put a bird who'd died of fatigue during flight inside it. Then they set it free. Afterward, the box smashed into the glass protecting the cockpit of a giant boat somewhere else. That cracked the box. But the crack went from here to there. And also to all the other boxes that I had already prepared. Because of this I realized what had struck that box. I spent the night sealing up the cracks with tape. I wasn't angry and I didn't feel too stressed. Sometimes, Nazmi, the box doesn't reach the star that we want, so we have to keep throwing boxes into space every evening. We have to throw them from the same place, with our eyes shut tight. Every evening."

Originally written in Arabic.

RUPTURE

BY BACHIR HILAL

Tallet al-Khayyat

I won't sign this report.

I am George, son of Abbas al-Majrouh the builder, nicknamed "The Boss" for the skill he claims he has in sculpting and building with stone, unmatched by anyone in Beirut, as he used to say and still does, all the more so when he's been drinking a lot: "I should be awarded a higher degree in engineering. God will never forgive my parents for not sending me to university; their own ignorance and helplessness meant they couldn't see my potential."

When I first became a Communist, he took my side and started speaking out against feudalism, the shaykhs, and the bishops. It wasn't unusual for him to insult Shaykh Pierre, saying he couldn't understand him because he "speaks like a fish" and needs to learn Arabic. Though my grandfather would get annoyed at that. "Give us a break, Abbas, must you anger the Phalangists and ministers and deputies?"

My mother Philomena was the sixth daughter of Father Tanios—son of Father Sam'an, son of Father Tanios al-Ha'er—who only had one son, my uncle Elia, who didn't even finish middle school. All he ever did was go fishing, play cards, drink, memorize local poetry, spend time with the wives of men gone abroad and the new widows who weren't too old, and help with the liturgy. According to people in the village, he didn't work, didn't marry, wasn't called to the priesthood, and would never die, despite his many accidents in the Italian cars he acquired one after the other. And despite the bullet that hit him in the foot hours after arriving in Beirut's hotel district at the head of a Phalange Party detachment from the village, causing him to withdraw injured—and half a hero—before he was transferred to office work in the central headquarters.

He learned about my communism two years before the war and didn't hesitate to tell me, "Someone whose grandfather and grandfather's grandfather were respected priests in the region—isn't it crazy for him to be a Communist? Tell me who you spend time with, and I'll tell you who you are."

He'd memorized this saying in school and repeated it every time he spoke to me: "*He who spends time with sinners sins, and he who spends time with the devout is devout.* Do you and your father need more misfortune? Had he not married into our family, no one would have acknowledged him in the village or the region, and no one would have given him work. You should leave politics and be successful, not because degrees are important. Look at me, I didn't study for a higher degree—that would have been a waste of time—and my social and financial positions are good. It was best for me to enter the school of life straight away. As for you, you need to study so we can find you a good government job later on. But you floundered even in choosing a specialty. Really, let me understand . . . what does *sociology* even mean? If you remain a Communist, you'll regret it. Your diploma will be worth as much as a pillowcase."

When the debates raged and he got angry, he often said to me, "You're still a boy who needs a lot of schooling in politics. Your social position is still that of a cockroach."

Me . . . a cockroach? That hurt. It reminded me of how small I was and how weak my father's standing was. I went away upset and sad, not wanting to insult my only maternal uncle. My mother kept saying that he wasn't reproaching me alone and that he'd only joined the Phalangist forces to protect her and the rest of the family after they were scandalized by me fighting alongside the armed Palestinian and Muslim groups. During the rare moments that she came to West Beirut to see me after the war started, I didn't ever share with her my suspicion that he'd wounded himself so that he wouldn't have to fight.

* * *

I was born in 1951, the thirteenth entry in the village register that year. Philomena told me I was born on the way to Mar Yusuf Hospital, after she spent two long, painful nights pushing me out despite my grandmother's prayers, incense, and the efforts of Zulaykha al-Zalaa, the midwife who'd delivered five sisters and brothers before me. Whenever someone asks her about me, Philomena repeats what she has always said when I'm in earshot, ever since I started disobeying her: that when I was born she'd anticipated my strange destiny that I'd be terrible, mad, or—and she would say *I hope* before the last word—a leader. And I would always answer her sarcastically that the family made a mistake in accepting the jinxed number thirteen for me in the registry.

He had chestnut hair. It was long and shaggy before Margot—the thirty-something French wife of Dr. Jalal al-Bahri, a well-known doctor from an important Beiruti family. He was also one of the people responsible for the party's clandestine organization. Comrade Abu Khalid, its main military leader, reported this to me, asking me to keep it to myself because of the sensitivity of the mission I'd been assigned.

Before this, I had never met Jalal or known him as a comrade. He had two clinics: one in the building which he owned and lived in, in the mostly upscale Tellat al-Khayyat neighborhood, which he opened up to inhabitants of less rich areas, serving the least rich of them; the second in a building facing the American University for his rich and paying clients, as Abu Khalid whispered to me when we went there two months before I became responsible for he and his wife's personal security.

"You must repeat only what everyone knows about him—he's an independent personality close to the national movement who was a candidate in the last parliamentary elections. Just so you know, we asked him to do this. Sunni Beiruti people are conservative and not very interested in politics, especially openly Communist politics. Most of them are businessmen, there are only a few literary and union names.

"Back to the issue I'm concerned with: this is what's useful from your nun's school education—you can speak to his wife in her native French to give her peace of mind. She's started going out less, fearing armed men in the streets and bombings and some of the gangs. She isn't like Lebanese women. I wish he'd never married her, she's one of his weak spots. He met her when he was studying in France. His family's like us, they don't care for her much, not only because in their view she's difficult and moody, but also because she hasn't had any children even though they've been together seven years. She also hasn't learned our language. She's only mastered a few words from a dictionary of food and drink, as well as greetings and farewells. Comrade: since the war intensified, he's taken care to accompany her when she meets her friends, to not let her go out alone. He's had to constantly deal with balancing his duties and meetings and her demands. He fears for her and she fears both for herself and him too. And while she's generally with the left, she isn't a Party member—and if she had been in a party, she might have chosen a radical leftist group who's against us. In truth, I feel she's searching for a sort of ideological luxury in the left, which the bourgeoisie to which she belongs hasn't been able to offer her. She made an aggressive critique of the Soviet comrades, saying that their regime is a failure. We have our critique too, but not to the extent that we would say that some of its small failings are reason to reject the collapse of the Socialist camp. Must we sacrifice socialism just for some jeans, rock and roll, and the bourgeois freedom of the individual? I mean, what do you want, the Soviets giving freedom to their class enemies and the Americans? Sometimes I wanted to ask him why the state, as a bourgeois state, authorizes the Party if we're its enemies. Is it because our opponents give us what we fight them with?"

In order to maintain his trust I don't answer him, and also because I already know his answer: they were obliged to—if we left them to their own devices the Party would still be illegal.

He continues, "We can't just introduce Margot to our comrades who have French education and culture, her influence on them could be negative. Comrade Jalal just laughs about this and tells us she can't be changed, saying, *We each have our own opinions and our independence and it's enough that she accepts me as I am.* His idealism sometimes annoys me. She doesn't know if she is living this war or living *in* it. She's started affecting Comrade Jalal's functioning, causing him to reduce his political commitments. Starting today, I'll send Abu al-Izz to accompany him wherever he goes—to his clinic and his meetings. You're responsible for guiding him, but you also must pay attention to the area around his house, the roads and streets leading to it. You'll be our permanent link, our connection to him. You'll send and transmit letters and other written messages. I want total precision, you must pass by the center whenever I call you, and you'll accompany his wife wherever she goes and help her with everything she asks from you. She's a little bit demanding; she's from a rich family like the doctor is. I'm sending you because I trust you and because you know French better than the other comrade-fighters."

After our introduction, Jalal told me that he'd assigned Abu al-Izz and me an apartment as luxurious as his own on the first floor of his building. Then silence. So Margot turned toward me, ignoring the presence of Abu Khalid, and informed me of a decision that I guess she'd made, that I would have to be inconspicuous to succeed in protecting them. Therefore I'd have to change my clothes and remove all obvious signs of belonging to the Party and my time in the trenches. Then with a nervous smile she turned toward Abu Khalid and said, "I don't know what you do in this Party, but I maintain my right to choose what I believe is appropriate for my security and my life."

I was speechless for a while that day, as the juices of anxiety and confusion seeped into my blood. It was the first time since my primary school days that I'd been subjected to restrictions on the way I looked. I'd considered this insignificant and trivial for many years. This was the first time since I'd grown up that I was taking an order not coming from my Party commander but from a woman who associates with people who I hate. Yet as soon as the interview finished and she and Jalal led me to a big apartment, with what I thought was calculated and patronizing kindness, I was unsettled by her raspy voice, which had become friendlier in the absence of Abu Khalid, and by the shape of her body. A flush of embarrass-ment rose to my face from recalling what we fighters used to repeat to each other—that the best way to break an uppity woman is to approach her sexually like a Soviet steamroller, to collect and dis-seminate massive force at one point and at one time.

"You have to be the lord of the raid, Abu Sakhr." That's what Comrade Abu al-Layl used to say when he came to the apartment to offer us a screening of erotic French films on his Super 8 camera or to meet one of his girlfriends. He was two years older than me, a student at the Faculty of Arts. We were squashed together with Abu al-Izz and other comrades in an apartment we used to call the Serail, in Cola, not far from the party headquarters in Tariq al-Jdeideh.

He would always say, "Let her fade away in your hands, like Yumna, Laure, and Lubna do in mine. Come on, don't you always hear them roar like wounded lionesses before one of them falls like a ripe apple and then treats me like a god? Oh Abu Sakhr, Newton could have learned from me."

When he'd say this I wouldn't tell him that my luck with women had been limited, because I wasn't handsome or brave. I'd only ever gotten to know women who my comrades didn't care about and had left to me.

My grandmother, the priest's wife—who I preferred to think of as senile and who favored my siblings and cousins over me from the time I was young—never stopped reminding me: "Look at your maternal uncle—tall and blond. He's like a superior-quality spear. Your shortness is inherited from your father and his father. God's wisdom created him to be near to the ground so he wouldn't tire himself from always bending over to lift up stones and carve them. Your mother wasn't lucky . . . she and her sisters, and there were a lot of them, they had to get married. Your grandfather the priest and I couldn't put everything we had toward the girls' dowry and leave your uncle with nothing."

I recalled Margot's incipient presence and would repeat to myself every evening: "I won't be a god for any beautiful woman." Indeed, if I think the opposite I risk transforming from a brave and faithful Party member whose nerves are calm in battle into an ordinary beggar for passion. Where's your revolutionary commitment, comrade? I need to stop thinking about her completely: *Wife of important comrade + beautiful + Western + rich + misfortune = zero luck.*

This wasn't the first time I'd been attracted to wives or relatives of comrades and friends. I must start a private journey to get control over myself before I show my hand. Hey, Abu Sakhr, what do you think about living in this apartment? The class enemy, even when he's a comrade, still loves his luxury—and you're enjoying it. How will you deal with a spacious apartment, decorated with the latest Western furnishings, instead of the trenches? Instead of feeling satisfied with ordinary filth when the shower's been cut off for days on end? Hey, Abu Sakhr, haven't you been given this fancy apartment, like some other comrades on the party's orders, to protect it from being burgled or occupied by other factions and gangs—or because it belongs to rich friends and comrades who left the country fearing for their families, their lives, and their jobs, or because its inhabitants were known enemies?

A fancy apartment belonging to a class enemy and Party comrade: what's the problem, Abu Sakhr? The Party is powerful. Intellectuals betray their class because they know that this is a historical trend and because they're good people, honorable people. When the time comes, everything will be in place: doctors, important government employees, and politicians from other parties whose army units we used to infiltrate. The Party is everywhere. Sometimes it's visible and some of what it does is underground. You've loved secrets for a long time. You are primarily a secret to yourself. Don't worry, you and Abu al-Izz won't have any trouble finding a cover. In front of your comrades in the Emergency Task Force, you'll say what Abu Khalid told you to: "The Party protects nationalist personalities to prevent assassinations undertaken by isolationist groups, the no-good Palestinian factions, and the Syrian regime—its commandos and the Baath party."

I'm with Abu Khalid on this—the Party should be true to its allies even if they are bourgeois. Do you want the Sunni leadership of Beirut to be secretly allied with the Phalangists?

The first thing I thought when I began my new mission of shadowing Margot was that I should go to sleep earlier. I should come up with a dream that would take me away every night. The war, battles, dead bodies, severed heads, imagining my own corpse and its putrid smell after days in the sun at the end of a hot Lebanese spring—this is not the material for a soft, dream-filled sleep. Thinking about women and drinking a lot of wine—I started actually preferring it during my mission—both had the power to anesthetize me like a tired bull. But which women? Those who I encountered didn't excite me or make me think about their bodies, the movements of their hands, the shape of their breasts, or the distant memory of sex.

Like Naheda, the tall, thin, fierce woman who fearlessly carried a gun and used to say to the comrades who desired her that she had canceled out her virginity "a long time ago—I gave it to heaven." She used to toy with me even more, saying that she didn't need "outside intervention. That way I'm never grateful to anyone." But she'd have sex with me as if she were following military orders—perfunctory, and at regular intervals. "This is a physical need, we shouldn't give it too much importance," she'd tell me, justifying herself as she quickly and restlessly picked up her clothes, put on her pants and belt, and strapped her gun to it.

As for Aida, my old college girlfriend, she'd returned to her family's peaceful village in the north. Friends told me that she'd developed an interest in makeup, jokes, and eating seeds and nuts all the time, so she'd gotten fat. She'd also started refusing to attend local Party meetings with the excuse that she was only used to working with students and that she was reconsidering her ideas. On the few times she visited me during the war, I felt her distant from me, not only in the newly unmeasurable size of her body, but also in her asceticism toward sex, and perhaps toward me. So in my mind, none of the warmth that used to sweep over me when she touched me remained, only reminders of an ancient coldness. I didn't start drinking until after she'd left, to try to forget. Then I'd wind up drunk, only to wake up hungover and go to the center with one thing in my head, to die in the dark and leave a will that said, *Put some apples on my body and write on my grave that I was the worst son of Adam ever to walk the earth and heavens. Oh my grandfather the priest, never accuse me of virtue and hating the lust of the flesh!*

Occupation: Internationalist, Arab Communist freedom fighter, holder of permission to drive a personal car, postman, and keeper of dark secrets.

When I drove her car, a blue Renault 20, for the first time, I opened the back door for her and she smiled and said, "I'm not a leader, a government official, or a diplomat—why are you doing that?! I'll sit next to you."

I didn't know what to do when escorting her around. "Come with me, don't wait in the car. If you're bored of our conversation, read this book in another room." Or she'd tell me during lulls in the artillery shelling that her friends' balcony in Ain el Mreisseh is nice and overlooks the sea.

At that time, I still couldn't recognize that she wasn't inviting me to be a kind of friend, that she only took notice of me because of her kindness. Her behavior was different from the comrade-leaders' instructions ordering me, as an escort, to act as her equal. They didn't care much about what we did. Hours passed with us waiting in places far from their meetings, languishing in cars—bored, anxious, staring at passersby—searching for a camouflaged assassination team, with our hands on our machine guns laid out on our knees, or standing in the doorways and entrances of buildings.

She asked me if I knew À *la recherche du temps perdu* by Marcel Proust. I answered that the French literature course we had in the Lebanese baccalaureate program stopped at Baudelaire. She smiled and said, "You all are a little conservative."

"He's the pioneer of the nouveau roman," she then told me when she gave me Alain Robbe-Grillet's novel *La jalousie.* "I should've started with *Les gommes,* which contains the declaration of this new literary trend, but I lost my copy, I'll look for it again."

When we were alone in the few repertory cinemas in the Hamra district, my breathing would get shallow as I monitored my silence next to her. I didn't dare turn toward her, except to look out of the corner of my eye, until I wished I were cross-eyed. My God, how unjust you are! I didn't want to interrupt this impossible happiness. This used to happen at least once a week. I'd feel less anxious when her friends would accompany us, as she'd be less likely to notice what my facial expressions gave away.

Three times, her breath came close to my face unintentionally. Two times because of cannon shelling coming from the other side, and the third a nearby explosion. This is how I tasted her perfume, the sweat of her fear, her summer shirt, her chest, the feel of her arms, and the viscosity of the gods. After those two minutes, taking refuge in my instinct to remain, she then emerged with a slow, gradual distancing of her two scrutinizing eyes—since her body was still whole—before exposing her smile: "Nothing, it's only a warning. I'm a statue, I'm a willing tool, I'm an ice-age nebula, please sympathize with me and do not look at me as a human being."

Margot didn't just introduce me to *Citizen Kane* and new cinema—*Death in Venice*, *A Clockwork Orange*, Truffaut, Fellini's *Amarcord*, and *The Godfather* by Francis Ford Coppola—but also to a more diverse world through the films we watched together on party missions, like *Battleship Potemkin* and *41 Bullets*. The language of books, movies, novels, and the faces of Margot's friends segued from my mission to my insides. A combatant doubting the war, its words, its beauty, and its weapons. A Party loyalist searching for something outside the party in passion, in madness, in silence.

She became all of my time. When I waited in "my" big apartment, empty of everything but her ghost. Or in her apartment when she sometimes invited me to share a French meal with her, or when I went out to survey the area around the house and speak to the people who knew me by my assumed name and knew that I was guarding the doctor's house and escorting his wife around, or when I lingered around reading in a room or on the balcony of one of her friends' places, or when I drove or exercised by her side on the Corniche near the lighthouse in the morning when the bombardments had decreased, or when I was swimming near her at Sporting because she invited me to: "Did you come to just sit there like that? Come on, enjoy the sunshine and water and forget the shelling." Or when I spied on her body, modestly and bashfully, watching her joking with her friends and acquaintances. She became all of my time that had changed. Even when Comrade Jalal conveyed his messages, fearing my incipient forgetfulness, I started asking him to write them down: "Comrade, I am afraid I won't do the job the way it should be done." He'd answer me, without suspecting the real reason, that he didn't like writing as it could be dangerous, though sometimes he'd give in to my request.

My eyes: hazel-colored, not at all like my Uncle Elia's green eyes that were a bit blueish. My maternal aunts, grandmother, and my mother always said that because of this, he alone deserved the most beautiful and richest young woman in the area. We lost him. But he didn't care. He had an adequate horde of women when he sadly approached fifty without having married or produced a descendant or heir. We kept searching and suggesting women to him but he always responded, "Why do you all want me to be chained to one woman for the rest of my life? I am a man who loves freedom and fun. Children . . . for what? What use are they? What use have I been to my father?"

Height: 165 cm. Very short, not fit for the police, only for the army corps.

Educated, enrolled as a second-year student in the social sciences at the UNESCO campus. Most of my professors are comrades in the Party or the Lebanese National Movement and aren't bothered by my repeated absences from classes. They understand who I am. I live off my work, officially a secretary in the department of social affairs, but I haven't gone to the office since the area it's located in became hostile.

Sect: means nothing to me. I scratched it off my identity card three years ago. In any case, I gave up using the card after "Black Saturday," and since then I've only used the card of a comrade in the Democratic Front. My name on that one is Mustapha Masoud. This means I have several assumed names: Steif to friends, Abu Sakhr to everyone else, and Abu Sukhur, the affectionate version, for my closest comrades. Comrade Kamel, who works as an Arabic-language professor at the Faculty of Arts in the Lebanese University and is responsible for bringing us culture, called me this when he saw me on my first military training mission in the south. "You, comrade, are a qabaday, your body is like a rock, so you are Abu Sakhr—father of the rock—not the rock of Saint Peter upon which Jesus built the first church, but Communist ones." My father and my grandmother again.

Abu al-Izz, I know you will tell Abu Khalid everything: my eyes won't carry the great emptiness coming, embroidered with death. I stare at it and it colors me in hell. I embrace its body stretched out in my words. From the beginning of this night, you ask me, "What if I were ill?" And I couldn't talk to you and answer your questions while I drank myself into a stupor. I know that you opened up an investigation and that you won't close it until you know everything. Therefore, note that I wanted you to talk to me about this. You will say that you didn't do it because you didn't know anything. Was it up to me to talk? The glasses of whiskey that I choked back all afternoon hit me like shelling in the Battle of the Hotels. A 60mm mortar cannon can damage a nearby building from behind, even when you can't see it directly. In this way, I aim my shot glasses at a place that I can't see myself and scorch it with gunpowder. Twenty, thirty shots that night became my only bridge to the spectators. It was as though, for all my desire and lust, I was nothing but a step on a tall ladder whose rungs broke each time I climbed up them, causing me to fall. Comrade, I want her to stay and I know it's impossible. I'll go mad, I'll kidnap her, but how and where will I go with her? I'll kill him . . . This won't make her love me, and the Party will punish me and never forgive me. I'll kill both of them and commit suicide. I'll press my hand against her neck and squeeze firmly while my lips speak to her lips in that sex that I imagine overflows in her sentiments.

Abu al-Izz, advise me on a good coffin made of oak. The Red Oak Tree, as the comrades call the Party. Not just an old piano box, like the one you play. I don't deserve either of these. As a lover, I am a dog. I love with no right to, and without hope. Abu al-Izz, I'll kill you if you relate this to anyone.

When Comrade Abu Khalid informed me that she was returning to France, I was like someone hit by a stray bullet: a bit of time passes before he reacts or responds, and only after he sees the hot blood spurting out does he cut off the flow. "Comrade Jalal's wife will travel tomorrow via the Damascus airport with the help of the French embassy, which will take care of everything. You will stay with him.

She recommended this when she learned she was leaving because she really trusts you and finds you effective. We made the decision that she will travel abroad because things are getting worse. Asad is going to reach Beirut, we're organizing our resistance, and there's no point in her staying and distracting us with minor issues."

When I left the center I was only thinking about one thing: her staying despite the bombings, her comrade husband, the Party, Abu Khalid, my grandparents, my uncle, Philomena, God, traditions, laws, and the war.

"Hello, George," she said in Arabic, opening the door to me, revealing what I'd told her a few days earlier about my real name, a one-time disclosure.

Jalal greeted me from the living room, "Welcome, Abu Sakhr," though he surely already knew my real identity.

"Will you eat supper with us?"

I lowered my gaze when she looked at me. "I'm tired. I don't know, perhaps it's an epidemic this summer."

"Okay . . . but come on in and relax a little bit."

"No, I prefer to go to sleep early."

"Then wait a moment for me," she said. I reached out my hand and she passed me a sheet of paper. "This is my address and my telephone number in Paris if you want to abandon your wars before they're over and complete your studies or work in better circumstances. I will do what I can to organize things for you, and Jalal will help you if you ask him to. I'm leaving early and I won't see you tomorrow." She grabbed my hand. "I'll miss your company, thank you for the lovely companionship."

Jalal stood up and said, "See you tomorrow."

What do you want, Abu al-Izz, dear comrade investigator? Now at the end of another glass, you can close the report for which you're the only witness. I've closed my life on an open identity. I lost the war, the Party, and my passion. I won't submit my resignation and you won't submit your official report. I'll return tomorrow to take care of Jalal, the apartment, the party, and the roads. Exhausted, I'll carry the burden of a long rupture with myself.

In my eyes open to blackness, suddenly
the last sky that I've seen awaits,
taking me toward the abyss,
the uselessness of a traveler without a destination,
a singer who suddenly lost his soul,
a toy car lost in the congested streets of the one playing with it,
only madness emerges from loneliness.

Originally written in Arabic.

PART III

WAITING FOR YESTERDAY

THE THREAD OF LIFE

BY HALA KAWTHARANI

Bliss Street

At nine thirty the autumn creeps slowly toward Beirut's night. The first hospital looks like a hotel with no guests, and the second one looks like hell. People are crammed into it, running toward life, breathing heavy, hanging on to its edges, to its fingernails, to sparks flying from it, and life shows them no mercy. She hurries to flee, her sarcastic laugh rumbles, and she becomes more talkative. She doesn't stop or stumble. Life goes on. It also happens that it stops suddenly. That occurs right away, after a huge explosion goes off in the narrow Beiruti streets, between ugly residential buildings and the gaps between them, gaps that used to be houses in the old days, unpreserved history whose value no one knows and no Beirutis care about.

Only minutes after the explosion, people are already wondering how the crime was perpetrated—from what was used to the details of its planning. They partake once more in a new horror movie. Was it a car bomb or a bomb planted in a tree or a handbag left in some prearranged spot? The place becomes famous, it becomes the location where life paused. The place becomes a hero in the eyes of the television cameras and petty politicians. Life ends outside the place where so many human lives were ended. Beirut suffers from a brief spell of amnesia, afflicted by both short- and long-term memory loss. The tape is wiped clean from beginning to end, and it starts all over again.

Dr. Rashid leaves the hospital. He had parked his car in a spot across from the political leader's house, near one of the area's three hospitals. This is the mansion-hospital to which it's difficult to move emergency cases, because the leader lives here and the roads around his house are always closed. Dr. Rashid knows that the leader's dogs eat breakfast at seven in the morning, then arrive in the neighborhood at exactly nine o'clock. The people in the area set their clocks by the leader's dogs' schedule. They sniff rocks and humans, walls and cars, shop entrances and buildings. The leader's life is always in danger. And the dogs are among those "responsible" for protecting it.

Sitting in his car, Dr. Rashid decides to walk instead. That way he won't have to worry about searching for a parking spot later. He is not in the mood to deal with traffic. He walks. Strange feelings of fear overtake him. For the first time, he experiences the horror he sees in the eyes of his patients. He never used to be afraid, and didn't pay attention to his patients' fear. His "professionalism" prevented him from reacting to their psychological pain. Experience also prevented him from having an emotional response. Observing large numbers of patients in their last stages of life, patients bidding life farewell, clinging to each breath, light, and voice. He sees young mothers saying goodbye to their children, fathers trying—after their last, incomprehensible words—to keep their children away from their final moments on earth. None of these scenes disturbed him before. What was happening? Why was he afflicted by this oversensitivity right now? How can he prevent his tears from showing? How can his eyes swallow them up before others see them? Who afflicted him with this reaction? What has he been injected with? What dream has changed him? What vision?

He walks down May Ziadeh Street. He'd fallen in love with the name of the street even before he was convinced to buy his apartment. It is near the hospital and close to his heart as well. It's important to him to fall in love with the places where he lives and rests. He's had enough of the sufferings of the hospital, the smells of disease and death. Thus, it's important that his apartment be comfortable, that he can find the life in it that he's been losing in the hospital.

He walks under the jasmine plants that extend over the walls of the Asseily Building. Gibran Khalil Gibran Street intersects with the street named for that other Lebanese literary figure, May Ziadeh. May and Gibran never met in real life. They only met on paper, in letters they exchanged. Gibran's attempts to meet May weren't good enough. They never met. His desire to meet her didn't equal her desire to meet him. But the two streets meet. There are jasmine plants on Gibran Street too. Dr. Rashid loves jasmine; he often boasts that he lives in the only jasmine zone left in Beirut. It is also a security zone, as they have started to call closed streets around the houses of political leaders who fear for their lives. These zones strangle the people of the country a thousand times a day. They've transformed the movement of cars in the city into a trap out of hell, or one long nightmare. He remembers that he was reading about battles on the nearby street named for Michel Chiha, the writer and intellectual. His leftist cousin was killed there by a bullet to his abdomen. He was walking between Michel Chiha, May Ziadeh, and Gibran Khalil Gibran.

He walks and tries to analyze the reasons for his strange transformation, rationally and scientifically. He's unable to produce a logical analysis. Was that the dream? He keeps walking, keeps thinking, saying hello to the leader's guards and the army troops who protect the area, the militarized zone.

Everyone here knows him. "Hello, doctor," "Greetings, doctor." He always returns these greetings.

It has only been four days since he changed, since the young woman arrived at the hospital.

He will be late meeting Nevine. He's no longer enthusiastic about their passion for each other. He had once nearly gone mad wanting to be near her. After he separated from his wife, he spent two years without thinking about throwing himself into another relationship. He was very cautious, fearing a drift toward another cycle of blame and reproach because of his continual absences. His time was not his own. He gave his life to time. He didn't fight it, wasn't able to fight it or laugh at it, because his profession was saving the lives of his patients and he wouldn't give up on the promises he made to them.

He forgets himself between the hospitals. He faces death boldly—this he fights, courageously holding onto his sick patients' bodies to keep them alive. He takes dangerous risks and triumphs. He gambles and wins. When he loses, he's expended all of his efforts. He would have fought until the end and surrendered nobly. Now when he looks at his body in the mirror, he stares at his face, searching for some kind of change. He asks: *What has changed? Where did this fear come from? Who injected me with this horror?* He starts to be scared of confrontation, scared to confront death.

He decides to amble around on the nearby streets. He doesn't answer Nevine's call. The ringing continues but he doesn't hear it. He's lost in his footsteps. He walks forcefully, drowning in his movement. Sinking. He was in the emergency ward the night they brought the young woman in. He saw his entire life in her face. He saw the secret of life in it. From the moment he beheld it, her face never left him. There were contusions and wounds above her left eye. He knew the face but didn't know where or when he'd seen it. It was as if he knew it well, as if he were a part of it. Her body was clinging onto the thread of life. She hadn't died yet. He froze his movements. Of course he didn't want her to die. But the reason was personal and not merely humane, this wasn't related to his professional duties alone. He wanted her to live for him. He wanted her.

She was wounded by gunfire from the war in a "mixed" alleyway whose residents belonged to different sects and different parties. A battle of flags was taking place in the alleyway. Which party would raise its flags? You can't take a battle of flags lightly in a potentially explosive neighborhood. They set off wars and bury young bodies and dreams. That night, the young woman had gone out to her car. At that very moment, bullets rumbled and blood streamed out of a vehicle near hers, quickly mixing with the autumn rain. Bullets penetrated the roof of the car next to hers and the reply came quickly. In shock because of what was happening, the young woman stayed in her car, covered her head with her hands, and bent over the steering wheel. But the gunshot pursued her. It didn't settle in her lung, though she couldn't escape either. She sank into a bent position and then into the calmness of the moment. Everything stopped, even the bullets. Her movements stopped. Her tranquil body stopped fighting against the gunfire crossing from one side to the other. They brought her to the hospital. They brought her to him.

He walks and listens to the sound of thunder. It's not yet raining. It doesn't rain gently here, even the rain has become violent. He walks, her face with him. If she woke up from her coma, he'd tell her his life. He'd tell her that he was born to see her.

He smells the calming scent of jasmine and descends toward the most beautiful of all Beirut's alleyways. Yet he's still battling a strange sensation of fear. He pushes away a lingering feeling that the leader's ferocious dogs, the guard dogs, are chasing him. He tells himself that he can feel their panting and that they are silently pursuing him. Then he tells himself: *There are no dogs here. The dogs are sleeping in their mansions.* He walks cautiously, aware of the crazy traffic, frolicking cars driven in the absence of any laws regulating the flow of traffic and protecting pedestrians from gratuitous death. How many lives have been lost in his hands before he could save them?

Why does he dream of her? Since he first saw her, he has dreamed of her every night. He feels that he has known her since birth, that her soul is like his.

He won't go back home now. Nevine will call him. Perhaps she'll decide to visit him or propose dinner together. He won't answer if she calls him again. She'll think he's at the hospital.

* * *

He turns left toward Bliss Street. Every time he passes by here he reads the writing on the wall of the medical gate entrance to the American University of Beirut's campus. They're all words that rhapsodize about old Beirut, the Beirut that has lost its architectural identity. He once read on one of the walls the expression, *Beirut Is not Dubai*. He also glimpses love stories written inside giant hearts sketched on the wall and the names of dead singers under drawings of their likenesses. As he approaches the wall, he glances at the top of the Gardenia Building, where Kamal—who once was his professor and now is his friend—lives. Dr. Kamal sleeps on the sixth floor but mostly lives in his clinic on the first floor. His age is now so advanced that practicing his profession has become almost dangerous, both for him and his patients. Dr. Rashid worries about him and finds it hard to convince his friend to retire. How can he ask him to retire from his most precious identity?

The lives of the AUB students add color to Bliss Street. It's the most beautiful street in Beirut in his opinion, despite its terrible traffic, lights, and noise. Heavily armed soldiers stand on the sidewalk. He's used to seeing this and always wonders if it doesn't frighten tourists and foreign students. The war is coming, the war never left. He feels he is always at war, fighting in wartime and fighting in peacetime. There they are imposing their clout by carrying their "legal" weapons. We should always be precise in describing the weapons used: there are legal and illegal weapons which different factions proudly use to govern their relationships—wars that are sometimes cold and sometimes hot.

The character of the weapon that disfigured her face—a face of such beauty he'd never seen before—doesn't matter to him. She will live. She must live so he can tell her that they'd met before. He would look after her. He fears he will lose her. He is now officially afraid of death, fearing the death of others before his own death. Previously he had enjoyed immunity to death. Now he was losing his immunity and she was the reason. He had resolved this matter after making peace with death.

But now, faced with death, he feels impotent. It's a game he hates, the game of life. He rejects it, but cannot elude it.

He left her sleeping in the frost, alone.

He passes by this place every day in his car. Today he is walking on the sidewalk which witnessed the most beautiful moments in his life, the series of romances which he experienced during his first years at the university. He walks, remembering the names of restaurants and bookshops that used to be here and have now had their spots taken by other restaurants, restaurants with global or "globalized" names that he can't enter. He won't forget his places—Uncle Sam's bookshop and Uncle Sam's restaurant too, Basha restaurant and the B-25 café. He heard so much about the restaurant called Faisal's, which in his father's years at the university was more famous than the university itself. It was just across from the main gate; writers and intellectuals gathered there alongside university students who were, according to his father's recollections, "more mature than students today—they went to the university wearing suits, respecting the opportunities made available to them, the opportunity to receive a university education." He wondered about his father's concern with the suits worn by his generation of university students, and the relationship between these suits and their academic achievements.

He turns left, going up toward Hamra Street. He passes Stars, the shop for musical instruments that somehow hasn't yet closed down. The imposing thick, white iron door next to Stars had been the entrance to a video shop that his brother's friend ran. It had lasted only two years before it closed. He continues a little farther, looks to his right, and then raises his head. That's where his childhood friend Manal lived, up on the top floor of the large building on the corner where the bar Under Water used to be. That's the first bar he ever entered and cast aside his self-consciousness around women. He remembers that the bar was through the second door after the main entrance to the building. The shop between the two doors sold used English-language books. Rashid was a shy boy, particularly self-conscious around women, and didn't brag about his wet dreams like his friends did. He would secretly rent adult films from the video shop near the bar so no one would discover his secret; meanwhile his friends, the other boys in the neighborhood, would watch the films together in one of their bedrooms, when their parents were out, of course. In the bar Under Water, Rashid abandoned his shyness about women's bodies, touching their secrets. His imagination was transformed there into flesh and blood, into stories words couldn't relate, indeed into the curves of "Lilly's" body. He remained self-conscious in front of Lilly both before and after they sat together. Only when she dragged him behind the wine-colored curtain in the back of the bar and put his hand between her breasts then moved it all over her body did he forget his shyness. He used to plan his trips to the bar on the weekends when Manal was away from Beirut with her family, at their house in the mountains.

In her East Side apartment on the top floor of the Sarmad Building, his childhood friend Manal committed suicide. She was twenty-two. During that time, he was practically living in the university library. He had passed his medical school exams. He hadn't seen her in months. At their last meeting in the Three Roses café, she seemed enthusiastic about a project renovating the interior of a clothes shop, showing him her designs. He noticed that she was calmer than usual. He thought that she had grown up and left behind the tumult that glistened in her eyes. Then came the news one Sunday morning. He was eating breakfast. He remembers every detail of the scene: His house phone rang. His friend Nader was on the line, a mutual friend of his and Manal's. Nader was sobbing. How did she get the rope? Where did she find the strength to tie it around her delicate neck? How did no one in the house notice that the sounds coming from her room weren't normal? She locked the door with a key and claimed that she would need some time alone, that she wanted to read without anyone disturbing her. She prepared carefully for her last night. She pulled the rope around her neck and jumped into the unknown. She ended. Since that day, he had put off thinking about what happened. He imagined her neck all blue and purple, and her face bloated with absence. He didn't want to explore the details; he didn't want to review their friendship in order to understand the reasons that she terminated her life.

He walks as though taking revenge on his memory. He takes big footsteps. The face that changed him appears once more to him. Yara. Her name is Yara. Her name suggests another place and time, before they came together. She must stay here, in the world that brings the two of them together. He can't explain his obsession with her. But he's dying to know everything about her. What was she doing in that alleyway? He knew she didn't live there. He'd met her mother. He was self-conscious in front of her agony and completely understood it, even before glimpsing her face. He had an understanding of the suffering of patients' relatives, but deep within himself he ignored this suffering. Her mother was in a state of hysteria. She oscillated between anger—which she translated to him through a torrent of insults directed against the country and its people—and sarcasm, which would sometimes prompt banter and laughter about her condition and that of her daughter. He saw no other family members, only her mother. He wished he could sit next to her, hold her hand, and transmit to her some of the warmth he felt toward her. He loved the sallowness of her face and lips, he knew them, he knew the shape of her eyes and the nightdress that covered her skin. He had seen her before, in that dream he can't forget. He dreamed it before he saw her, before he was afflicted by the ever-present disease of fear.

He dreamed about a chair that he put next to her bed in the intensive care unit. Now he walks, holding her hand bound with tubes that provide her with life.

He walks in his Beirut. This city is like a giant village, a village unlike any other village, or any other city. He used to say that despite its new ugliness, Beirut still enjoys a certain charm that he doesn't know how to explain. He doesn't say this anymore. During his walk he searches for a charming setting. By day he tends to move between less ugly parts of the city and those with actual charm, if that's the right way to put it. He lives in what are called Beirut's "bubbles." There are neighborhoods in the city he hasn't visited since he was a schoolboy at the end of the seventies and the beginning of the eighties; there are other neighborhoods he's never visited at all.

He carries Yara with him, perhaps he doesn't feel afraid for her. How can he fight fear when it is percolating inside him, becoming a part of him? Perhaps it is a temporary state. He saw her wounded face in his dream before he saw her in real life. In the hospital he succeeded in hiding his shock. Then when he was alone, his obsessions and fears were born. Was the day's exhaustion enough to make him hallucinate or was he experiencing the symptoms of some disease? He raises his hand to his face, then sticks it on his forehead. He needs to sleep. Perhaps he will wake up tomorrow and have lost this terrible fear. He needs to pass by and see her tomorrow, because he is the surgeon who saved her from death as her mother keeps saying. He laughs. What kind of savior-hero do others think he is? What kind of savior-hero does he himself think he is? He walks. He is no longer able to move quickly. Tomorrow he will see her. Will she regain consciousness tomorrow? Perhaps he'll wake up tomorrow and be cured from this disease, from this beautiful curse.

He walks right through the chaos of a long Beirut night. He listens to the distant sounds of fireworks, as if they're faraway explosions that keep repeating. This violence is the expression of joy; this violence is the expression of all kinds of emotions. He is walking through Beirut while it's shedding the veneer of civilization. How can a respected doctor like him be so lost? He walks quickly like a man searching for his mind. He tells himself that tomorrow he will resist her pallid face and closed eyes. He will resist her lips that are searching for the kiss of life. Tomorrow he will resist fear. Why is he now fighting against night and its mysteries? He should go up to his apartment to collect himself before sleeping. He misses dreamless sleep, unless Yara decides to visit him. What is this loss that tortures him? He feels her lying beside him. She is here sleeping in his bed just like she is sleeping in the hospital—absent, infatuated with absence, haggard, and beautiful. He wants to sleep, and doesn't want tomorrow to be like today. This is what he's gotten used to in Beirut. This is what he learned from it. He should sleep now to live tomorrow, another Beirut day.

In the morning he has to shower quickly. He has to be at the hospital before eight. He doesn't think while putting on his clothes. He's still exhausted from wandering around yesterday. He is also afflicted by the exhaustion of the long years that came before this. He glances up at the sky as he leaves the building. The Beirut sky is so beautiful! The color of the sky here is spectacular. He looks up the whole time walking from home to the hospital. When he turns left the dogs bare their teeth. They arrived early from their morning excursion and have already started their security patrol. The dogs are in charge, he has to smile at them and fully acknowledge their extraordinary capabilities and their terrifying appearance.

When will he hear Yara's voice? When will he contemplate her eyes, open to the world? He ran all night long. He ran in his sleep, listening to himself panting. In the dream he arrived at the fourth floor of the hospital. He dashed through the corridor leading to the intensive-care unit. The lights were out. For the first time he recognized the darkness in that room, as if it were abandoned. Darkness enveloped the place and there was no sign of the young woman at all, nor of her mother. There was no one there to ask about what happened to the injured woman who was here just a few hours earlier. Then he woke up to the sound of the alarm clock.

When he reaches the fourth floor, his colleague who had been monitoring her was being paged. Her heart suddenly got tired; his heart almost stops. He still doesn't understand why he cares so much about her. It's as if his heart is suspended with her heart. He feels an exhaustion that he's never experienced before. He peers out the window of his clinic in the hospital at the Beirut sky, muttering, "Oh Beirut sky, save me." Then he carries on with his day. Her face is an enigma, and she is slipping through his fingers. When he enters her room, he tries to evaluate her sleeping face. If she wakes up, he'll have a brand-new life.

Originally written in Arabic.

WITHOUT A TRACE

BY MOHAMAD ABI SAMRA

Raouché

I stopped walking in the middle of a path in the public park. Images, ideas, echoes of words sunk into my wandering consciousness. I was struck by the memory of a laughing, silent face, but I don't know whose. Absentmindedly, I glimpsed a feeble sunbeam on a row of trees at the end of the street where I begin my evening walk a bit before sunset every day. A young woman on a bicycle, wearing fancy exercise gear, passed me by. Then she crossed back in front of me and gave me a curious glance, making me realize I was standing frozen like a statue in the middle of the empty path. I smiled and waved at her, while she wound away on her bike down another path, fading from sight.

Why did I smile at her? Did she notice the wave of my hand, or did it simply pass into oblivion? Like my words and movements that had sometimes started coming too late recently, it was as if a little opening had swallowed it up before it was completed. Suddenly, involuntarily, I burst out laughing. And in the little opening I noticed my own reflection in the image of that other unknown laughing face that had returned to my wandering consciousness just moments before.

When did that long, carefree laugh stop emerging from within me? I thought while quickly turning down the narrow pathway into which the bicycle woman had disappeared. I couldn't find any trace of her. In the shadow of her absence, a bygone memory emerged. It involved my little sister Vera, whom I have not seen for years, whom I rarely call, and who rarely calls me from Paris. I'm not even sure what time and place this was.

Fast and fading, the years retreat and vanish in time. Though my body started to become sluggish without me noticing, every moment became a nice memory—like my smile and the wave of my hand. They remained precariously suspended in emptiness. Like people wandering through the public park without a trace. Like my face, giggling in the forgotten memory, which caused more than half of my life to flash by in an instant. Like the laugh, which escaped from me involuntarily just a moment ago, but which had died years before I left Beirut for Los Angeles—more than twenty years ago now.

I exited the gate of the public park. The cool, light evening breezes revived the damp skin on my face. I walked along the sidewalk, heading toward my little but recently renovated ground-floor apartment in an old three-story building.

The glow of lampposts hung motionless over the street and sidewalk. The men and women passing by, myself included, were few and distant from one another. We were a mysterious being, strange and unknown, in a transient present which perhaps makes it forget itself and who it is. Perhaps the transient present extracts it from itself or preys on it, so it separates from its life. I enjoy this fleeting presence of humans, similar to how I enjoy the frozen, suspended memories that float through my vagrant vision when I pause in front of my living room window each morning. It's an external scene that the windowpane keeps me separated from—faraway, distant, invisible, present only in my seclusion, no one can see me but myself. Every morning, I stand behind that pane of glass, separating myself from the things in that static, outside world that makes my vision wander. I imagine myself a person in an Edward Hopper painting that I've inhabited and has inhabited me, by virtue of how much I've stared at it. I begin to think the painting depicts and narrates moments from my life.

In my Beiruti adolescence, I isolated myself from my parents and other people. I started seeking aesthetic inspiration from Edward Hopper paintings I discovered in a catalogue of his works among the books at our house in Sanayeh. Like the women in his drawings, I would sit on the chair or the bed, frozen all alone in time and place. The chair, the bed, and other things in my room were haunted by the shadows of inanimate objects, lit in the catalog's pictures by an unknown source. They enticed me. It was the power of the deep pain in the women's eyes staring out into that bleak, illuminated void, emanating from the emptiness that the paintings depicted.

Throughout my entire life in Beirut, nothing ever suggested that people in the city desired their time, bodies, things, and places—even their intimate ones—to be devoid of the presence of the noisy outside world and all its reverberations. Rarely did I come across someone accustomed to living in voluntary isolation—of the self, body, things—internally, in dark solitude. Whenever I recalled the Beirut which I left, it seemed to me that people lived, and I lived like that too, under the gaze of others—whether those people were actually present or not—haunted by other people's words, looks, and echoes. I remember myself among them merely as a black bee buzzing inside a hive, as I would write on the first page of my diary days after arriving in Los Angeles.

Here I am now, in the living room of my small house, lighting a candle for my sixtieth birthday. One candle, one glass of champagne on the side table, and me in my exercise clothes, wondering what to do, where to sit in the weak light shining from the corner. It is as if I'm reliving exactly the same birthday for the second or third time: a candle, a glass of champagne . . . nothing. No one else but me, taking a long rest on the rocking chair, absorbed in my daydreams.

The light of the lamppost, which pours out brilliantly on the asphalt outside, keeps me company. It spills through my window, dim and evanescent on the furniture whose edges are embroidered by the nighttime shadows. For a long time I haven't been able to bear beauty and its daytime colors, so I notice the darkness of the shadows in my house which don't leave a trace, or a memory, for anyone but me. Even that memory of the public park has repeated itself since I started taking my evening strolls there years ago: Passersby exchange greetings and kisses. I'm used to their faces and they're used to mine, leaving no memories or traces. Sometimes one of their faces appears to me like an image suspended in spacious, silent emptiness. It's as if time has simply been standing still or frozen since I entered the park that first time.

On the rocking chair, I close my eyes, swinging back and forth until I lose the sense of direction, time, and place. With the rhythm of the chair's two wooden rockers on the fur of the soft carpet beneath me, I swing and fly in the nighttime space of a city with few lights. I hear the echoes of my earlier, giggling laughter, which I imagined arose from my mouth and all of my body like crystal balls of air and light, illuminating the nightlife and the faces of the people I used to sit with in Beirut's cafés. Was my face also illuminated during these sessions and evenings at home before the long nights of the wars in Lebanon?

Suddenly I remember the first man in Los Angeles whose bed I spent the night in. I forgot his name many years ago, but the years haven't erased the memory of the morning in his kitchen where we drank instant coffee with milk. The silence was warm and thick in the big kitchen, resembling the sensation of sleep. My body relaxed in a dark calm. I was stretched out naked on the sofa, wrapped in a white sheet pulled back to partly expose my breasts and thighs, with luxurious and artificial negligence, like women in advertisements. My legs were resting on the chair close to the table on which the man whose name I've forgotten was sitting, naked except for his baggy, multicolored underpants.

I don't know if my feelings of disconnect from the world truly date back to our morning session in the kitchen, or if they were from the long gap in time separating me from that moment we lived together. But here I am now on a rocking chair soaring above the scarce city lights on my sixtieth birthday. From the outside, our silent scene recurs in my mind; I hear the echoes of the man's voice asking me if the day before had left strange feelings in me that perhaps the passing of days made even stronger and more present in my body.

That was the first time in my life a man had asked me such a question. It revealed his sensual desire for me, converting it into an old, fleeting memory. His question allowed me a sensual answer about a blurry, abstract thought which used to recur in my inner consciousness and which I couldn't put words to: chance encounters lead us, we meet and we part with trivial memories, so that life is and remains trivial, just like a passing memory of chance encounters.

The man smoked greedily and ecstatically in those moments. It was as if the tobacco which filled his lungs and was exhaled through his mouth granted his feelings and words a redoubled strength, making our dark morning meetings in the kitchen a lust-filled ritual emanating from our strange bodies that had lain together the night before. I kept silently soaring in the eyes of this stranger. One time he got up from the table and approached me. I hadn't anticipated that he would pour the milky coffee ever so slowly over my naked shoulders and lick it from my breasts with his orange tongue.

Sitting and snuggling, we came together on the sofa when I asked him in a faint lust-filled voice about his female colleague, the journalist who'd interviewed me while he was photographing me the previous evening at the Armenian Club, where my first exhibition of paintings in Los Angeles was opening. He whispered in my ear that they were siblings of Armenian descent and my whole body started trembling, reaching an orgasm for the first time in more than a year, since I had emigrated from Beirut. My spasms began transmitting like a storm in all my senses, every part of my body, followed by waning flashes of lightning that illuminated the darkened screen of my vision.

I postponed my shower for the second time. I turned on the computer and wrote: *How long has it been since I've heard a voice, my own or someone else's, in this house of mine? It's as if I haven't talked to anyone or heard anyone talking to me except outside for a long time.*

An apparition of the Virgin emerged in my imagination; it stopped me from writing and made me laugh. The crown of thorns of Golgotha on the Messiah's head, then on my mother's head, and a bloody tear streaming down her pale, deathly white cheek. My father slowly ripping the Virgin's dress off her chest, while she smiled at him, thrusting her tongue out and moving it between her lips, exactly the way I'd sketched her in my room a few days before my trip to Rome on a scholarship to study drawing. While I was outlining her angelic face, I kept hearing echoes of my mother's words—that she would lose me, that I would lose myself, that I would disappear, all alone in Rome, and never be heard from again. That I would never come back. Her words made me laugh. An impudent smile hung on the face of the Virgin and I drew her tongue licking her lips.

The evening of my trip, I hung my picture of the Virgin on the living room wall. My mother was extremely anxious, but her sadness and trepidation were concealed behind a mask of happiness put on to greet well-wishers who flocked to our house. We sat together in the living room, with our entire family. I purposely sat under the picture of the Virgin that I'd drawn, and during certain moments that evening I tried out the expressions of the Virgin on my own face. That evening I met our Armenian neighbors and others, our relatives who I hardly knew, some of whom I'd never even met before. I stood at my mother's side to receive and greet them, but from time to time that evening I had to rush to my room, so that I could unleash the laughter that took me by surprise and get control over it in order to answer the old ladies' questions about what I would be doing in Italy: how would I live there all alone? They would look at my mother while directing these kinds of questions at me. But it was my grandmother who occasionally took charge of answering. One of the times when I left the living room I heard her say, "She will draw, she will study drawing, she will become a great artist," and when I turned around I saw her pointing at the picture of the Virgin hanging on the wall.

At that point, my father rushed over to me when he noticed I was bursting into a fit of uncontrollable laughter. He took my hand and led me to my room, where I thought he would lock the door and start scolding me. But he surprised me by letting out a chortle that I'd never heard before. In turn I unleashed my own resounding laugh. He hugged me and held me to his chest, whispering in my ear in his pitiful French that I could laugh as I wished in the streets of Rome and to never let a man own me or rob me of my desire to laugh.

After many years, on one dark, dreary Beirut evening near the beginning of the wars in Lebanon, I managed to elicit one of those rare giggles from my father that I so often wondered when, where, and with whom he allowed to escape. Why did he never do this with us at home? I will never forget that moment when he was sitting alone on the balcony on one of those miserable Beirut evenings. Each one of us was alone in our own room, after we learned that the fire raging for days in the port had burned down his nearby factory and its imported goods. He'd put a glass of whiskey on the table in front of him on the balcony and started drinking, drinking and smoking without stopping, staring at the stray clouds of smoke rising up from the warehouses of the distant port.

I was worried, after he'd been sitting like that for nearly two hours during which I'd left my room a few times to check on him, and he didn't even notice me standing barefoot in the wide-open inner door leading from the balcony to the living room. Finally, I moved quickly from the door and leaned against him on the wrought-iron railing of the balcony. After a moment of shared silence, I told him that I would never let anyone or anything own me or rob me of my laughter—not in Italy and not in Beirut. I saw him peer at me through faint darkness, before letting out that rare laugh whose darkly murderous bitterness I didn't recognize until days later, when a heart attack overtook him on the morning of a sunny winter day on that very same balcony.

* * *

So here I am lying down in bed, in my bedroom in Los Angeles. Memories of myself in the room of a Kurdish poet I'd met in Beirut thirty years ago blur together. I can imagine him now in a room in Sweden. In another room, perhaps in a sanatorium for mentally ill people, in some country I don't know, I imagine the Iraqi painter who left the scar on my forehead. Through my Kurdish poet's thoughts about me, I saw my youthful face and his older gaze during our many rendezvous in Beirut. How different my face is now from how it was when I was young. If my life had led me down another path, to another destiny, would it have been possible for me to be different from how I am now?

No, I am not nostalgic for anything. I still steer clear of tender feelings, just as I used to do in Beirut whenever their echoes would reach me, like from the stories told by friends during the war. They would recount what went down with them—the life of their country and its people before the war. At that time I didn't feel that I had a past that I was cut off or uprooted from, or that I would long for. It was as if the war didn't besiege me, in the way they used to say that it had besieged them. I lived time and moments spirally, like now—with nothing behind me, without a trace, a lineage, or roots binding me to places and times that my friends in Beirut felt they were disconnected from, regretting the demise of those things and proclaiming their nostalgia in their stories.

In coffeehouse sessions on Hamra Street and evening gatherings at home, they used to talk about different villages, towns, regions, and neighborhoods. But it was strange to me: I didn't understand their distinctions except for the names. At the many party meetings I attended of what was called the Artists' and Intellectuals' Cell of the Lebanese Communist Party, I didn't understand anything at all. Nothing they said about the reasons for the war—its parties, battles, and regions—spoke to me. None of this altered my view of the war and its fighters. The announcements by the person in charge of the Party cell, while playing with the hairs of his long beard, would incite my sarcastic commentary. If I understood some of its ideas and hollow rhetoric, I would conceal my sardonic laughter, which I used to let out raucously whenever I heard a speaker unleashing his tirades at massive partisan rallies in Beirut. If rallies like this were paying tribute to the Party's martyrs, I would conceal my giggles amidst the screams of party members crowded around with their slogans and applause for the speakers, before turning to my journalist girlfriend without whom I never attended a rally, and saying to her, "Look, look at him on the podium—he's about to blow someone up or kill someone. Is he carrying a gun? Look, come on, let's get out of here." My friend would manage a shy, scared smile and her reluctance to applaud like everyone else made me envious.

My cynicism of the idea of the martyrs grew after the armed groups started showing off their dead—counting them, glorifying them, and competing for greater numbers. When the expression "the Party's martyrs" became popular and spread throughout the Communists' daily speeches, I told my comrade friend that this had become a registered trademark, which we've all shared in creating and promoting. I, for example, designed recruitment posters in the communal studio allocated by the party leadership to amateur artists who were party members, and their friends. The studio was in a working-class Beirut neighborhood mostly filled with Druze and Christians. The other Communist artists and I were the ones who set up the studio, and we worked for months there drawing and designing posters of martyrs and training the beginners. But it quickly turned into a headquarters for the fighters, a refuge to hold meetings, and somewhere to sleep after the intensification of battles after the war spread throughout the whole city.

When I entered the studio for the last time on the morning of an intensely hot summer day, all of my senses were invaded by a smell that froze my body in its place. I felt that it had crashed into a gelatinous, organic material, with my eyes as wide open as they could be, so I closed them and stopped breathing. In vain I took steps to repel this odor that I could smell emanating from inside my skin, so I ran outside. I couldn't forget that smell from the main room of the studio that morning. Along with the weapons, rounds of ammunition, and piles of military clothes and shoes strewn around, bodies of fighters—naked except for underpants—covered in regretful sleep, were piled up on filthy mattresses made of naked sponge foam.

Whenever I remember a scene, incident, or person from those Beiruti days, my ears are provoked by echoes of a song about the mothers of martyrs, whose words I've forgotten. I've totally erased them from my memory. It's a song inhabited by time, place, and language, like space or a floating rhythm that the whole world swims in. The closed, claustrophobic world of everyone I knew and who knew me in Beirut those days at the beginning of the war. But how can forgotten words remain a stronger and deeper presence in my memory than things and faces and scenes? It's as if words, if they are forgotten and erased, leave a void behind them inhabited by a mysterious physical force that can't stop memories and their moments. A poet who was a member of the Party's intellectual cell wrote the words to that song. He used to be in love with me. Perhaps that's because I was the only woman in the cell. All of them, one after the other, tried to get together with me. The singer of the song offered his deep love to the martyrs, with all the passion of his spoiled, childlike voice. Once he offered to take me home in his car after we'd left a meeting at the cell leader's house. On the way he started flirting with me and invited me to dinner at a restaurant on Hamra Street. I asked him, giggling, "You are dedicated full-time to loving the martyrs, why do you love me? How can you?!" I had an aversion to his sharp, high-pitched voice, as if he were a teenage schoolgirl softening her tone when addressing a teacher who confused her in class.

Dusty, gray, and sticky, like that oily layer on the skin of my Party journalist friend's face, moments from those Beirut days at the beginning of the war are present in my memory now. I used to figure that the day's hot, mucous-like stickiness would only soil me as a curious spectator. That stickiness would be kneaded in things and objects, like vomit, as if it were its original material. As if it were a coagulated substance in the bodies of humans and their relationships, meetings, words, and voices; in streets, places, and houses at all times. While they slept and when they woke up late in the morning, a magnetized tinfoil fog would stain the city's low-hanging sky. They would walk on the ground with heavy aborted footsteps, as if they were battling through a womb's serum mixed with urine and dirt on the asphalt on sticky days, and nights when opaque, scarce lights resembled a carbon fog on faces . . . I moved through these moments with my journalist friend, as if she were my blind guide born of the womb of that world, as if I were a guide for her slow emergence onto its shores.

Was I truly a spectator standing on the shores of this world that Beirut drowned in years before I left it? Were there even shores over there? I don't know.

I didn't step into the small, glass shower stall. Naked, walking barefoot in the corridor to my bedroom, the feel of the threads of the small silk rug in front of my wardrobe sent soft tremors from my feet to the edges of my naked body. With my own eyes I glimpsed the anonymous person, the narrator of imaginary scenes of my life, my nakedness illuminated by the dusty light emanating from two old lamps covering the glass of two small wooden bedside tables. The dusty light behind me drowned things in the room in still, concealed shadows and I imagined the light intimate and pale on my naked back. I passed the palm of my hand ever so slowly over the small dark-blond freckles on my shoulders. All of the men whom I've gotten naked for have rubbed their lips on these freckles that the Beiruti-Baalbaki painter once told me were stars extinguished on my skin. He was the only one of my men in Beirut who I'd responded to, agreeing to be—though I was fifteen years younger than him—an extramarital lover who didn't ask him one question about it.

I reach my hand out to open the drawer of my wardrobe and I suddenly realize that it's this painter who is the one now inspiring me to remember the scenes of my life. Months ago, I learned that he'd died in Beirut. I push my hands between my clothes hanging in the wardrobe. The mild, refreshing cold—my neglected clothes cool in their sleepy, intimate neutrality—slinks from a long black dress onto my hands and skin, so I take it out, unfold it, and hug it to my chest. Its soft cloth revitalizes my breasts while hanging on my naked body all the way down to my legs. Here in this very room, I'd put it on fifteen years earlier, and was overwhelmed by my breasts, back, and naked arms reflected in the mirror. So I'd put on a black sweater and went to my mother's funeral. And isn't this also the same dress I'd worn in my role as a "lady of the night" on my rendezvous with my Kurdish poet in Beirut?

Is this one of the many dresses that my colleague and only friend from the art institute left at my parents' house when I let her stay with us, after my sister Vera left for Paris?

The institute was a residential building on a small hill near the Raouché coast and its famous rock. After being the only female teacher at the institute where all the other professors were men, I met my friend after the administration contracted her to teach lessons missing from the full-time professors' schedules. During the first five years of the war, the female teachers all immigrated or retired—one after the other—until not one other remained in the institute.

Years before I started teaching I heard stories from my artist and journalist friends about the institute in the time before the war, all of which centered around its professors who had once been students there. From the strands of these stories, I concluded that they were men from modest backgrounds and families, new to the city, who in their school years had mixed with female students of urban families who could afford luxury. These young women would enroll in the institute for a period of time, and their liberation would take on an affected character. They paraded beauty, the feminine body, and its elegant fashions in the theaters of public daily life. In the time before the war, the institute was one of these theaters. It mixed liberation, the glitter of art, and the fashion parade—and this made its students stars who diffused their glamorous, intoxicating brilliance out of the reach of the eyes and imaginations of the male students of more modest backgrounds. These men were obsessed, infatuated, and crushed by their female colleagues' charms—for example, their burning love and infatuation with the girls working in beauty salons and clothing shops, imitating the cinema and singing stars of the 1960s. But what truly surprised me was that in the stories of their burning passion for their female colleagues, the former-student teachers would identify them by their family names, saying that this one or that one was a girl from one family or another, as though they were announcing the brand names of luxury goods. I found it strange that this or that narrator would say that he had forgotten the name of his female colleague, a student whom he had been obsessed with and blindly subservient to for a year or two or three . . . He'd sat with her in classrooms, drawing studios, the institute cafeteria, and the city's coffeehouses. I surmised that the young women of the stories were nothing but reflections of their notable families' lives of luxury and affluence in the eyes and imaginations of young men hungry for lives of luxury and affluence. They didn't touch those girls except when they were alone daydreaming and masturbating. I said that once, giggling loudly, during a session where which some of the institute's male teachers were telling these old stories, shortly after I had started teaching just at the end of the first years of the war, 1975 and 1976.

At that time, academic life in the institute—teachers' meetings, relationships, and daily get-togethers—had started to become colored by creeping rivalry, discord, and rumors circulating among the professors and students who belonged to political parties and armed groups fighting in the streets. A few days after I began teaching—and I didn't want to do this, but I reluctantly submitted my request to the institute administration for contractual teaching hours, my answer to the insistence of the leader of the Communist Party's intellectual cell—I heard that my request would have been denied were it not for the intervention of the party leadership and its pressure on the administration. At first I was the only female teacher, so the presence of another woman in the institute delighted me—from the moment I saw her in a long black dress, with slits up the side and revealing the top of her chest. Soon, my initial, fleeting encounters with her alerted me to the need of having *any* woman at my side in this sexist place. Days after this female colleague started teaching, rumors started to spread around the male professors that she was the lover of a failed lawyer from a modest background, who had risen through the ranks of an armed group to help to establish both it and its leader who had been a cleric before his disappearance three years after the beginning of the war.

When she told me during our second meeting that she'd spent years in Paris studying drawing and sculpture, I didn't believe her. Nor did I believe her tale about her prosperous family who owned land and orchards in Sour. Nor that armed Communists blew up their abandoned mansion after they'd fled to Paris. She used to come to the institute as though she were being forced there. I then bumped into her several times stepping out of or into her fancy car, which made me want to flee, feeling an aversion to her slow, swaying, stylish way of walking in evening dresses which she wore even when teaching. Then I started thinking that her skin, under the flashy cloth of her dresses, exuded a stickiness like the saliva that dripped from the mouths of the male teachers whenever they saw her. Their lecherous saliva would be smeared on the ground around her feet and these sticky smears would pile up on top of others that had been left on the tiles long before. So, whenever I ran into my only female colleague, I'd quickly move away as though I smelled a terrible odor before she even stopped to initiate a conversation.

But a captivating smell wafted from her body and her car when we escaped to my parents' house on the day two bombs exploded on a street near the institute. On the steps in the middle of a crowd of students, I heard her angry and trembling voice behind me, calling me to wait for her. She clung to my arm and asked me not to leave her to drive her car through the streets all alone. As soon as we had walked two or three steps into the crowd, she turned around quickly, shouting, "Institute full of animals, I hope you all die! Go back to your mosques, a curse on your fathers, you dogs!" Then I saw her slap a young bearded man behind us. I dragged her by her arm down the stairs, and she told me in a low voice trembling with rage that he'd forced his hand between her thighs. At the entrance to the institute she dug her fingers into my arm and I hugged her to calm her anger. That alluring scent wafted into my nose and I heard applause all around us, only then realizing that the students were enjoying the sight of us hugging each other. We entered her car, not far from the institute's gate, just a little before nightfall. Sitting behind the steering wheel, she said that after today she'd never return to this house of vice. I was struck by her bold, violent movement, hitching her black dress up to the top of her thighs before quickly launching the car in a way that scared me more than the loud blast of the explosion I'd just heard. She turned toward me, saying that he—that bearded young man—hurt her with his violent grabbing of her underpants and almost ripped them from under her dress.

The streets of Beirut were thunderstruck by a sudden fear, haunted by passing ghosts who disappeared as fugitives a few moments before. Its asphalt seemed somber, vibrating like metal under the screeching of our speeding car's tires, a long, extended thrust into the terrifying daytime silence. As far as I could see, a spectacle of buildings almost devoured us, declining and drifting away, as though they were collapsing in silence and vanishing behind us. Suddenly, my driver closed the car window and burst out screaming. She careened forward, reeling between the two sides of the street before crashing a front wheel against the curb. A new explosion stopped my friend's hysterical screaming, causing her to hunch over the steering wheel, which she hugged with her arms. When she lifted her head after a few moments, I told her that my parents' house was nearby and we could go spend the night there.

In the dark light of my room, in front of the mirror on my wardrobe, I put the long black dress forgotten in my closet since my mother's funeral on my naked body. A clear, sudden flash of that captivating fragrance blows over my senses, and blurry images of my colleague and I in my parents' house in Beirut are reflected in my imagination. In a large mirror on the walls of my room in the old house, a vision of my colleague removing her long black dress, then putting on one of my housedresses. My skin shivers tautly under the cloth of my dress, and I lift it off my thighs and pass two strange hands over them, as if I'm passing them over my colleague's thighs. Like a phantom from drawings I sketched during my innocent isolation in my Beirut adolescence, departing her body, her cold skin revealing thin, symmetrical bones. Irritation from my old housedress on that skinny body snuck onto my skin, on the days when I drew myself all naked and stretched out on the white sheets of my bed. I approached the mirror on my wardrobe, eyes closed. I kissed myself on the lips and listened to the echoes of my lust-filled gasps for air, from which a remote voice pronounces my name.

I try in vain to remember my colleague's name. Its letters are scattered, remote, and don't come together on my tongue. This smooth gap in my memory pulls me backward and makes me take a few steps away from the mirror on my wardrobe; I notice in its depths a blurry vision of our naked embrace. The taste of her scent in my mouth. I take the straps of my dress off my shoulders, and its cloth slowly falls from my chest and bends over at the top of my round butt. It's as if my hands, without me, touched the pleats of the cloth, pushing it to the ground so that it piled up around my feet. Two moist lips kiss my belly button, and I bend down to embrace the woman's head, my fingers playing with her short, boyish hair. With two thin arms she hugs my thighs and she passes her rough tongue, anointed with saliva, slowly over my skin. I'm intoxicated all the way to the roots of the hair growing out of my head. I open my eyes and hear myself repeating my colleague's name. Cold little drops of sweat drip from under my arm, and from the strip of kisses between my breasts they descend toward my side. I bend down, pick up my dress from the floor, and a dizziness burns in me.

The light is strong on the surface of the mirror around my body. Suddenly, I remember the face of my friend and colleague and her rosy, puffy cheeks, a colored hijab tied tight around her hair, the top of her forehead, and her neck presenting itself as a stranger to her body and self. I remember her in a scene that took place in front of a mirror in my parents' house, practicing with laughter to put on the hijab and tie its edges around her face, while informing me that the director of the art institute had spoken to her about wearing it and his desire to marry her secretly. They'd be married by a shaykh he knew, rent an apartment in Beirut for their secret life, and he'd appoint her a full-time professor at the institute.

Before this, when he first approached her, we spent evenings at my parents' house laughing and talking about him and his behavior. She told me that once she took him out in her car on Beirut's seaside Corniche, and with his outstretched hand and thick, short, trembling fingers he started skimming and touching the cloth of her dress. The image of a man's hand creeping up toward a woman's thigh under the cloth of her dress in a car aroused me, and I asked my friend what she did at that moment. She told me that she turned to her side and saw an impassive bald head, belonging to a man who'd let his blind, detached hand approach her dress and leg, both of which she felt were detached from her. The idea of a blind hand and its movement detached from a man's body, together with a bald head stationary like a stone sculpture, with its suppressed, fearful desires, suggested to me that I had found the necessary shades and features to complete the canvas that I had started painting.

In that vast living room with its high ceiling, I turned to my friend who was stretched out on an old sofa. I loved the sight of her in an open bathrobe, revealing her long, thin legs. I came close to her, started running my hand slowly over the blond fluff of her legs, and felt a slight trembling in her skin, a little rough to the touch under my hand. She didn't turn to me and she didn't look at my hand. It was as if she were submitting to a distraction that completely detached her from her body and her presence at my side. To bring her back from her reverie, I observed that the toupee on the director's head would take fifteen years off of his life—that was the age difference between the two of them—and that her secret marriage to him would add fifteen years to her life, so they would be the same and could produce secret children.

My friend laughed and got up from the chaise longue, saying, "All male children, I will bear twins after twins, and not like the four female children that his cousin my co-wife bore for him in his village in the south where they live in his parents' house." I was hearing the word *co-wife* for the first time and I imagined an old blind woman in a painting of the Greek countryside.

But I followed my friend's words and thoughts, telling her, "You'll visit her there and help her go on a diet. With his fake hair and marriage to you, the director will rekindle his desire for her and not divorce her. He might also regain his Communist commitment from the days when he was a school teacher in the village, before he left the Party and travelled to France to get a doctorate in philosophy, which led to his appointment as director of the Art Institute."

After a while my friend told me that she invited him to dinner at a seaside restaurant and he told her that in his doctoral dissertation he had analyzed manifestations of the Nietzschean philosophy of power in the personality in Imam Ali ibn Abi Talib's book *Nahj al-Balagha*, or *The Way of Eloquence*, and in Imam Khomeini's school of Islam. After the two of them had left the restaurant, my friend continued, he dared to put his hand on her thigh where her dress was pulled back, as she was driving the car. I laughed, telling her that he was remembering the revolution of power in his dissertation, but just as quickly she shouted, "No, no . . . he wasn't remembering anything!" Then she laughed, saying that he asked her to end her relationship with me because I was an Armenian slut. Suddenly, I begged her to bring him to my place one evening. She liked the idea and I realized that she—with no explanation—had already intuited what I was thinking. We would agree on the nature of the evening and its purpose, even down to the implications of her conditions—that she would leave us alone at home, the director and me, and she would depart at the end of the night.

Months had passed with her staying with me at my parents' house. On the evening of the invitation, I intentionally put on a long sky-blue dress whose thin cloth revealed my body's curves. When I opened the door to them, I swallowed laughter upon seeing a pile of jet-black hair on the director's head. I welcomed them and brought them into the living room, congratulating the director on his new hair, but I surprised him and myself by saying to him, with a smile, that his baldness used to entice me. He stared silently at my face for a moment before moving his gaze onto my body and stabilizing it at the tops of my thighs, and I asked him if he liked my dress. My friend answered that the dress—her dress—was more beautiful on my body than her body, saying to the director, "Look, look, isn't she just like Mary Magdalene—why don't we use her as a drawing model at the institute?" Then she turned on the large crystal chandelier hanging from the high ceiling, and the lights of its many lamps were diffused throughout the expansive living room. I wanted to say that women's bodies seem bald when they are free of clothes, but I turned quickly toward the door of my room, explaining that I would change the dress I was wearing for another one. The director mentioned that we were alone in the house, that no one among us was a stranger, and that his wife wore a red dress like mine after she went into the hotel room and took off her white wedding gown. I nodded and headed toward a seat in the living room. But I quickly stopped, since a new scene suddenly loomed in my imagination: the director on a bed in a hotel room, tearing a see-through red dress off the body of a woman. It then occurred to me that I was the woman whose dress was ripped off on the bed, here in my room, after my friend had left at the end of the evening.

Originally written in Arabic.

THE DEATH OF ADIL ULIYYAN
BY **ABBAS BEYDOUN**
Ras Beirut

The café was almost empty. Two men were sitting at a corner table playing cards with unusual silence for a game around which crowds of spectators usually gather and work their tongues. They seem to be playing more from boredom than anything else, faced with empty tables and pervasive silence. I sat down and after a while one of them, a young, khaki-clad man, approached me. As he walked over, I could make out that he was older than I had suspected from a distance. He shook my hand and asked me what I wanted. When I ordered tea, he told me that the water had been cut off since the morning and it would be better to order a Pepsi. I agreed, in order to avoid further conversation, but the man kept standing right there in front of me, not moving. He stared at me as though waiting for me to recognize him. Then he told me that he knew me. He said he was Samir Uliyyan, the son of Adnan—Adil Uliyyan's brother—who had apparently told them a lot about me; I am Jahal Mazhar. He told me that Adil had come back from Beirut ill, that they had found something in his stomach. I asked him where Adil Uliyyan was living, and he said that he had built a place in Rweiss, on some land he had bought there.

I didn't meet Adil Uliyyan until we'd both moved to Beirut. I'd moved here before him, to attend the American University. I rented a house and settled down in the city. But I'd heard what had happened to him in Beirut and most of it was what I would have expected: cruel machinations and scams. He traded in elections. He'd go up to a village and choose a candidate who he was convinced could be the victor. He'd use his influence over certain officials, telling them he had to have a certain amount of money. It's not important what the ballot boxes said plainly the morning of the elections, he would capture the amount needed to win, then disappear. I heard that he'd belonged to influential parties during the war, struggling within them to achieve a certain rank, rallying around and causing trouble until the party leadership got tired of him and kicked him out. But he always found his way to another party, wreaking havoc within it until they too were exasperated with him.

During the war, he was well suited to join in the killing, quickly becoming one of the war's rising stars. He spent three months in a military training course and returned from it an officer in the Pioneers of the Revolution unit. As a military man, he could do what he liked. He could refuse orders. He could call on anyone he wanted, mobilize people around him. He could also organize big operations: stealing cars and coming away with a diverse fleet; his comrades had a habit of driving these cars wildly and wrecking them, creating excellent parts at low prices afterward. They would also sell furniture from houses they'd pillaged, and extort the rich and influential in exchange for protection.

The war destroyed political parties and organizations; military wings prevailed, as did the logic of war itself. As soon as killing starts, as soon as human life becomes cheap, then everything is allowed. As soon as people acquire the right to annihilate human life, they become lowly gods who consider everything available, and any material possessions as offerings for themselves. They become idiots, using their whole lives to snatch up whatever comes into their hands. They exist only to expand their authority, committing all sorts of transgressions. After the second or third operation they are liberated from any type of self-reflection and start to believe in themselves—of course, most of the time not giving value to anyone else's opinion. It can't hold up. From the moment people start to cross lines, thought becomes weak and can't defend itself. Each individual must build his authority with his own hands, necessitating an increasing number of transgressions.

Adil Uliyyan—according to what I'd heard of him—did this. I heard that he was extremely reckless and killed more people with his own hands than all the rest. He once walked up to a customs officer in the Beirut port and emptied a cartridge of bullets into his head in front of a group of people. From that time on, no one dared oppose him anymore, even his comrades started to fear him like they would a god. He had killed a man in cold blood and he did it for show. His aides completely submitted to him out of fear; in the beginning, their way of thinking united them. Of course, a way of thinking is only useful as an excuse, an empty excuse. What really unites and equalizes people is fear. The one who inspires fear is the master—but this equality is frightening, since no one knows who will be the first to initiate something, who will be the first to transgress. Adil Uliyyan was the first, and it cost him just one murder. From that time on, he profited from everything. A relatively guaranteed sum came to him from every operation; it was protection money from the aggressors, the ones who extorted money through their racket.

One day, fear caused someone to raise a gun and empty it into Adil Uliyyan's body. The man went into hiding after that. It was said that he had fled to Brazil, but afterward Adil Uliyyan was bedridden and when he recuperated he was no longer himself. He staggered when he walked, his body shaking violently, his limbs trembling. Despite this, the person who shot him didn't come forward and feared him even in this state. He had no doubt that Adil Uliyyan could still kill him. His disability made him even more terrifying: those trembling limbs could strangle a person, suck out his bone marrow, squeeze his heart. People waited for him to do something but he didn't budge. In this way, he remained the very image of fear itself. He was fear trapped in a shaking body—his fingers quivering; his two eyes open and ready.

Samir Uliyyan told me that after they found something in Adil's stomach, he moved from Beirut to Sanawbariyeh to rest there. I didn't know if I should visit him; it is true that we had been . . . I don't know how to put it . . . friends. I'd meet up with him from time to time, until we both left Sanawbariyeh. We were friendly when we were first becoming men; but we were comrades, nothing more. Every day we'd cross the village together. He was a liar and I wasn't. He was outgoing and I was shy. But those were the days of our innocence. Even in all his lies and exuberance, Adil was innocent back then. Who would think that an idle lie could transform into a crime? Who would imagine that shyness and indecision could transform into intrigue? But innocence can show through lies, it can show through shyness. It can be idle chitchat, it can boast, it can rave deliriously and go into a coma. No one knows what it will lead to.

I didn't know if I should visit Adil Uliyyan, or if we should even meet again. After all that time that had passed, it would be like a conspiracy, a meeting of the smuggler and the thief. What would the two of them have to say to each other? What could members of the war generation have to say to one other? Who will they accuse if time turns against them, if they end up as miserable criminals, miserable smugglers, miserable thieves? They won't accuse either God or destiny, since they know that they are acting without either of them. They won't accuse anyone of treachery, for this is what they have to expect. They have gone so far with their own treachery that they have even forgotten what treachery is.

Despite all this, I still wanted to visit Adil Uliyyan. I thought that perhaps he had something to give back to me. I thought that he owed me something; I didn't know what it was but the time we spent together had somehow indebted him to me. When I first met him, he was writing, or imitating really, using the very same hand to do it that he'd used to empty bullets into the customs officer's head. I had a shameless desire to hear him narrate this . . . a shameless desire that I was ashamed of when I realized it. I wanted my roaming comrade to narrate it to me as though it were a lie that I couldn't possibly believe even if we'd been sitting in a holy place that compelled us to tell the truth. To tell it like he invented his love story with the curate's daughter.

Can we go back to those places that prompt us to the truth, and still lie? Can we narrate our lives as though they didn't happen? They did happen, but what is left of them in our souls is no more than a lie.

I decided to go visit Adil Uliyyan.

Rweiss isn't far away; it's a rocky cliff at the edge of the village. When I arrived, I didn't have to ask where Adil's house was. There were three floors with wraparound balconies and tinted glass, crowned with red tiles. Inside the flower garden was a wall and in front of the wall was a square of pavement where three cars were parked—a Cadillac, a Chevrolet, and a Peugeot. I rang the bell and a Sri Lankan servant looked down at me from the balcony. I asked her to tell Mr. Adil that Jalal Mazhar was here. After that, the gate opened and I entered, walking toward the house on a path paved with cobblestones.

The servant opened the door and led me to the spacious living room, which was surrounded by plate-glass windows on all sides. The sofas, tables, and walls were all gilded. After a bit, a taller-than-average, well-built woman, wearing a tight-fitting green dress, came down. Her black hair hung to her shoulders. Scrunching her eyebrows, she said that she was Rosette—Adil's wife. When she realized that I didn't know who she was, she said that she was from the village and had heard all about me from Adil. She'd married young, moved to Beirut, and from that time on seldom returned to the village, so she'd never met me. But she knew who I was. She sat down in front of me on a gilded sofa, crossed one leg over the other, and offered me a cigarette from her pack of Kents. When I refused, she took the cigarette herself and lit it. She told me that Adil was in his room on the second floor; he'd just finishing shaving and would be down shortly. I mumbled a nervous question about his health and she replied that the doctor had reassured them—it would definitely be a long process, but the illness had been found early and he was responding well to the treatment.

Rosette showed me around, answering my questions about how the house was organized. As I had guessed, the first floor was essentially a huge living room with groups of sofas scattered throughout with a bar at the far end. The second floor was for the family—bedrooms, a dining room, and a family room. The third floor had a large kitchen, a pantry, a sitting room, and guest rooms. We went up in a glass elevator. This was a vacation home, Rosette started to tell me. I could only imagine what kind of palace the family lived in during the rest of the year. We didn't encounter Adil on our tour around; he was still in the bathroom. Back on the first floor, I expressed the desire to wander around the flower garden, and Rosette seemed eager to accompany me. I looked at the flowers; the gardener readily volunteered to name the ones I couldn't identify. We went back inside and sat down in the living room.

After a while we heard the elevator door open. Rosette and I stood up and stared at it. A tall man I didn't recognize stepped out. I assumed that this was Adil Uliyyan. He was the same height and had the same dark coloring that I remembered. But those two things were all he still had. He was mostly bald with little hairs scattered across his head. His face was covered in wrinkles; deep trenches in his face gave it a permanent scowl. He walked extremely slowly, one step after the other. He made a great effort to lift his torso, though this couldn't hide the fact that his back was starting to hunch over. Rosette hurried to his side but when she tried to hold his hand he rejected her with a wave. I felt hesitant about approaching him, so I let him walk over to me. When he reached me, he stopped for a second to secure his footing. He extended his hand to me with the same deliberateness. That's when I noticed how emaciated he was.

He said, "Welcome," nothing more. He was facing a round sofa and started to fold his body slowly to settle down on it with exaggerated composure. He wasn't swaying, but he looked like someone who was trying hard not to fall down. His eyes were sunken and moved in their sockets with the same slowness as his body.

"The war . . . took us . . . young men . . . and . . . alienated us so often . . . from where we came . . . afterward . . . left us back . . . on our trash heaps . . . on purpose . . . you . . . they towed . . . your boat . . . for you . . . I . . . I . . . as . . . you see . . . I was . . . I became . . . a cripple."

Adil tried to appear as if he were in charge of his mind and body. As he sat on the sofa he recuperated somewhat. He was exercising his control over the situation. I don't know what he'd prepared for this meeting but he'd certainly known about it beforehand from his brother's son Samir. He was definitely struggling to appear worthy of his mansion, but his words seemed to make him feel regretful, his eyes moist with tears that wouldn't fall. Then he asked me, "Do you still read? I still write. Rosette, bring me the file."

After his tearful moment, she was pleased to comply. Rosette walked upstairs to the second floor and came back with two thick, leather-bound volumes. Written on the first one in gold letters was, *Secret Conversations of the Dust*. *The Tenth Floor* was written on the second in the same lettering. Adil handed me both books, then took out a thick notebook that contained reviews of his books. I flipped through it and my eyes passed over words like *"the great novelist," "the creator," "the innovator," "He delves into the depths of the human soul," "soaring," "an incredible imagination," "penetrating wisdom," "masterful philosophy," "modernity and postmodernity," "innovation," "avant-garde literature," "the revolutionary soul," "destruction and ruin," "deeply rooted structure."*

The pages I was holding in my hands were replete with all kinds of praise and commendation, though the clippings displayed a pitiful absence of either well-known or meaningful names. Adil then handed me his treasure—a stack of translations into French, English, Italian, Spanish, and German—not with prestigious publishers, but that doesn't matter. By all accounts, Adil Uliyyan had been able to start from nothing and put out a book. It cost him less than his garden did. He bought the book and its publishers for a price less than what he paid for his fleet of servants. I thought that everything in the world must be off-kilter if it occurred to someone like Adil Uliyyan to play at this kind of game.

Then he handed me two more books from the stack. One of these was *Modernity in Adil Uliyyan's Fiction* and the second, *The Thought of Adil Uliyyan*. Two professors—neither of whom I'd ever heard of—had written them. There's no doubt that he'd given each of them a little money. I imagined him slipping it into each of their pockets while making a show of the fact that money was not the issue here, that it's best to negotiate with your eyes closed.

But I don't follow literary criticism and I don't know if Adil Uliyyan has a standing in literature . . . or indeed if any of these "critics" made any difference or not. It would be strange if all of this praise was merely there hidden away in his file, and had come to pass without anyone noticing it. It would be stranger yet if Adil had succeeded in exploiting his writing in the same way he succeeded in his other ventures. What will remain of literature if it becomes a matter of financial exploitation? The cost of fashioning a writer like Adil Uliyyan would be less than that of opening a shop. Adil didn't actually admit that he'd paid for the book and I didn't expect him to do so either. But this was his sole exploit about which he never mentioned money.

He remained on the sofa all taut as a bow. He was wearing a thin black jacket and gray trousers. His shirt was hanging loosely off his body and was fashionably untucked. He handed me the articles written about him page by page, waiting for me to read each one before returning it to the file for safekeeping. While I was reading, he observed me with steady eyes. I gave him the pages back without comment, though while reading all of this extensive praise a sound escaped from between my teeth, which he received with a gratified smile. When I stopped flipping through the papers, I told him that I didn't understand criticism and critics but they'd praised him a lot. He was content, pleased with what I'd said. It seemed to me that his body relaxed a little. He wanted me to know that he wasn't merely a person who couldn't control his body and who was practically keeling over in front of me.

Finished with the papers and books, he started reminiscing about when we were friends, the days back when we were young men. He had more memories than I did—and I doubted if some of them had even happened. Perhaps they were his own inventions. In his narratives, he was the hero of the story and I was merely his sidekick.

He narrated to me—or rather to his wife—the story of the cemetery guard who would have kicked us out, had he not resisted. I knew nothing about this story. Nor the one in which we were confronted by four men while going down to the river. That time, it seems, he outwitted them and we escaped. These stories had me at a loss. But when he started in on the tale of his imaginary adventures with the curate's daughter, my bewilderment disappeared. I realized that Adil Uliyyan was the very same liar I once had known.

He finally reached an old story that he was still proud of and wanted his wife to hear. It's the story of a practical joke he played on me. We were sitting beside a natural spring, one of those places that feels like it's inside the earth, perpetually dark. We arrived there at the end of a day's outing during which we'd eaten a picnic lunch outside. He took out two plates, gave me one, and told me to do as he did. I don't remember the reason he gave but I assented in order to please him—I couldn't say no to my friend on the trip that day. He scooped up water from a little stream and I followed. He started dipping his fingers into the water on his plate, passing them under the plate, and then rubbing them all over his face. I did the same. He repeated this and I imitated him until we stopped. Then we left. We crossed the village square together and then parted to go home. I didn't yet know that my face was stained with charcoal; there had been sooty charcoal under my plate that had stuck to my damp fingers. Even now—almost forty years later—Adil's still proud that he was with me when my face was covered in soot in the middle of the town square and everyone laughed at me. This was the go-to episode that he'd recall whenever we met.

Up until this day, I'd never known him to have the ethical disposition to be ashamed of himself for putting a friend in this kind of situation, one that started out as a joke but turned to malice. His smugness about his own cleverness and the success of his prank has remained the same—from when he was fifteen until now that he's over fifty. From this incident, something childish developed within him and remained there. No doubt this same childish thing was also present in the cartridge of bullets he emptied into the head of the customs man. And no doubt this childish impulse has accompanied him on all his exploits and malicious deeds. He's the child who plays practical jokes to get attention—amusing people or terrorizing them, there's no difference.

From that day on, whenever I'd meet Adil Uliyyan he'd retell this story in front of his wife, as though by doing so he could relive it in the present and make Rosette and his daughter Line, who sometimes sat with us, laugh at me. He kept returning to it until I felt that he was humiliating me once again, and that I was a victim of his prank anew. I told him that he hadn't grown up yet. That he's still a little boy playing jokes and that he needs to get a life instead of ruminating over these kinds of stories. He recoiled a little bit when I said this, but it didn't stop him from retelling the story the very next time we met. What really surprised me was how pleased Rosette was by how I spoke to him. Indeed, the way she looked at me while I was talking encouraged me to carry on . . . The same was true of his daughter Line. The two of them paid me full attention while I talked. They wanted me to keep going and from that time on they started welcoming me warmly, as though I had become part of the family.

The voice of a woman on the other end of the line told me that Mr. Adil wanted to speak to me. Adil then took the phone, his rattling voice coming over the wire, laughing and congratulating me on my grandmother becoming a saint. He said that no doubt some of her saintliness would stick to her children and grandchildren. The whole family would become holy. Despite his playfulness, I could sense anxiety in his voice. He told me that he wanted to see me. Could I find the time to come by his place that day? What about stopping by in the evening so we could drink tea together? I dressed carefully: a brown leather jacket with light-colored jeans; it's appropriate to maintain a proper appearance in front of Rosette.

When I got there, the servant came and told me that "Baba" was waiting for me in his room. I went up to the second floor and Adil called me into the family room. He told me that Rosette and Line were out shopping. I felt a bit frustrated; it would have been better if Rosette were sitting with us. I liked it when she was there, or at least I didn't like to be alone with Adil. He was in his dressing gown and slippers and was stretched out on the long sofa that was the only one of its kind in the room, as if it were designed just for him. Struggling to stand up to greet me, he motioned me to the sofa across from him. I entreated him to remain seated and walked over to shake his hand.

We stayed silent for a while, until Adil pressed a button in the arm of the sofa and a servant came. He asked her to make tea. Then he started talking about my grandmother, picking back up where we'd left off that morning on the phone. He wanted to start the conversation between us like this, forging a path through laughter. When the tea arrived, Adil lifted his glass, and as he brought it close to his mouth, he said that he wanted to confide something very important. I promised him that it would remain between us, but I told him explicitly that I don't like carrying around people's secrets because it makes me feel an unbearable responsibility; I don't want to share anything with anyone that isn't my business. I really didn't feel any desire to know his secret and hoped that he would leave me free of this burden. But all my excuses only loosened his tongue. He stretched out even more on his sofa and told me that there was something he didn't want to take to the grave with him. He didn't know what motivated him to confide it in me. But the day before he'd cooked up an idea in his head and decided to just do it; there was something he wanted to get off his chest, something boiling deep inside his heart he wanted to let out.

He said, "You know that when I was first in Beirut, I belonged to the Pioneers of the Revolution. And as you know, this unit had a strong moral code. Before long, people in the organization started stealing cars. I acted against the rest of the group and refused to join in, but it was war. The rules just fell away of their own accord, without anyone noticing. The group's harsh discipline helped in stealing cars. Murder was easy. Before we all became isolated, we organized together and we killed because of sectarian identity. Then sniping started on the other side and it soon moved to our side. Soldiers became proxies to do anything and everything. It was war and we had to win at any cost.

"One day, Commander Suleiman called us in. There were ten of us. He said they were sending us to train as snipers. We learned to target anything, any person who crossed through the little square box that we saw through the sights of our guns. I learned fast. No target escaped me. We went up to the roofs or top floors of buildings in Chiyah and we started sniping across in Ain al-Rummaneh. For me, it was fate that moved people into the little square box. I had no hand in it; I was simply working in the service of fate. You will ask me if I looked into the eyes of any of my victims. I will tell you that it's not possible to see eyes in the sights. It's a game of fate. So when someone fell on the first shot it meant that his time had run out and we couldn't do anything for him because this was his fate. I don't want to hide from you—I don't feel any guilt. Those people who kill for sectarian identity listen to their victims' pleas. We listened to nothing but our bullets and looked at nothing but what they hit. It's sport, totally clean killing. I didn't read the newspapers and didn't want to know my victims' names. I didn't want to see their pictures. I'm not the one responsible. They're the ones who walked into my sights, into the little square box. If someone took one step backward and was saved, that wasn't my doing, it was because it was his fate. They used to talk about their victims; I never did. As soon as the event happened I washed my hands of it. I acted as if I didn't do it. In the end I succeeded in convincing myself that it wasn't me who did it. It's an instant, and I'm not even totally convinced it happened.

"Once a man and his son walked by. I targeted them in my sights. Then I noticed that his son sort of resembled my daughter. I noticed that the man looked like me. Out there were two people who looked like my kid and me; I suddenly didn't want to kill them. But they were inside the little square box. I wanted at least not to target the child. But fate intervened and the child fell. At that moment, I felt that I became my daughter. That I had targeted myself. I quickly ran downstairs from the top of the building to the street; people were still gathered around. I took another road. I fled. That time, I felt I was a coward. I fled from fate, from *my* fate. It was condemning me. When that coward emptied his gun into me, I immediately remembered the child falling down. It was as if my own shot had come back to hit me, as if it were ricocheting back at me from that place."

A stormy morning froze Beirut. Adil Uliyyan didn't stumble but rather fell flat onto the floor. He cried out but the thunder drowned his cries before they reached the family room where Rosette and Line were talking about the weather. Rosette noticed earlier the color draining from Adil's face. When she went into his room to check on him, she found Adil on the ground, pinned against the bed, his mouth agape, unable to speak.

She tried to lift him into bed. But it was difficult for her to raise his body, and his unconscious state made him even heavier. She rang the bell for the third floor and two servants came down. They yelled when they saw Adil unconscious, which alerted Line, who then hurried into her father's room. When she saw him on the ground, she froze for a moment. Then she shook herself out of it and took a step to her mother's side. Her mother helped the two servants manage to finally get Adil into his bed. Everyone waited for the ambulance to come after Rosette phoned the Red Cross. Line's brooding silence made her anxious.

The house was completely still, including the servants who went quiet too after noticing how calm the two women were. The ambulance arrived and Adil was moved onto the stretcher. Rosette went with him and Line followed in her own car.

Samir Uliyyan informed me that Adil had been moved to the hospital in Ras Beirut; he was also quick to inform me that Rosette had asked about me and that she wanted to see me. I had been intending to visit Adil in the hospital anyway, and so I visited the very next day.

As soon as Rosette and Line saw me they erupted into sobs. I must be the one remaining person who reminded them of Adil. I am the lone, distant comrade who could still be called a friend of his.

Adil never regained consciousness. He died on the seventh day, the day on which God rested. Rosette and Line left the southern suburbs.

A whole summer passed during which I heard nothing of Adil's family. In October I received a package. When I opened it, I found a jumble of papers full of Adil's creative ramblings, all pretentious analysis and philosophizing . . . his thoughts on writing. But a single paper with large handwritten words stopped me in my tracks: *I am not evil. Everything I did, or claimed I did, was simply intended to be terrifying.*

Originally written in Arabic.

SCENT OF A WOMAN, SCENT OF A CITY

BY ALAWIYA SOBH

Khandaq al-Ghamiq

I t was half past seven in the morning. I didn't get out of bed, I didn't hear the usual church bells across from my house in Hamra. Instead I woke up to the chimes of my mother's voice saying, "The day's almost over and you're still sleeping. If I were the ministry, I wouldn't pay you one cent. It's seven thirty and you're still lying around in bed." My mother's rosary of words continued until I got up.

My mother can tell the time without a clock. She lifts her finger to the sun to tell the time; I don't know how she does this. And I don't know how to use an alarm clock either. I've bought clocks many times, but they are soon destroyed or lost without me knowing why. My friend says that my relationship with time isn't normal. I smiled when she said that and then asked her what time it was. She responded, but just as quickly I forgot what she'd said and so I asked her again. She smiled and patiently answered once more, but perhaps I didn't hear. One of my bad habits is that I always ask questions but don't bother listening to the answer. My mother asks and answers herself when she can't find someone else to talk to. She told me that she'd listened to all the news reports while I was sleeping, and that a woman had been found dead in Khandaq al-Ghamiq.

I didn't pay attention to what she said and tried to not care. Words like these weren't strange to my ears.

I opened my eyes wide and I felt an intense swelling in them and all over my body. The exhaustion I felt was like the one you feel at the end of the day. My God, how will I feel by evening? Morning blends into evening, day into night.

I opened the window to cold shadows. The rain was heavy and the howling of storms reminded me that the earth was still turning.

Nature is there in the seasons, but winter grayness has a scent that rises from the street and enters the house, a scent like the one I smelled yesterday evening that's remained suspended in my nose and on my body since. Before I entered the house and locked the door on another day and another world, I'd tried to walk down the street a bit to take in some air—but the air was not air.

The scent of the Beirut evening was strange, the scent of passersby clung to me. It was not the scent of people's exhaustion and their old sweat; instead the scent resembled that of dead bodies, the scent of death which emanates from their faces and eyes. In the evening, I wanted to explain this to my friend, but I was afraid that he'd call me crazy or tell me go to a nose doctor—"Perhaps your sense of smell needs curing"—so I didn't say anything to him. When I awoke to that very same scent in the morning, my fear grew—perhaps the smell of Beirut had changed, but I didn't want to believe it. Or perhaps the scent was emanating from *me*.

I observed myself in the bathroom mirror, the scent rising from my face and sticking to the glass like vapor. I thought at first that my breath had stuck to the mirror. I wiped it with my sleeve but the vapor returned to fog it up. I couldn't see the full reflection of my face; my features were obscured by the vapors of death on the mirror, resembling the death in the city, and resembling the scent of yesterday's passersby. I tried to convince myself that the problem resided in my nose.

Then I tried to ignore the whole thing, as I had gotten used to facing my problems with instant forgetfulness, but that didn't help either. I kept telling myself that perhaps I was imagining everything. But I kept hearing my mother's voice repeat: *The crime didn't happen in that place.*

* * *

Through practice, I started forgetting the whole war, not even believing it. Whenever I want to forget something, I sleep. Similarly, whenever it wants to forget, Beirut sleeps.

Sometimes it seems to me that the war didn't happen. One day city people grew bored of peace, and since they liked to forget, they went to sleep. The city started sleeping on the night of April 13, 1975, and all the people dreamed of war.

It was perhaps the first time in history that thousands of people shared a single dream.

It was really quite strange. I used to always say that to my friend.

"Oh girl, when will you grow up?" he would say, smiling. "What came before the war was a dream, my dear."

But I didn't believe him, because I'm more than a thousand years old, if we're following the Islamic calendar. He smiled again when I said that to him. Then he said, "Why isn't the dream that old?"

Of course, I didn't sleep through all those centuries. But my grandmother told me I was born dead, that I was murdered at birth all those years before by my grandfather's grandfather.

Why he killed me at birth I don't remember.

My grandmother says that the past is our roots and that the murder of women and girls in infancy is an open secret throughout our land.

But another friend informed me about a woman whose father killed her in childhood because she was too beautiful. She was four years old and looked as if she appeared from a fairy tale. He feared that someone would rape her and so he decided to kill her first.

I grew anxious when she told me this story. She continued, "Perhaps he was afraid of his desire for her—do you think that desire can lead to murder?"

I didn't answer. I thought, *I'm not beautiful.* So then why did my ancestor kill me in infancy years before? I don't remember. But I remember that I was afraid he would kill my sister's daughter when she was born in the hospital. We didn't know if my sister would have a boy or a girl, and I waited impatiently and anxiously throughout her labor.

The nurse came out and walked right by me without saying anything so I grew even more worried. I walked up to her and asked, "Is it a boy or a girl?" But she didn't answer. So I asked another nurse nearby. She looked at me and didn't answer either. I thought that something had happened to my sister.

I lost it. I stormed into the operating room and asked the doctor. He said, "It's a girl." I informed my mother. She said that the nurse was right, the person who informs someone about the birth of a girl shames herself before God for forty days. The nurse who hadn't replied to me still had a look of shame on her face.

My sister was as beautiful as the white rose on her bed. But I remain full of shame. My mother told me that the news report said that the woman was found dead with her limbs cut off. The security forces' said that the corpse was unidentified. The incident was believed to have taken place elsewhere. I told her, "Strange. Are you sure?"

She said that the news reported it. With a curious expression, she added, "If the girl hadn't done anything, no one would have killed her." Then she continued, "What's wrong? You don't look right. You look ashamed."

I didn't answer. I turned my face from her and peered out the window, once again feeling ashamed.

The scent kept filling my nose; I thought that it was coming from my mother.

My mother's scent was like that of Beirut today, neither that of the village nor of the city. I remember that my grandmother's scent was different—perhaps it was the scent of the village. I used to be able to distinguish the scent of her house from that of all other houses. I remember when I was young, the beautiful scent would fill my nose upon merely entering her house. I used to search through her little room to try to figure out the secret of her scent, but I never could. I thought about this a lot. I asked her about the secret to her house's scent, and she would smile and lift the scarf up off her face and her red cheeks, a trace of beauty and a halo of light and goodness bringing fragrance from between her eyes.

Today I see many women covering their heads like my grandmother did, but I don't smell her scent on them when they pass me. I don't smell the scent of love that used to waft from my grandmother's face. I smell a scent of hatred.

Her face was as open as her heart and the scent of her house was a boundless scent of serenity. I didn't know the secret in the beginning, or its explanations weren't clear to me. Now I realize that it was the scent of eighty years in the house. A delicious scent that radiated from her face and the yellow calicotome flowers in her hands. The scent of her generous eyes. I still know that scent even now.

The scent is a secret.

The secret is that I smelled the scent of a woman one day, crossing Hamra Street. More than two years had elapsed since my grandmother had passed away, and for a flash of a second I thought she was still alive.

I followed the scent and I followed the woman. She grew afraid and quickened her footsteps. I walked faster too but I still couldn't glimpse her face. Her scent filled the street. I kept getting closer to her, she was rushing and I was rushing, then she started to run. I forgot everything and ran after her, but then she disappeared among the passersby. Her scent remained in the street though. I was really sad because I'd lost her. When I told my friend about it, she advised me to visit the doctor right away. Then I was even sadder, because she didn't understand me.

I was even sadder yet when I left the street in the heavy rain. The storm twisted around Beirut and made the scent of trash rise in the street. The trash scent was strong in the evenings, when my friends and I would careen all around the city in a car, laughing. The refuse of one street is different from that of every other street. My friend said that nature was also found in the scent of garbage. The scent in this street seemed profound. The wind stirred up leftover bits of food into the air, then we moved to another street where groups of people who are always fighting each other live.

My friend observed, "These two groups of people are only united by the scent of garbage." When we crossed into a posher area, he said, "This is the scent of bourgeois trash." We laughed until we almost died . . . either of laughter or of that scent.

I felt sick when I saw the mounds of rubbish rising up out of pools of water and I crossed the street. It didn't feel like morning. The morning meant that a new opportunity—washed and clean— would augur another day.

The morning was dead in my eyes.

The street wasn't how I once knew it. For a long time now, the morning has been overshadowed.

Years ago, I used to sit in the Wimpy coffee shop in Hamra in the morning and look out the window at the people on the street. I felt that Beirut was waking up from its slumber little by little, movement crept along little by little, and noise crawled by little by little. The sight of the workers was beautiful, when they were rushing to their jobs. Now there aren't any workers left in the city, nor does the city wake up to the sound of their shoes. Armed fighters have taken over everything. Workers are now clothing vendors or fighters on the many front lines. Whenever more battle lines are drawn, more workers disappear. The city wakes up today without mornings to indicate the start of work. At least the scent of morning is no longer present, so people don't wash the traces of the day before off their faces; they continue to live yesterday.

I don't like yesterday.

Yesterday's scent was on my body, on Beirut's body, and the scent of the news of the crime against that woman was in my chest.

The scent of people's eyes resembled each other, though the eyes of faces were alone and sad and closed like those iron gates placed in front of the doors of houses.

People feel that they are isolated from one other. Bodies move. As if they are beings with no relationship to each other, though they say that people group into different types of clusters. I don't believe this, and faced with this feeling I almost hope that my eyes will be dead.

But the scent of death emanating from the passersby unites them. Before, the street used to take on the scent of people along with the scent of the buildings.

I used to walk on the sidewalk, even though there wasn't really a sidewalk anymore. Just as inhabitants of the houses in Beirut changed, the sidewalks changed. The houses in the city disappeared and the sidewalks disappeared. The sound of shoes on the sidewalk couldn't be heard anymore, only the sound of selling. Every vendor takes a share of the sidewalk, sitting there with his wares. Clothes hang on Beirut's sidewalks and walls and from balconies. It seemed to me that the city had changed a lot, or perhaps had disappeared. They say that time is more powerful than anything else. Things change but people only yearn for the past. They only believe their memory.

The past is the origin and the origins are lost.

A sense of loss pervaded everything, and I almost got lost. Where was I going? I forgot that I am also a worker. The sound of my shoes didn't rise up anymore, only the voice of a taxi driver. He screamed at me and I walked over to him. I approached the car as if I wanted to flee from my exhausted head, the exhausting street, and the exhausting city—the closed faces like the locked iron gates in front of the houses.

For a long time, the doors to houses weren't locked. I remember that our neighbor didn't lock her house out of embarrassment, so it wouldn't seem like she was in a conflict with my mother. My mother also used to do that. The two houses were always open except when there was a fight between the two families. Now all doors are locked. Perhaps anger blinds people's hearts, or perhaps fear. But the city is locked up on itself, people are locked up on themselves, each sect on itself, each face on its features.

Metal doors are heavy. I shut the metal door to the car, sliding into the backseat.

I told the driver, "Good morning."

He smiled, saying, "Good morning."

After the taxi had driven for a while, a woman got in. Her body was wrapped up in gray and her face was covered in a gray cloth hung around her ears on both sides. She said loudly, "Salaamu alaykum." The driver answered, "Salaamu alaykum." Then he glanced at me in the rearview mirror, reminding me that I hadn't said Salaamu alaykum. He suddenly got mad at me, his face turning angry. "Where's the salaam, the peace?"

"Perhaps it won't come to us," the woman said. I didn't think anything more of it then. I was only thinking about getting to the place where the crime had occurred, and that the woman sitting next to me didn't have a scent like my grandmother's.

"Where's the salaam from?"

I tried to press myself harder against the door on my side of the car.

The driver almost crashed into the beggar who always stands in the middle of the street. This man has a strange shape. He looks as if he's balancing precariously on a tightrope with one foot.

One of his legs was longer than the other. One eye higher than the other, one hand longer than the other, and the right side of his mouth was raised up higher than the left. He seemed blinded by fear. He was shaking violently. Sometimes when he approaches the car with his hand outstretched to take money he looks like he might topple over. He can't balance. He is a lump of a ruin, or a lump of a little war of destruction. Again and again I'm afraid that I'll hit him with my car and he will fall on the ground dead. His appearance frightens me so I always try to change my route home so I won't crash into him.

I used to feel that I hated him. He made me nervous whenever I saw him. I don't know why I grew afraid every time I glimpsed this young man.

For a split second I almost screamed at the driver—I thought he was going to hit him—but I quickly put my hand over my mouth.

What are you thinking, girl? I was really afraid of this.

I rested on the metal car door and felt like crying. But I was too embarrassed to cry there in the car. They wouldn't understand and would ask me what was wrong. How could I say that I really want the driver to kill this beggar who I'm afraid of? In the best-case scenario, they would call me insane. Perhaps they would say, *She's right.* For sure, I'm more afraid of what their answer would be.

I thought of going to the doctor and telling him about this. But if he diagnosed me as abnormal, I wouldn't be able to explain it to him. Killing scares me, and even the *idea* of killing terrifies me. My eyes overflowed with tears, I almost wept aloud.

Another male passenger looked over and I turned my head away. Then I really did cry and everyone in the car started staring at me. My crying grew much louder.

My grandmother used to say that crying doesn't bring sadness, but rather washes your heart, that crying is relief.

Why did I want to kill that shaky, scary man? Perhaps out of weakness—because everyone else is killing. People who aren't killing in the city don't feel their own existence. For a moment I sensed the secret of my hatred for that man. It was like looking at him in a mirror: I observed people in the road, they all looked like him. The walls of the city, the roads, and the country and its economy—everything was him. He was a summary of what's inside all of us.

All of us resemble him inside. The country is this man. So I'm scared of him. I am scared of the truth. The ugly truth. I don't like it. We all shake like him and the earth beneath our feet shakes like him too.

Again and again, I've changed my route so I won't run into him, but it's in vain. Whenever I go out on the street I see him there. Even though he can barely walk, you see him wherever you go. So I avoid looking at him, and when I'm driving I close my window whenever he approaches. I tremble when he knocks on the glass with his fingers, and the moments when I stop in traffic feel like an eternity.

My fingers had pins and needles, as if my blood couldn't reach them, as if all the blood was pooled in my head. I smelled the scent of blood in the taxi. I looked around me but didn't find any trace of it. The scent of blood increased when the driver turned on the radio.

I heard the report about the woman again. The broadcast said that she was found murdered on the steps of a building, her features unidentifiable, and there were bullet holes in her belly and neck.

From the backseat of the taxi I glimpsed my reflection in the rearview mirror. My features seemed indistinguishable. I wound my fingers around each other and crossed my legs because I had to go to the bathroom; whenever I'm scared I have to go to the bathroom. I fell silent. In the beginning the news didn't arouse anyone's curiosity.

The woman was talking about how expensive things are; she said, "Plastic flip-flops cost fifteen lira!"

Someone else sitting in the car interrupted her, saying, "Now it's the women's turn. They've finished everything else and now they've started in on the women."

Silence reigned. Then another man's voice followed: "Good man, women are like cats, they have nine lives, nothing harms them. So many men have died, there are lots of women in the country. However many are lost, there will still be more women than men."

The woman who was sitting in the backseat with us said, "Every time a woman is killed, there is a good reason behind her death. God punishes she who sins. The fate of the sinner is death."

"Yes indeed," they all replied.

I remained silent and backed farther into the corner.

I remembered my friend's story. She told me that when she was a girl, a man entered their house asking for her father's protection. This man had killed his mentally challenged sister. Her family had sent her to someone's house to work there. The owner of the house assaulted her. When her belly grew big, without her knowing why, her brother shot her and took refuge in my friend's father's house, asking for his protection. My friend was upset when she told me about this, saying, "What makes me sad is that my mother was praising the guy, *God bless your hands, you noble man!*"

For a moment, I thought that the news of the woman on the radio was the same person who my friend had told me about. I had almost forgotten about that incident from so many years ago. But I remembered that for the woman who was found killed, there was no mention of an investigation into a possible rape or assault. They found not a baby, but bullets in her belly.

But where did they find these women to kill? Though the man said that there were so many women in the country, they aren't here anymore.

My friend says they are floating apparitions, resembling gray tents from head to toe. My grandmother used to tell me that women haven't been present since the time of her grandfather's grandfather who killed her in infancy because he didn't want anyone to be disgraced like that woman.

I believed my grandmother was telling me a bedtime story on that distant day. In my dreams I saw the neighbors' daughter entering a white room where I lay stretched out on a bed. The neighbors' daughter was wearing a beautiful long white dress as if she were a bride. I only knew her from having seen her on the balcony. In the dream, she gave me a sad look, then waved her hand. She left through the door and locked it behind her. With this sound of the door closing, I woke up to gunfire. I got up quickly and went to the balcony. I saw the girl's corpse lying out in front of her house, the women and men of the street gathering around her. Her brother had shot her. They said that she was having a relationship with someone, her brother saw her with him. His mother's voice rang out through the street: "Run away, get out of here before the police come!"

That day I told my mother about the dream. She said that the white dress symbolizes death. "My daughter, your dream frightens me."

The words of the woman in the car and her enthusiasm about the crime against the dead woman reminded me of that girl's mother's voice. For an instant, I thought that she was her mother, especially when the broadcast said that the woman was wearing a white dress.

My grandmother says that age is a lie. The coming days are an echo of the past and its shadow.

The past is truth and the truth is the infant girl murdered at birth centuries ago. But I don't believe the news. Is it possible that the scent of blood can remain on the body for centuries?

The scent of my body has remained for centuries.

The scent of my body rose and filled the car. The people in it started coughing. I coughed too, and the dust of my breath reached the driver's mirror. He pulled his head back and turned toward me in anger.

I knew he couldn't understand my features. They had lived through centuries. Today they have the city's scent. Everyone coughed again. I coughed too, and my heart stopped beating before I reached the place where the incident happened. My body had become unidentifiable.

Everyone was scared and filled with shame. They started exchanging glances with each other. When we got to the scene of the crime, the man sitting next to me opened the door and threw me out on the ground. The car took off quickly.

I stretched out on the ground, and before closing my eyes and passing out, I realized that I was the woman who was found murdered. My grandmother's voice was ringing in my ears and my scent covered the whole place.

The scent of the city covered my outstretched body.

Originally written in Arabic.

SAILS ON THE SIDEWALK

BY MARIE TAWK

Sin el Fil

She went up the stairs, careful as usual not to stumble on the broken steps. It's a long walk up to the sixth floor. She put the bags she was carrying on the landing to rest a little. She leaned against the edge of the big wrought-iron window that's cracked in more than one place. Electricity lines hung suspended and sagging between the buildings. A drab flock of pigeons flew near the cypress tree that soared up above the buildings. Desiccation had begun to grip it from the top and some of its branches were dead. Will this affect all of its branches or will it endure in the same condition it has been in for the past few years? Why had she never noticed this before? She felt a sudden fatigue; she had to hurry up and prepare dinner.

It was a worthy occasion. She was going to talk to Farid about everything. (She liked to pronounce his new name, not what he called himself as a child but what he did now after coming back from Australia: *Freddy*. This was nicer, it made her feel that he'd become a new person.) She was going to talk to him about their life together, and she would try to come closer to his world because the few memories that she's preserved of him have become cloudy. All that she can recall is his beaming smile, which bewitched all the young women, and his huge, round, black eyes that added magic to it. She also remembered how he came back happy after watching a scary film in which the heroine, who he said resembled her, had been hanged. She asked him why he was happy about her death projected onto the big-screen heroine—did he hate her that much? He didn't reply. She also didn't forget his lightning-quick visit through Beirut, his insistence on seeing her, and how she couldn't be bothered. She was completely absorbed in another world, a severely blind one. She then learned that he'd married a foreign woman soon after he'd come back, and they'd divorced four years later.

She opened the door. She headed into the kitchen to put the bags on the counter, then went back into the living room. White sheets covered the sofas, like it was wartime or summer vacation. After her father died, her siblings emigrated and her mother moved to the mountains, so the house was left to her free-ranging loneliness. She threw herself on the sofa. She felt dizzy, so she got up to open the window and take in a bit of air.

She wouldn't ever again hear her father cough as he walks up the stairs. She was so used to hearing it, she couldn't have known that this cough would become the portent of nothingness. She wouldn't be anxious anymore because her father didn't answer the phone all night long. She'd nap awhile then wake up a little panicked, dialing the number again and waiting for him to answer. In the morning, he would answer her call with his shaky voice, accompanied by a strangulated cough, saying that he'd gone to sleep early and didn't hear the telephone ring. She later considered these the first signs of his imminent death, and also fully recalled the nerve-wracking waiting for Philippe—her ex-sweetheart—to respond at the other end of the line.

The cold was severe; she closed the window. What should she prepare for dinner? The best thing to do would be to call Farid and ask him. After a bit. Nothing here called for hurrying. She found her habit of perpetual hurrying absurd. She went into the bedroom: books filled the shelves; some of them had yellowed pages, some emitted an old vanilla scent. What would be the fate of her books? Soon nothing would connect her to this world, which she built or destroyed, brick by brick. She opened the cupboard: her own clothes and some of her mother's. In the corner, a navy-blue suit of her father's that she thought he'd been buried in, believing that he'd only owned one. And navy blue was indeed what he'd been shrouded in. She drew it close and inhaled; it still carried his scent. How did her mother forget to get rid of it, especially since she always said, "The clothes of the dead should never be mixed with the clothes of the living"? She saw him in her sleep. She knew in her dream that he'd passed on, so she wanted to ask him about his new residence. She was sitting near him in the backseat of his car; for the first time he wasn't the driver. She was planning to ask him about . . . he didn't even once turn to look at her. He was morose and angry, knowing that she'd ask him about his death. He merely waved his hands at her nervously, saying, "You're still rushing around." He didn't utter the word that he usually used: *frantic*.

Right now, though, she wasn't "rushing around," but lifeless.

During her drive down to the seaside Corniche with Hyam, she started telling her friend to hurry, with Hyam imploring her to stay with her a little longer.

"I wanted to call you yesterday, but I decided not to. I didn't want to bother you. Lamia . . . you've seemed preoccupied for a while."

"I'm trying to change my lifestyle. It's the second time that Farid's come to Lebanon. I don't want to engage in any more stupidity."

"Rest assured, there can't be any greater stupidity than what you were doing back when we first met! If you'd killed someone . . ."

She was surprised by the way Hyam was speaking to her. Why all this hostility?

"Hyam . . . are you all right?"

"No—and I wanted to tell you about my new resolution to put an end to all stupid things."

"Did you fight with Nazih again?"

"No one deserves me. Do you remember that day when we were preparing food and he refused to help us? How could he just sit there all surly and superior, refusing to be with us?"

"Perhaps he wasn't feeling well or was tired . . ."

"None of us feel well; we're all tired . . . There's something else there . . . I'm thinking about divorce."

"Funny, when I'm thinking about marriage."

"It hurts me to leave him, I'm afraid of him faltering . . . What keeps me there is his weakness. When he gets stronger, I'll give up on him. Later, when he's doing better, I'll leave him right away, with no regrets."

"Really nice. You help him to get stronger and he gets stronger for you, then you leave him?"

"I can't leave him when he's in this condition. My whole life is just a postponement of divorce."

"What if he stays the way he is?"

"I don't know. This is what confuses me. Perhaps the only solution is that we live apart, and through this I'll find some kind of space that can make me love him more."

"My God, I'm lost . . . You've lost me in all these twists and turns!"

"Sorry."

"For what?"

"That I've confused you along with myself . . . I can't bear to either separate from him or stay with him."

"Would you consider separating, at least for a little while?"

"The thought haunts me. I don't know if he would agree."

"What do you say we finish this conversation tomorrow?"

Lamia reminded her friend that she'd invited Farid to dinner and needed to get home soon. Hyam turned to her, exploring her face with a piercing look.

"Is this serious with Faird? Are you sure? This quickly? Don't you want to wait a little?"

"I want change; I can't keep vacillating . . . You always criticize me for how my life has stagnated. In the best of times, you look down on my patience on the one hand, and on the other, my impulsivity. Why have you changed your mind all of a sudden?"

"I don't know, perhaps because I'm preparing for an imminent divorce."

Lamia opened her locked desk drawer. She kept it locked to ensure that her mother wouldn't pry. It was funny because the one day she forgot to lock it, she noticed in her mother's mocking smile that she'd gone through it. Her mother waited more than a year to ask her about the pictures of the man she'd found in the drawer.

She answered, "Salma took these photos when shooting one of her films in school."

"So why are you in most of them?"

"Because Salma wanted me to be the star."

"Yes, she's right, you were so beautiful."

"Every monkey is a gazelle in its mother's eyes!"

"So what is it that I'm always hearing about the reasons you haven't gotten married?"

"And now we've gone back to the same old song."

"But you're my only daughter . . . I want to celebrate your wedding with you. All of your girlfriends have married and had children. What's your story? Fine . . . That letter signed by your old high school friend, saying, *May God keep this bitter drink far from us* . . . What does that mean? What drink? You know . . . it's the war's fault; it meant that I couldn't protect you. I was forced to stay in the mountains with your siblings. And you lived with your crazy girlfriends. All of the neighbors used to tell me, *Umm Joseph, these girls are raising hell in the neighborhood.* Your whole life I couldn't learn anything about you or from you. Sometimes I'd be thinking, *Is this my daughter? The one who I gave birth to? . . . Or not?*"

Her mother had stopped asking these questions a long time ago. Clearly, she'd lost hope.

Perhaps the only good thing for her in this war was the freedom of living far from her parents. The constant cutting of the phone lines was a ready-made excuse to justify many things. She, Salma, and Hyam moved from one car to another around Beirut, undeterred by shelling and checkpoints, without any impediments. Salma would deal with falling shells as if they were fake—simply there as a backdrop to allow her to photograph the expanse of the entire city. She didn't believe it possible that she could be killed or injured. She brooked no fear. If she sensed any fear in you, she would give you a look that would chill the blood in your veins.

Back then, Lamia had grabbed the photos from Philippe, the "hero" of the film—whether cynically or jokingly, it doesn't matter. As usual, he threw himself on her bed, eyeing her. Then he said to her out of the blue that he never stays with any woman for more than two years. Two years in the best of cases. She didn't reply.

He did what he said he would. He didn't stay with her even one month beyond the two years. When she added up the period of time between when they met and their breakup, the precision of his calculations amazed her. Those beams of the setting sun started to dim, carrying her days on their wings. Hyam came over to comfort Lamia and Salma picked up her letters to deliver them to Philippe by hand or send them by post (she learned only afterward that Salma would actually throw them in the trash can). That summer, she didn't change out of her winter clothes, nor did she change her winter bedclothes. Beirut's fiery summer heat, with its sun and bombs, couldn't warm the cold inside of her. Nothing protected her in the barren field that was her bedroom except her dressing gown and her covers. If it weren't for the war, her winter couldn't have gone on for so long and she would have enjoyed her love that ended before it even began.

Other forgotten memories surfaced from her "secret" stash of photos. They showed the blondness of Philippe's stubbly beard, contrasting with his black hair and eyebrows and the shadows of his thick eyelashes. She recalled passing her hand over the freckles on his lower lip slanting down toward the fluff of his beard, the spot she touched stinging her own face. She drew back, and he grabbed her by the hand and threw her on the ground of the cement rooftop. There were stars above her eyes, glittering in a small pool of rainwater. She remembered him sitting on the sofa beside her, snatching pieces of fig from the plate in front of him, peeling them and scraping off the bits stuck on his fingers with his teeth. He seemed far away when he was united with her body (she was aware that after he got up, she'd put the same clothes back on that she'd worn earlier to greet him in, preparing for the moments of their encounter one by one, like someone replaying a scene in a film, and trying as much as possible to simulate his confident, slow caresses sliding from her legs up to her shoulders).

Philippe put his hand on her freezing shoulders. He liked to touch them; that's what he told her.

"Will you put your hand on my shoulders next autumn, once you've gone? Will you feel pleasure when it's cold?"

He encouraged her not to think about this.

"But why? Does this have to happen? Isn't it up to us?"

"What do you want me to say? No matter what I say, you are going to be sad . . . If you'd only met someone else . . ."

"Could you stop offering condolences? I know I'm the only one here mourning our relationship."

"Perhaps this misery comes from those dark clouds. Haven't you noticed how thick they are? How could you expect me to have hope?"

Everything that he said bothered her. She didn't know what to do when faced with his complaining and infectious despair. In another picture, he was sticking his tongue out at her, a pink tongue folded in thirds.

"What do you want, a *happy end?*"

She stuck her tongue out at him now. "I just want some kind of *end.*"

The pizza that she'd insisted on preparing for Philippe that hot spring day had a taste she'd never forget. She was half-sleeping, half-awake, so the ring of the phone surprised her. Even today, she still remembers his number because of the frequency with which she'd dialed it on the old black phone, turning her finger again and again so that it hurt and she had to switch to dialing with a pen instead. Perhaps the broken telephone lines ignited their love rather than impeded it.

She'd promised Philippe that she'd make a pizza for him. She left her house, went down to the street, leaving the Sayyidah neighborhood in Sin el Fil, taking the shortcut to Mar Elias. A small truck was stopped at the intersection, loaded with large cylinders of gas that looked exactly like the one she saw just before the explosion that destroyed most of the neighborhood. Afraid, she glanced away and didn't head down that street. Before turning on her heels, she looked back once more: a year had passed and the specter of death was still looming over this stricken neighborhood. She took another road, passing in front of the church to reach Ghazal Street. She was crossing the muddy wasteland when shelling started raining down on the area. No doubt it would be described as a new "security setback." She retraced her path along the sidewalk to her house at full speed.

She prepared the dough while hoping that the madness would calm down so that one of the grocers would feel secure enough to open his shop. She was also worried about her two girlfriends who lived with her. Salma finally returned home, looking flustered. She'd continued studying on the West Side despite the threat of death hanging over her at every checkpoint when she traveled between the two Beiruts.

"Why are you so pale? What happened?"

She paused to collect herself, then said, "Three armed men stopped me and asked me my name. They told me, *Walk with us,* while pointing their machine guns at my stomach. Then they made me get into a small car. It was the first time I felt afraid, mostly because they were looking right at my chest and I wasn't wearing a bra."

"Oh my God, you and your bra!" Nazih said, trying to lighten the mood.

"As soon as I got in the car, I buttoned up my blouse and covered the book I was carrying with my arm. The men were morose. I asked them why they were kidnapping me, as I have nothing to do with politics. *What do you want from a poor girl like me?* They answered all together, *Poor girl . . . ?* I said, *Yes, really . . . poor girl! Every day forced to go through checkpoints just to pursue my studies.* They asked me, *Why don't you go to university on the East Side?* I answered them, *Because I want to know the real Beirut, the diverse Beirut. On the East Side there's only one party and one sect.* They didn't say a word. I felt cramped and unhappy in this small car, especially with the machine gun thrust into my waist. I had a collection of Muhammad Abdullah's poetry with me which I began reciting aloud. They laughed but at least moved the machine gun away from me. Then the car stopped in front of the party's headquarters. At that moment, I finally lost my mind and told them, *You and everyone else! The whole world's at war, even my parents and family, so I became a member of your party—and then you arrest me! Really? I was expecting a fighter from the other party to plunge a machine gun into my belly . . .*

"I unbuttoned my blouse then because I was no longer afraid. They told me, *This news just reached us: a Maronite girl from the East Side is going to the Corniche at Raouché and learning from the fighters there how to make TNT and put it into jerricans.* Then I told them that they should thank me for my work, so that I could fight against Israel. *By the way, you all don't fight against it as you should be.* One of them said to me falteringly, *We believed you were a spy!* I answered, *Could a spy to work in the light of day on the Corniche in sight of everyone?* Afterward, he started to respond to the arguments I'd made, in which I'd intended to exaggerate, by proposing that I work as a spy for them, bringing them news of the other party. So I told them, *Let me go, I won't be anyone's spy, not even Lenin's himself.* Then I got out, slamming the car door behind me."

"And Hyam, why hasn't she come back yet? Have you heard from her?"

"I saw her in the café at the university and she told me she would stay at Nazih's place."

"What a day! I went out to the shops and everything was closed."

"Your problem is simple to solve. It seems like the shelling is dying down. Let's step out to buy what you need and celebrate your special guest."

This is Salma's favorite line. She works hard to make the shelling die down. That time the Russian Grad missiles all but destroyed the entire neighborhood, the balconies of the building facing ours fell off and she said, "Don't worry, it's far away."

Lamia missed Salma so much since she'd moved to Sydney. In any case, one of the good things about the trip she has planned with Farid is that she'll get to see Salma, her friend for life. Lamia didn't know why, but when thinking about Salma, she would remember her feet more than any other feature: her childlike feet clambering through fields and up trees, her two legs plowing through streets, wandering sidewalks, penetrating alleys, going up stairs, climbing up dirt berms as though they were small hills. Her feet were balanced, like a boat between the shores of a city totally given over to its madness; they rose up tearing apart roads and checkpoints, and they pumped blood through its severed arteries. Her old feet were there on the asphalt, deaf to everything that might startle the ear and heart, pursuing the traces of the one she loved so as to touch his shadow. It was as if this young woman was soaring in an earthly flight that could never weaken. But once her feet suddenly betrayed her in the middle of the street, forsaking her, making her unable to take even a single step ahead. That time, she and Hyam were forced to pick Salma up and put her in the car as though she were actually paralyzed. She started screaming, saying that she didn't want to go home and that she couldn't bear to see her husband all devoted to his pigeons, or escaping into the garage, claiming to be absorbed in his drawing while all he was doing was smoking and drinking beer.

"He even pushed me to argue with our next-door neighbor, saying that she was a lying, gossiping woman, after she told me that she saw him going into my house with that whore of a woman during the summer holiday. If only I hadn't listened to what he said and fought with the neighbor, I would've been able to find out more details."

"More than what you know? What's the point? Then you'd be destroyed!"

"And let this destroy *me*? I will destroy his comfort and that whore's as well . . ."

She declared with total impudence that before marriage she'd wanted to establish a relationship with a man with experience.

"And your husband, what about him . . . ?"

"As usual, he told me that jealousy would blind my heart. Before marriage, we'd agreed on an open relationship with no conditions. But what kind of free love can you have with kids? Lamia, please rub my knees for me, I can no longer feel them . . . And my head hurts, give me a scarf to wrap around it . . . Why doesn't he love me anymore?"

"Haven't you had enough of this question? Salma, be as strong as you always have been. You've survived worse."

"This man is displacing me in my own house, he's made me unable to stand up. They imagine me, Salma, to be debilitated and disjointed, only able to ask one question." She lowered her aching head like a woman bereaved, then added, "But why doesn't he still love me? Does that trivial woman understand love better than I do? She's certainly no Claudia Cardinale . . . I've brought women who are much more beautiful than her to my husband so he could film their bodies."

"Then think of her as one of the young women who you brought to him and forget the whole thing."

"She left her fiancé for him . . . Who does she think he is? I've only just agreed to marry him."

"It's good that he's no longer entitled to anything. Why did you want to know about his affairs in the first place?"

"Tonight I'm going to meet that filmmaker who liked my movie—and I think he also likes me."

"But you're half-paralyzed, you can hardly stand up."

"I'll stay at your place, Lamia—and tell the filmmaker to bring me back there. You have to take me to pick up my daughter from the nursery . . . You know, Lamia, I'm losing my strength. I'm sad when I think about how much I've chased love. All of this effort, in vain. He doesn't even ask how I'm doing! My failure is massive. I've forgotten how to laugh. I've lost the joy of living, the pleasure of feeling the ground underneath my feet. I imagine him with his whole body curved around her, staring at her mad with love, with me sitting in front of them. This is terrorism, this is a direct assault on my being."

"I can't believe what I'm hearing . . . You, Salma, who are so—"

"Sometimes I think about calling the two of you—you and Hyam—asking you to send me flowers or candy or fruit so I can feel some kind of warmth. Lamia, you want the truth? I think your failure means nothing compared to mine. Every day I feel the same way you did that evening when it became clear that everything would end between you and Philippe."

"You still remember that evening?"

"Now even more than ever. Your only concern was preparing Philippe's pizza. You didn't pay much attention when I told you about my kidnapping by the party's 'comrades.' We didn't know that on that very evening we would do brave and fearless deeds in battle with members of the Other Party! Yes, we swept away passion and weapons in one fell swoop that night, and we were careless."

Despite her pain, Salma burst out laughing and said, "By day, the machine gun was waiting for me and by evening you were waiting for Philippe while your mad admirer Samir was waiting for him with his gun. A group of armed fighters surrounded Philippe at the entrance to the building. You started pacing around like a madwoman, asking me, *Why is he late?* I don't know what inspired me to go out and see what was happening on the street. I found Samir in front of the building in a military uniform. He turned toward me and said, *Tell your girlfriend I won't let him enter this building and he won't be able to cross this street, no matter how quick he is. I told him that were he to return it would be his last stand. I instructed my guys to follow him home and watch his every move.* Then he added, *Tell your girlfriend that it is she alone who is able to keep this bad seed away from all of us. Tell her that my situation in life has improved and that I've been in love with her since high school. He doesn't love her.* I responded, *Why don't you come yourself, Samir, and let her know all these things?* But he didn't dare climb the stairs to our place, despite all the influence he claimed to have."

"Yes, calls and threats were enough for Philippe to be humiliated like this in front of my house . . . and the man with bullets and influence to meddle in my life . . ."

"I cannot forget your face or how you looked on that night, your back hunched over all of a sudden. We tried to intercede with someone in the party who had more influence than Samir . . . We went to him in the morning and we felt reassured when we saw him, because he was an older man. But he started to scoff at everything that you were saying. *My girl, you are pursuing an already lost cause. He's not for you.* My God, he started admonishing us so we'd understand that we were all under close surveillance. And we went back the way we came, like this, defeated. I knew that the season of your sadness would begin when the 'joy' of Philippe's marriage to someone else became a reality."

"Come on, let's stop worrying about this and live our lives."

"Lamia, I'm living a failure like yours right now, but I'm thinking about getting out of it, whereas you didn't want to leave it behind. You needed a house, not university, not friends, not family; you found a thousand pretexts to not see anyone. How stupid you were!"

* * *

In any case, pretty soon she won't be stupid anymore. She'll marry Farid and turn a new page in her life.

She put the pictures back in the drawer and went into the living room. She opened the window and leaned against it. The roar of the powerful electric generators reached her. This feeling of exhaustion returned: an exhaustion of bygone years, a delicious exhaustion which gripped her when Mousa, Philippe's friend, came for an unexpected visit. She started to feel her sadness passionately because he came to offer her comfort. She sat on the sofa, listening to his pleasant words, stealing looks at his childlike hands and his sturdy neck.

She recalled the day when the three of them—Lamia and Philippe and Mousa—were together and Mousa offered his hand to help her cross over a pool of water, then he turned toward Lamia and said, practically in a whisper, "I can see that the two of you will no longer be together, from now on."

A painful sweetness emanated from him. He started showering her with calls in the afternoon and their conversations would stretch out long into the evening. She left the cover of the sofa where he'd been sitting crumpled up in the same position for days. It made her happy to think about his presence there in front of her as permanent. She'd sip what remained in his cup, after he left, as though it were a kiss. Once, she was standing in front of the window and he called to her from the stairs, smiling. His smile made her understand that she'd replaced one love with another. If only she were able to delete those evenings from all the memories of her life, when she'd lean out the window and see his broad feet climbing the stairs to visit her without warning. He'd sit on the sofa and start laughing his sweet laugh, continuing his story about Prince Myshkin. His fluttering eyelids melted her. Each flutter was some kind of colorful bird that she'd approach only to have it fly off, away from her, to parts unknown.

What was it in his voice that made her loneliness dissipate, bringing joy to her heart and removing it from its labyrinth? His gentleness entranced her in the beginning. Then ever so slowly he started assailing her with dark thunderbolts. What did he want from her? Nothing, he told her, adding that he didn't get involved in the lives of women who he has affairs with. Sometimes he'd call her and ask her strange questions, like the number of times her ex-lover had sex with her. Why did he even care about that? His questions perplexed her: What did he want? For her to announce her love for him? Would that be enough? Did he want an intimate friendship? She awoke from her daydreams panicked by the ringing telephone. Farid's voice surprised her, drowning her thoughts of Mousa, "Darling, I'll be a little late."

She opened one of the unsent letters to Mousa she had kept, as though to complement the miserable pleasures that her life kept from her.

You don't want to influence the lives of the women who you have affairs with? That's fine. This sentence is enough for me to not want to see your face again. You know something? I turned that sentence over in my head thousands of times and didn't consider asking you what you really meant by it. You don't know the dark thoughts that invaded me and made me dead inside. As soon as I would try to get close to you, you'd let me know that there wasn't any benefit for me in being in your life, freely offering hints, marked by pain, almost as though you were completing the thought to yourself: Or in anyone's life.

Should I have endured your dark thunderbolts, vagueness, and forgetfulness?

Did I learn anything else from you? Are you truly able to leave me in peace?

I feel like a sad, raging bull, ready to fight, but the stabs it's receiving on all sides have made it feel hollow.

I feel truly exhausted. Nothingness is the most exhausting thing.

She put the letter in an envelope. She decided to finally send it by post. She passed her tongue over the sticky line. It tasted bitter. No, she won't send it. If only Salma were here to take care of this. She'd know how to, like she used to do in the past.

"Salma, why did you throw away all the letters I wrote to Philippe?"

"Because I believed this was the only way to avenge you."

"But you made me believe that he had no feelings . . ."

"And he doesn't . . . My husband has no feelings either. I'm going to arrange another meeting with that film producer."

"I won't destroy myself like you did. It'll be an open marriage like we agreed it would be: step by step."

"But won't you wait a little bit until you can stand on your own two feet?"

"I won't wait. This isn't the first time he's betrayed me with random women whom he's found along the way. Carrying on like this you're harming your children."

"Spare me the sermon. Even you, Lamia, didn't you say that you would've loved Philippe until the end of time, that you would've waited for him for a hundred years? Even after he sold you out for the cheapest possible price?"

"But he didn't sell me out. He had to pull back because Crazy Samir the militiaman would've killed him. Samir sent me a letter that said, *If you open your door to him one more time, I'll push him right through the gates of hell.*"

"You know what? Today I can't even believe this whole story . . . How did Samir know that Philippe had been coming over to your place?"

"He was definitely spying on the house."

"So he would spend all day and night guarding the entrances to the street? Who knows, perhaps a mutual friend told Samir what time your dear beloved would come. Believe me . . . there was a mutual friend. Perhaps Philippe was happy about this development and seized the opportunity to flee, using the party thugs as an excuse—something beyond his own desire or free will."

"But who was restraining him? Holding his freedom hostage? Who was blocking him?"

"You portrayed him as an exemplary person, tormented and honest, you only ever spoke about his sincerity. He didn't remain sincere, though. Why didn't he stand up for you?"

"With those murderous beasts after him?"

"They only wanted to frighten him . . ."

"He had a right to be scared—I would have done the same thing had I been in his position . . . He is free!"

"Of course he's free, but the problem is that he shackled you with your feelings . . . He didn't end things there but instead distorted your view of life and men. This shriveled you up—you! Someone who had been full of life and brimming with confidence. You started your life with the wrong person and this ruined everything."

"And you . . . ? Aren't you doing the same as I did? Then surely what you're saying isn't true, and at least I knew love."

"In my opinion, all you knew was stubbornness, sadness, and loneliness that got you nowhere . . . Yes, he was *very* sincere! The whole time you used to talk to us about how he didn't want to be tied down to any one woman, and then, all of a sudden, he was engaged. Then he got married with everyone there watching—all of his friends and ours too . . . He's worse than my husband, taking everything he could and not giving anything at all. After all these years, I charge him with having planned this all with a mutual friend of his and Samir's, encouraging Samir to threaten him so he could run away like the wind."

"Could someone really plan to act so despicably? What are you ranting on about? It seems to me that your husband's cheating has made you delirious!"

"But with clear vision. Never make justifications—of any kind—for a man. And Philippe's the one being charged here."

"Wow, the girl's gone mad!"

"No, I'm not mad. Only I can no longer trust anyone, not even you, who deluded us into believing you were unique, suffering, tortured—but no more than two years had passed when . . . Didn't you fall in love with his friend Mousa? Did you think I didn't know? Why didn't you try to marry him?"

"Who told you that he wanted to get married?"

"Your egotistical beloved made it seem as though you weren't suited to marriage and you believed him, you believed the lie. You constantly compared him to Philippe and that's how you distorted your relationship with Mousa for no reason. After this, you did the worst thing. You fell in love with a married man!"

"But I don't know his wife!"

"What's the difference?"

The doorbell rang. She awoke in a panic, not only because of the ringing but because Farid had arrived before she'd prepared anything for dinner.

Farid was there in front of her, with his big, sparkling eyes. He engulfed her in his arms and his scent filled her nose: this strange mixture of expensive cologne and washing powder wasn't familiar to her . . . She found the scent pleasant, perhaps because it wasn't like other scents she knew. The cologne seemed like a disinfectant. Then he put his hand on her backside, forcefully, lifting up her buttocks.

"How I love a woman's full bum!"

She started to laugh vibrantly and was secretly happy because he'd praised her butt.

"Do you know, Lamia, I love you for your happiness? When you were small, you were so joyful. I would watch you bite into an apple as though it were the last apple on earth. Do you still eat them like that?"

"Like what?"

"You used to plunge your teeth into an apple and bite into its core, sucking out its juices voraciously. Hearing that sound from far away would make me salivate. So many times, I'd bite into an apple trying to imitate you and not succeed. This made a big impression on me. Could you eat one right now just for me?"

She started to laugh. "I didn't know you were paying attention to what I was doing."

"I remember another time: You'd finished cleaning the porch and you were sitting on the stairs in the shade to cool off. Then you brought a plate of apricots and put them down in front of you on a little stool. The colors of the apricot stones were reflected in your skin. Then your female cousins came, Salma was one of them. They sat down and ate apricots and gossiped. I used to gaze at all of them and wonder which of you was the prettiest. I used to feel that you all had one face that was repeated over and over."

She felt like he was talking about another woman. Had she really been that happy? She took pleasure in this image of a young woman surrounded by a bevy of other young women who resemble her. As if she were a memory of a paradise lost. *Yes, Farid will take me far away and he'll help me. He'll be busy with his scientific research and I'll be busy with my children. I'll discover a new continent; I'll be in his big house in Sydney, far away from all this muck.*

She saw white sails in tranquil, sparkling harbors, as though they were an extension of a road that continues when asphalt turns into water.

"It's my luck that you didn't marry. I've wanted a woman like you in my life for so long. Happy and strong. Perhaps you were satisfied when I came to you the first time. You didn't even visit me or pick me up at the airport. I'm the one who took the initiative and came to visit you all. You were unfazed by my visit and remained distant, standing on guard. You are still as proud as you were as an adolescent and perhaps even more so."

"It seems I still have high expectations," she said. "Your pride frightened me."

"How did you manage to put aside fear and find the courage to encroach upon my world once again? I thought you'd arrived at this age without marrying because of your pride. You know that as a woman advances in age, there is no longer a justification for these high expectations."

She sighed deeply. She looked at the open suitcases in front of her with her carefully ironed and folded clothes inside them.

"You'll have to excuse me; I haven't found time to prepare dinner yet . . ."

"Don't worry about it. Let's go to a restaurant around here."

"Should we go to a Lebanese place?"

"Doesn't matter . . . In Sydney, we're used to all kinds of cuisines . . . We should settle the wedding formalities and leave right away. If you could see Sydney, if you could see the harbor, the beauty of the sails. I don't know how people can bear to live here."

"You should give it a little time . . . But wasn't Beirut worse on your first visit? You came during the height of the war—it was destroyed, dead, soulless."

"I don't feel any change. Maybe because I blocked this out. Now, before we marry and leave the country, we should discuss the most important thing: I have two daughters. As you know, their mother left them because she wasn't able to look after them and I wouldn't allow them to live with her. Will you agree to have them live with us, or should I have them stay with their mother?"

"Where's the problem? Of course I want them to live with us."

"I know you are an understanding and good person."

"This is how I'll build my family . . . I'm still young enough that I might be able to have a couple of children . . ."

Faced with Lamia's enthusiasm, Farid started biting his lips. "This is the only point that we really have to discuss. I don't want more children. I've suffered a lot. I can't stand to have another child in my life."

Why did he not care about her opinion? Who was she to him? Did he want to withhold the one dream that she still had left? Seeing the face of a child, holding it close to her chest, inhaling its fragrance and kissing its toes, one by one.

Lamia went into the bedroom to change her clothes, with Farid following.

"Lamia, what's wrong? Can I come in? Your face is pale . . . What's wrong?"

"Nothing, my head hurts a bit . . . Tomorrow we can go to a restaurant . . . or the day after tomorrow . . . I have a headache and I want to be alone."

She took off her clothes, sadly calm. She no longer wanted anything. Now all her dreams have come to nothing: the miniature white sails slipped away with the road and remained suspended in the harbor; the hand of the little boy and his tiny red sweater have disappeared far away, behind her eyes shrouded in tears. He no longer brings her little bunches of flowers or puts paper sailboats in the pool in front of their house.

After he was gone, she opened the window to banish the last traces of Farid's cologne that still lingered in the room. It would take her some time to get herself together again. She thought she heard the ringing of a telephone, which evoked in her neither the desire to get up, nor the slightest bit of curiosity. No doubt it's Farid, wanting to check on his bride's "mood." She couldn't picture him as one day being her life partner. "High expectations" are a beautiful thing; she won't substitute them for a sliver of hope.

She breathed out a great sigh of relief. She would grow old peacefully, without hopes, with quiet despair. The sails set off, never to return, and the honking of car horns returned in the street. She didn't know how late it was when, half-asleep, she picked up the phone near her bed.

"Hello, Lamia?"

"Yes, who's this?"

"Lamia, it's Nazih."

"Nazih? Did something happen? Is Hyam all right? Are you both okay?"

"Why is your voice shaky? Have you been crying?"

"No, I was sleeping."

"Are you ill? It's still early . . ."

"No, I'm not sick . . . Have you sorted out your troubles?"

"Lamia, I just wanted to tell you before it's too late: you are my ultimate love."

Originally written in Arabic.

ABOUT THE CONTRIBUTORS

MUHAMMAD ABI SAMRA (b. 1953) is a Lebanese novelist and journalist. He is currently the director of the weekly investigative journalism section of *Nahar* newspaper, a field he has been working in since 1977. He has published many novels and other collections of writing.

Hachem Mouawieh

TAREK ABI SAMRA (b. 1983) is a short-story writer and freelance journalist born and living in Beirut. He writes in both French and Arabic. He holds a BA in clinical psychology and is currently pursuing a master's degree in the same field.

NAJWA BARAKAT was born in Beirut and has lived in Paris since 1985. She has worked as an independent journalist for various Arabic newspapers and magazines as well as the BBC and RFI. Barakat has written five award-winning novels in Arabic, most of which have been published by Dar al-Adab in Beirut and translated into a number of European languages. She has also written one novel in French, *La locataire du Pot de Fer*. Since 2005, she has run writing workshops to discover previously unknown talents.

ABBAS BEYDOUN (b. 1945) is a Lebanese poet, novelist, and journalist, born in Tyre, Lebanon. He has published numerous volumes of poetry, which have been widely translated; English translations of his poetry have appeared in *Banipal* magazine. He has also published six novels, two of which have been translated into English. Beydoun has been cultural editor of the Beirut-based newspaper *As-Safir* since 1997.

Iman Humaydan

BANA BEYDOUN (b. 1982) has been writing poetry for ten years. She published her first poetry collection, *The Guardian of Illusion*, in 2012. She studied cinema at the Jesuit University in Beirut and the Sorbonne in Paris. She has also directed a number of short films, including *A Moment Alone* (2001), *Sanayeh Bath* (2004), and *Ninar* (2004). She currently works as a journalist in Lebanon and is a film critic for the newspaper *al-Akhbar*.

LEILA EID is a Lebanese novelist and poet born in the Shouf, Lebanon. She lives in Beirut where she works as a journalist for the national news agency. She has published a novel, *Pub Number Two*, and two collections of poetry, *From Where, I Don't Know* and *Sometimes I Dance*.

RAWI HAGE is a writer and a visual artist, born in Beirut and currently residing in Montreal. His first novel, *De Niro's Game*, won the IMPAC Dublin Literary Award, among other major prizes. *Cockroach*, his second novel, was also a finalist for many prestigious awards. His latest novel, *Carnival*, is about the beautiful, twisted existence of life in the modern city, told from the perspective of a taxi driver, and was a finalist for the Writers' Trust Award and won the Paragraphe Hugh MacLennan Prize for Fiction.

Tameem Hartman

MICHELLE HARTMAN is a literary translator from Arabic and French into English, and associate professor of Arabic literature at the Institute of Islamic Studies, McGill University. Her translations include Muhammad Kamil al-Khatib's *Just Like a River* (cotranslated with Maher Barakat), Alexandra Chreiteh's *Always Coca-Cola* and *Ali and His Russian Mother*, and Iman Humaydan's *Other Lives* and *Wild Mulberries*, which was runner-up for the Banipal Prize for the best novel translated from Arabic in 2009.

BACHIR HILAL (b. 1947-2015) was a lawyer and writer born in Lebanon. He wrote a weekly column on political issues for the Arabic daily newspaper *al-Hayat*. His short stories and poetry have been published in the culture sections of many Arabic-language newspapers. He moved from Beirut to Paris during the Lebanese Civil War.

Gerwig Epkes

IMAN HUMAYDAN is a Lebanese writer, creative writing instructor, translator, editor/publisher, journalist, and cofounder and current president of the Lebanese PEN association who splits her time between Beirut and Paris. Her novels *B as in Beirut*, *Wild Mulberries*, and *Other Lives* have been translated into English and other languages; her most recent novel is *Three Ounces of Paradise*. She is the screenwriter for the acclaimed film *Here Comes the Rain*, and coauthor of the documentary *Asmahan: Une Diva Orientale*.

HALA KAWTHARANI (b. 1977) is editor-in-chief of the pan-Arab weekly *Laha* magazine. She is the author of four Arabic novels: *al-Usbuʻ al-Akhir* (*The Final Week*), *Studio Beirut, Ali al-Amerkani* (*Ali the American*), which won the 2013 Sharjah Book Fair prize for Best Arabic Novel, and *Karisma* (Charisma), all published by Dar al-Saqi. Kawtharani holds an MA in Arabic literature and a BA in political studies from the American University of Beirut.

Eva Zayat

ZENA EL KHALIL (b. 1976) has lived in Lagos, London, New York City, and Beirut. A visual artist, writer, and cultural activist, el Khalil works in a variety of formats ranging from painting, installation, performance, mixed media, collage, and writing. She has exhibited internationally, and held solo exhibitions in Lagos, London, Munich, Turin, and Beirut. Her memoir, *Beirut, I Love You*, was translated into several languages including Italian, Spanish, Swedish, and Portuguese.

Raphaël Lucas

MAZEN MAAROUF (b. 1978) is a Palestinian poet, writer, and journalist born in Beirut. He has published three collections of poetry: *The Camera Doesn't Capture Birds, Our Grief Resembles Bread,* and *An Angel Suspended on the Clothesline*. His poetry has been translated into many languages, and the South Lebanon Council honored him in 2009. His first collection of short stories is forthcoming.

ALAWIYA SOBH (b. 1955) was born in Beirut and has published novels, poetry, literary criticism, and journalism. Her novels have been translated into several European languages and have won a number of important literary prizes. She frequently lectures about women's issues, among other subjects, throughout the Arab world and beyond.

MARIE TAWK is a writer and renowned translator currently based in Jbeil (Byblos), Lebanon. She has published numerous literary translations from French into Arabic, as well as from Arabic into French. She recently translated chapters of Jonathan Littell's *The Kindly Ones* from French into Arabic in the *Nahar* newspaper's cultural supplement, and she has published a number of her own short stories and literary criticism in Lebanese newspapers and journals. Tawk is currently working on her first novel.

THE AMAZIN' SARDINE is the author of *An Ever-Receding Tide*. He has been performing under this nom de plume for several years. In his performances, he always strives to be the devil's advocate and impersonates unsavory characters to elicit a reaction from his audience and push them to reconsider established truths.

HYAM YARED (b. 1975) is a French-language Lebanese novelist and short-story writer. Her three novels have won numerous prizes. Her most recent novel is *La Malédiction* (*The Curse*), the story of a modern-day Middle Eastern Medea. She is the president of the PEN association's Lebanon chapter, where she is engaged in the struggle for freedom of expression for all writers, especially those imprisoned or subjected to other forms of intimidation and censorship.

Translator's Acknowledgments

I would like to first acknowledge Ibrahim Ahmad's thoughtful, consistent, and enthusiastic support of this project. I would also like to thank all of the authors of the stories in this collection who were helpful and insightful in their comments and suggestions. Sincere and deep thanks are owed to Iman Humaydan, who continues to teach me so much about literature and language itself. I also would like to express a sincere debt of gratitude to Bader Takriti for working so hard to help me finish the translations, as well as the careful readings of Katy Kalemkerian.